'Dick's plastic [illegible] ant to know about the insi[illegible] out. In his tortured topog[illegible] mindscapes that we ourselv[illegible] mpsed and thought real. Di[illegible] behalf. It is our duty to read the repor[illegible] home *James Lovegrove*

'Dick quietly produced serious fiction in a popular form and there can be no greater praise' *Michael Moorcock*

'One of the most original practitioners writing any kind of fiction, Philip K. Dick made most of the European avant-garde seem navel-gazers in a cul-de-sac' *Sunday Times*

'The most consistently brilliant SF writer in the world'
John Brunner

'Dick's abundant storytelling gifts and the need to express his inner struggles combined to produce some of the most groundbreaking novels and ideas to emerge from SF in the fifties and sixties'
Waterstone's Guide to Science Fiction, Fantasy and Horror

'In all his work he was astonishingly intimate, self exposed, and very dangerous. He was the funniest sf writer of his time, and perhaps the most terrifying. His dreads were our own, spoken as we could not have spoken them' *The Encyclopedia of Science Fiction*

Also by Philip K. Dick

NOVELS

Solar Lottery (1955)
The World Jones Made (1956)
The Man Who Japed (1956)
The Cosmic Puppets (1957)
Eye in the Sky (1957)
Dr Futurity (1959)
Time Out of Joint (1959)
Vulcan's Hammer (1960)
The Man in the High Castle (1962)
The Game-Players of Titan (1963)
The Penultimate Truth (1964)
The Simulacra (1964)
Martian Time-Slip (1964)
Clans of the Alphane Moon (1964)
Dr Bloodmoney, or How We Got Along After the Bomb (1965)
The Three Stigmata of Palmer Eldritch (1965)
Now Wait for Last Year (1966)
The Crack in Space (1966)
The Ganymede Takeover (with Ray F. Nelson) (1967)
The Zap Gun (1967)
Counter-Clock World (1967)
Ubik (1969)
Galactic Pot-Healer (1969)
Our Friends From Frolix 8 (1970)
A Maze of Death (1970)
We Can Build You (1972)
Flow My Tears, The Policeman Said (1974)
Confessions of a Crap Artist (1975)
Deus Irae (with Roger Zelazny) (1976)
A Scanner Darkly (1977)
Valis (1981)
The Divine Invasion (1981)
The Transmigration of Timothy Archer (1982)
Lies, Inc (1984)
The Man Whose Teeth Were All Exactly Alike (1984)
Puttering About in a Small Land (1985)
In Milton Lumky Territory (1985)
Radio Free Albemuth (1985)
Humpty Dumpty in Oakland (1986)
Mary and the Giant (1987)
The Broken Bubble (1988)

SHORT STORY COLLECTIONS

A Handful of Darkness (1955)
The Variable Man (1957)
The Turning Wheel (1977)
The Best of Philip K. Dick (1977)
The Golden Man (1980)
Minority Report (2002)

THE COLLECTED STORIES OF PHILIP K. DICK

1. Beyond Lies the Wub (1987)
2. Second Variety (1987)
3. The Father Thing (1987)
4. The Days of Perky Pat (1987)
5. We Can Remember It For You Wholesale (1987)

Do Androids Dream of Electric Sheep?

Philip K. Dick

This edition published in Great Britain in 2007 by
Gollancz
An imprint of the Orion Publishing Group
Orion House, 5 Upper St Martin's Lane, London WC2H 9EA

A CIP catalogue record for this book
is available from the British Library

Typeset at The Spartan Press Ltd,
Lymington, Hants

Printed and bound by
CPI Group (UK) Ltd, Croydon, CR0 4YY

www.orionbooks.co.uk

To Maren Augusta Bergrud
August 10, 1923–June 14, 1967

And still I dream he treads the lawn,
walking ghostly in the dew,
pierced by my glad singing through.

Yeats

Auckland

A TURTLE WHICH EXPLORER CAPTAIN COOK GAVE TO THE KING OF TONGA IN 1777 DIED YESTERDAY. IT WAS NEARLY 200 YEARS OLD.

THE ANIMAL, CALLED TU'IMALILA, DIED AT THE ROYAL PALACE GROUND IN THE TONGAN CAPITAL OF NUKU, ALOFA.

THE PEOPLE OF TONGA REGARDED THE ANIMAL AS A CHIEF AND SPECIAL KEEPERS WERE APPOINTED TO LOOK AFTER IT. IT WAS BLINDED IN A BUSH FIRE A FEW YEARS AGO.

TONGA RADIO SAID TU'IMALILA'S CARCASS WOULD BE SENT TO THE AUCKLAND MUSEUM IN NEW ZEALAND.

Reuters, 1966

One

A merry little surge of electricity piped by automatic alarm from the mood organ beside his bed awakened Rick Deckard. Surprised – it always surprised him to find himself awake without prior notice – he rose from the bed, stood up in his multicolored pajamas, and stretched. Now, in her bed, his wife Iran opened her gray, unmerry eyes, blinked, then groaned and shut her eyes again.

'You set your Penfield too weak,' he said to her. 'I'll reset it and you'll be awake and—'

'Keep your hand off my settings.' Her voice held bitter sharpness. 'I don't *want* to be awake.'

He seated himself beside her, bent over her, and explained softly. 'If you set the surge up high enough, you'll be glad you're awake; that's the whole point. At setting C it overcomes the threshold barring consciousness, as it does for me.' Friendlily, because he felt well-disposed toward the world – *his* setting had been at *D* – he patted her bare, pale shoulder.

'Get your crude cop's hand away,' Iran said.

'I'm not a cop.' He felt irritable now, although he hadn't dialed for it.

'You're worse,' his wife said, her eyes still shut. 'You're a murderer hired by the cops.'

'I've never killed a human being in my life.' His irritability had risen, now; had become outright hostility.

Iran said, 'Just those poor andys.'

'I notice you've never had any hesitation as to spending the bounty money I bring home on whatever momentarily attracts your attention.' He rose, strode to the console of his mood organ. 'Instead of saving,' he said, 'so we could buy a real sheep, to replace that fake electric one upstairs. A mere electric animal, and me earning all that I've worked my way up to through the years.' At his console he hesitated between dialing for a thalamic suppressant (which would abolish his mood of rage) or a thalamic stimulant (which would make him irked enough to win the argument).

'If you dial,' Iran said, eyes open and watching, 'for greater venom, then I'll dial the same. I'll dial the maximum and you'll see a fight that makes every argument we've had up to now seem like nothing. Dial and see; just try me.' She rose swiftly, loped to the console of her own mood organ, stood glaring at him, waiting.

He sighed, defeated by her threat. 'I'll dial what's on my schedule for today.' Examining the schedule for January 3, 1992, he saw that a businesslike professional attitude was called for. 'If I dial by schedule,' he said warily, 'will you agree to also?' He waited, canny enough not to commit himself until his wife had agreed to follow suit.

'My schedule for today lists a six-hour self-accusatory depression,' Iran said.

'What? Why did you schedule that?' It defeated the whole purpose of the mood organ. 'I didn't even know you could set it for that,' he said gloomily.

'I was sitting here one afternoon,' Iran said, 'and naturally I had turned on Buster Friendly and His Friendly Friends and he was talking about a big news item he's about to break and then that awful commercial came on, the one I hate; you know, for Mountibank Lead Codpieces. And so for a minute I shut off the sound. And I heard the building, this building; I heard the—' She gestured.

'Empty apartments,' Rick said. Sometimes he heard them at night when he was supposed to be asleep. And yet, for this day and age a one-half occupied conapt building rated high in the scheme of population density; out in what had been before the war the suburbs one could find buildings entirely empty . . . or so he had heard. He had let the information remain secondhand; like most people he did not care to experience it directly.

'At that moment,' Iran said, 'when I had the TV sound off, I was in a 382 mood; I had just dialed it. So although I heard the emptiness intellectually, I didn't feel it. My first reaction consisted of being grateful that we could afford a Penfield mood organ. But then I realized how unhealthy it was, sensing the absence of life, not just in this building but everywhere, and not reacting – do you see? I guess you don't. But that used to be considered a sign of mental illness; they called it "absence of appropriate affect." So I left the TV sound off and I sat down at my mood organ and I experimented. And I finally found a setting for despair.' Her dark, pert face showed satisfaction, as if she had achieved something of worth. 'So I put it on my schedule for twice a month; I think that's a reasonable amount of time to feel hopeless about everything, about staying here on Earth after everybody who's smart has emigrated, don't you think?'

'But a mood like that,' Rick said, 'you're apt to stay in it, not dial your way out. Despair like that, about total reality, is self-perpetuating.'

'I program an automatic resetting for three hours later,' his wife said sleekly. 'A 481. Awareness of the manifold possibilities open to me in the future; new hope that—'

'I know 481,' he interrupted. He had dialed out the combination many times; he relied on it greatly. 'Listen,' he said, seating himself on his bed and taking hold of her hands to draw her down beside him, ‘even with an automatic cut-off it’s dangerous to undergo a depression, any kind. Forget what you’ve scheduled and I’ll forget what I’ve scheduled; we’ll dial a 104 together and both experience it, and then you stay in it while I reset mine for my usual businesslike attitude. That way I’ll want to hop up to the roof and check out the sheep and then head for the office; meanwhile I’ll know you’re not sitting here brooding with no TV.’ He released her slim, long fingers, passed through the spacious apartment to the living room, which smelled faintly of last night’s cigarettes. There he bent to turn on the TV.

From the bedroom Iran’s voice came. ‘I can’t stand TV before breakfast.’

‘Dial 888,’ Rick said as the set warmed. ‘The desire to watch TV, no matter what’s on it.’

‘I don’t feel like dialing anything at all now,’ Iran said.

‘Then dial 3,’ he said.

‘I can’t dial a setting that stimulates my cerebral cortex into wanting to dial! If I don’t want to dial, I don’t want to dial that most of all, because then I will want to dial, and wanting to dial is right now the most alien drive I can imagine; I just want to sit here on the bed and stare at the floor.’ Her voice had become sharp with overtones of bleakness as her soul congealed and she ceased to move, as the instinctive, omnipresent film of great weight, of an almost absolute inertia, settled over her.

He turned up the TV sound, and the voice of Buster Friendly boomed out and filled the room. ‘—ho ho, folks. Time now for a brief note on today’s weather. The Mongoose satellite reports that fallout will be especially pronounced toward noon and will then taper off, so all you folks who’ll be venturing out—’

Appearing beside him, her long nightgown trailing wispily,

Iran shut off the TV set. 'Okay, I give up; I'll dial. Anything you want me to be; ecstatic sexual bliss – I feel so bad I'll even endure that. What the hell. What difference does it make?'

'I'll dial for both of us,' Rick said, and led her back into the bedroom. There, at her console, he dialed 594; pleased acknowledgment of husband's superior wisdom in all matters. On his own console he dialed for a creative and fresh attitude toward his job, although this he hardly needed; such was his habitual, innate approach without recourse to Penfield artificial brain stimulation.

After a hurried breakfast – he had lost time due to the discussion with his wife – he ascended clad for venturing out, including his Ajax model Mountibank Lead Codpiece, to the covered roof pasture whereon his electric sheep 'grazed.' Whereon it, sophisticated piece of hardware that it was, chomped away in simulated contentment, bamboozling the other tenants of the building.

Of course, some of their animals undoubtedly consisted of electronic circuitry fakes, too; he had of course never nosed into the matter, any more than they, his neighbors, had pried into the real workings of his sheep. Nothing could be more impolite. To say, 'Is your sheep genuine?' would be a worse breach of manners than to inquire whether a citizen's teeth, hair, or internal organs would test out authentic.

The morning air, spilling over with radioactive motes, gray and sun-beclouding, belched about him, haunting his nose; he sniffed involuntarily the taint of death. Well, that was too strong a description for it, he decided as he made his way to the particular plot of sod which he owned along with the unduly large apartment below. The legacy of World War Terminus had diminished in potency; those who could not survive the dust had passed into oblivion years ago, and the dust, weaker now and confronting the strong survivors, only deranged minds and genetic properties. Despite his lead codpiece the dust – undoubtedly – filtered in and at him, brought him daily, so long as he failed to emigrate, its little load of befouling filth. So far, medical checkups taken monthly confirmed him as a regular: a man who could reproduce within the tolerances set by law. Any month, however, the exam by the San Francisco Police Department doctors could reveal otherwise. Continually, new specials came into existence, created out of regulars by the omnipresent dust. The saying currently blabbed by posters, TV ads, and government junk mail, ran: 'Emigrate or degenerate! The choice is yours!' Very true, Rick thought as he opened the gate to his little pasture and approached his electric sheep. But I can't emigrate, he said to himself. Because of my job.

The owner of the adjoining pasture, his conapt neighbor Bill Barbour, hailed him; he, like Rick, had dressed for work but had stopped off on the way to check his animal, too.

'My horse,' Barbour declared beamingly, 'is pregnant.' He indicated the big Percheron, which stood staring off in an empty fashion into space. 'What do you say to that?'

'I say pretty soon you'll have two horses,' Rick said. He had reached his sheep, now; it lay ruminating, its alert eyes fixed on him in case he had brought any rolled oats with him. The alleged sheep contained an oat-tropic circuit; at the sight of such cereals it would scramble up convincingly and amble over. 'What's she pregnant by?' he asked Barbour. 'The wind?'

'I bought some of the highest quality fertilizing plasma available in California,' Barbour informed him. 'Through inside contacts I have with the State Animal Husbandry Board. Don't you remember last week when their inspector was out here examining Judy? They're eager to have her foal;

she's an unmatched superior.' Barbour thumped his horse fondly on the neck and she inclined her head toward him.

'Ever thought of selling your horse?' Rick asked. He wished to god he had a horse, in fact any animal. Owning and maintaining a fraud had a way of gradually demoralizing one. And yet from a social standpoint it had to be done, given the absence of the real article. He had therefore no choice except to continue. Even were he not to care himself, there remained his wife, and Iran did care. Very much.

Barbour said, 'It would be immoral to sell my horse.'

'Sell the colt, then. Having two animals is more immoral than not having any.'

Puzzled, Barbour said, 'How do you mean? A lot of people have two animals, even three, four, and like in the case of Fred Washborne, who owns the algae-processing plant my brother works at, even five. Didn't you see that article about his duck in yesterday's *Chronicle*? It's supposed to be the heaviest, largest Moscovy on the West Coast.' The man's eyes glazed over, imagining such possessions; he drifted by degrees into a trance.

Exploring about in his coat pockets, Rick found his creased, much-studied copy of Sidney's Animal & Fowl Catalogue January supplement. He looked in the index, found colts (vide horses, offsp.) and presently had the prevailing national price. 'I can buy a Percheron colt from Sidney's for five thousand dollars,' he said aloud.

'No you can't,' Barbour said. 'Look at the listing again; it's in italics. That means they don't have any in stock, but that would be the price if they did have.'

'Suppose,' Rick said, 'I pay you five hundred dollars a month for ten months. Full catalogue value.'

Pityingly, Barbour said, 'Deckard, you don't understand about horses; there's a reason why Sidney's doesn't have any

Percheron colts in stock. Percheron colts just don't change hands – at catalogue value, even. They're too scarce, even relatively inferior ones.' He leaned across their common fence, gesticulating. 'I've had Judy for three years and not in all that time have I seen a Percheron mare of her quality. To acquire her I had to fly to Canada, and I personally drove her back here myself to make sure she wasn't stolen. You bring an animal like this anywhere around Colorado or Wyoming and they'll knock you off to get hold of it. You know why? Because back before W.W.T. there existed literally hundreds—'

'But,' Rick interrupted, 'for you to have two horses and me none, that violates the whole basic theological and moral structure of Mercerism.'

'You have your sheep; hell, you can follow the Ascent in your individual life, and when you grasp the two handles of empathy you approach honorably. Now if you didn't have that old sheep, there, I'd see some logic in your position. Sure, if I had two animals and you didn't have any, I'd be helping deprive you of true fusion with Mercer. But every family in this building – let's see; around fifty: one to every three apts, as I compute it – every one of us has an animal of some sort. Graveson has that chicken over there.' He gestured north. 'Oakes and his wife have that big red dog that barks in the night.' He pondered. 'I think Ed Smith has a cat down in his apt; at least he says so, but no one's ever seen it. Possibly he's just pretending.'

Going over to his sheep, Rick bent down, searching in the thick white wool – the fleece at least was genuine – until he found what he was looking for: the concealed control panel of the mechanism. As Barbour watched he snapped open the panel covering, revealing it. 'See?' he said to Barbour. 'You understand now why I want your colt so badly?'

After an interval Barbour said, 'You poor guy. Has it always been this way?'

'No,' Rick said, once again closing the panel covering of his electric sheep; he straightened up, turned, and faced his neighbor. 'I had a real sheep, originally. My wife's father gave it to us outright when he emigrated. Then, about a year ago, remember that time I took it to the vet – you were up here that morning when I came out and found it lying on its side and it couldn't get up.'

'You got it to its feet,' Barbour said, remembering and nodding. 'Yeah, you managed to lift it up but then after a minute or two of walking around it fell over again.'

Rick said, 'Sheep get strange diseases. Or put another way, sheep get a lot of diseases but the symptoms are always the same; the sheep can't get up and there's no way to tell how serious it is, whether it's a sprained leg or the animal's dying of tetanus. That's what mine died of: tetanus.'

'Up here?' Barbour said. 'On the roof?'

'The hay,' Rick explained. 'That one time I didn't get all the wire off the bale; I left a piece and Groucho – that's what I called him, then – got a scratch and in that way contracted tetanus. I took him to the vet's and he died, and I thought about it, and finally I called one of those shops that manufacture artificial animals and I showed them a photograph of Groucho. They made this.' He indicated the reclining ersatz animal, which continued to ruminate attentively, still watching alertly for any indication of oats. 'It's a premium job. And I've put as much time and attention into caring for it as I did when it was real. But—' He shrugged.

'It's not the same,' Barbour finished.

'But almost. You feel the same doing it; you have to keep your eye on it exactly as you did when it was really alive. Because they break down and then everyone in the building knows. I've had it at the repair shop six times, mostly little malfunctions, but if anyone saw them – for instance one time the voice tape broke or anyhow got fouled and it wouldn't stop baaing – they'd recognize it as a *mechanical* breakdown.' He added, 'The repair outfit's truck is of course marked "animal hospital something." And the driver dresses like a vet, completely in white.' He glanced suddenly at his watch, remembering the time. 'I have to get to work,' he said to Barbour. 'I'll see you this evening.'

As he started toward his car Barbour called after him hurriedly, 'Um, I won't say anything to anybody here in the building.'

Pausing, Rick started to say thanks. But then something of the despair that Iran had been talking about tapped him on the shoulder and he said, 'I don't know; maybe it doesn't make any difference.'

'But they'll look down on you. Not all of them, but some. You know how people are about not taking care of an animal; they consider it immoral and anti-empathic. I mean, technically it's not a crime like it was right after W.W.T. but the feeling's still there.'

'God,' Rick said futilely, and gestured empty-handed. 'I *want* to have an animal; I keep trying to buy one. But on my salary, on what a city employee makes—' If, he thought, I could get lucky in my work again. As I did two years ago when I managed to bag four andys during one month. If I had known then, he thought, that Groucho was going to die . . . but that had been before the tetanus. Before the two-inch piece of broken, hypodermic-like baling wire.

'You could buy a cat,' Barbour offered. 'Cats are cheap; look in your Sidney's catalogue.'

Rick said quietly, 'I don't want a domestic pet. I want what I originally had, a large animal. A sheep or if I can get the money a cow or a steer or what you have; a horse.' The bounty from retiring five andys would do it, he realized. A thousand dollars apiece, over and above my salary. Then somewhere I could find, from someone, what I want. Even if the listing in Sidney's Animal & Fowl is in italics. Five thousand dollars – but, he thought, the five andys first have to make their way to Earth from one of the colony planets; I can't control that, I can't make five of them come here, and even if I could there are other bounty hunters with other police agencies throughout the world. The andys would specifically have to take up residence in Northern California, and the senior bounty hunter in this area, Dave Holden, would have to die or retire.

'Buy a cricket,' Barbour suggested wittily. 'Or a mouse. Hey, for twenty-five bucks you can buy a full-grown mouse.'

Rick said, 'Your horse could die, like Groucho died, without warning. When you get home from work this evening you could find her laid out on her back, her feet in the air, like a bug. Like what you said, a cricket.' He strode off, car key in his hand.

'Sorry if I offended you,' Barbour said nervously.

In silence Rick Deckard plucked open the door of his hovercar. He had nothing further to say to his neighbor; his mind was on his work, on the day ahead.

Two

In a giant, empty, decaying building which had once housed thousands, a single TV set hawked its wares to an uninhabited room.

Their ownerless ruin had, before World War Terminus, been tended and maintained. Here had been the suburbs of San Francisco, a short ride by monorail rapid transit; the entire peninsula had chattered like a bird tree with life and opinions and complaints, and now the watchful owners had either died or migrated to a colony world. Mostly the former; it had been a costly war despite the valiant predictions of the Pentagon and its smug scientific vassal, the Rand Corporation – which had, in fact, existed not far from this spot. Like the apartment owners, the corporation had departed, evidently for good. No one missed it.

In addition, no one today remembered why the war had come about or who, if anyone, had won. The dust which had contaminated most of the planet's surface had originated in no country and no one, even the wartime enemy, had planned on it. First, strangely, the owls had died. At the time it had seemed almost funny, the fat, fluffy white birds lying here and there, in yards and on streets; coming out no earlier than twilight as they had while alive the owls escaped notice. Medieval plagues had manifested themselves in a similar way, in the form of many dead rats. This plague, however, had descended from above.

After the owls, of course, the other birds followed, but by

then the mystery had been grasped and understood. A meagre colonization program had been underway before the war but now that the sun had ceased to shine on Earth the colonization entered an entirely new phase. In connection with this a weapon of war, the Synthetic Freedom Fighter, had been modified; able to function on an alien world the humanoid robot – strictly speaking, the organic android – had become the mobile donkey engine of the colonization program. Under UN law each emigrant automatically received possession of an android subtype of his choice, and, by 1990, the variety of subtypes passed all understanding, in the manner of American automobiles of the 1960s.

That had been the ultimate incentive of emigration: the android servant as carrot, the radioactive fallout as stick. The UN had made it easy to emigrate, difficult if not impossible to stay. Loitering on Earth potentially meant finding oneself abruptly classed as biologically unacceptable, a menace to the pristine heredity of the race. Once pegged as special, a citizen, even if accepting sterilization, dropped out of history. He ceased, in effect, to be part of mankind. And yet persons here and there declined to migrate; that, even to those involved, constituted a perplexing irrationality. Logically, every regular should have emigrated already. Perhaps, deformed as it was, Earth remained familiar, to be clung to. Or possibly the non-emigrant imagined that the tent of dust would deplete itself finally. In any case thousands of individuals remained, most of them constellated in urban areas where they could physically see one another, take heart at their mutual presence. Those appeared to be the relatively sane ones. And, in dubious addition to them, occasional peculiar entities remained in the virtually abandoned suburbs.

John Isidore, being yammered at by the television set in his living room as he shaved in the bathroom, was one of these.

He simply had wandered to this spot in the early days following the war. In those evil times no one had known, really, what they were doing. Populations, detached by the war, had roamed, squatted temporarily at first one region and then another. Back then the fallout had been sporadic and highly variable; some states had been nearly free of it, others became saturated. The displaced populations moved as the dust moved. The peninsula south of San Francisco had been at first dust-free, and a great body of persons had responded by taking up residence there; when the dust arrived, some had died and the rest had departed. J. R. Isidore remained.

The TV set shouted, '—duplicates the halcyon days of the pre-Civil War Southern states! Either as body servants or tireless field hands, the custom-tailored humanoid robot – designed specifically for YOUR UNIQUE NEEDS, FOR YOU AND YOU ALONE – given to you on your arrival absolutely free, equipped fully, as specified by you before your departure from Earth; this loyal, trouble-free companion in the greatest, boldest adventure contrived by man in modern history will provide—' It continued on and on.

I wonder if I'm late for work, Isidore wondered as he scraped. He did not own a working clock; generally he depended on the TV for time signals, but today was Inter-space Horizons Day, evidently. Anyhow the TV claimed this to be the fifth (or sixth?) anniversary of the founding of New America, the chief U.S. settlement on Mars. And his TV set, being partly broken, picked up only the channel which had been nationalized during the war and still remained so; the government in Washington, with its colonization program, constituted the sole sponsor which Isidore found himself forced to listen to.

'Let's hear from Mrs Maggie Klugman,' the TV announcer suggested to John Isidore, who wanted only to know the time.

'A recent immigrant to Mars, Mrs Klugman in an interview taped live in New New York had this to say. Mrs Klugman, how would you contrast your life back on contaminated Earth with your new life here in a world rich with every imaginable possibility?' A pause, and then a tired, dry, middle-aged, female voice said, 'I think what I and my family of three noticed most was the dignity.' 'The dignity, Mrs Klugman?' the announcer asked. 'Yes,' Mrs Klugman, now of New New York, Mars, said. 'It's a hard thing to explain. Having a servant you can depend on in these troubled times . . . I find it reassuring.'

'Back on Earth, Mrs Klugman, in the old days, did you also worry about finding yourself classified, ahem, as a special?'

'Oh, my husband and myself worried ourselves nearly to death. Of course, once we emigrated that worry vanished, fortunately forever.'

To himself John Isidore thought acidly, And it's gone away for me, too, without my having to emigrate. He had been a special now for over a year, and not merely in regard to the distorted genes which he carried. Worse still, he had failed to pass the minimum mental faculties test, which made him in popular parlance a chickenhead. Upon him the contempt of three planets descended. However, despite this, he survived. He had his job, driving a pickup and delivery truck for a false-animal repair firm; the Van Ness Pet Hospital and his gloomy, gothic boss Hannibal Sloat accepted him as human and this he appreciated. *Mors certa, vita incerta*, as Mr Sloat occasionally declared. Isidore, although he had heard the expression a number of times, retained only a dim notion as to its meaning. After all, if a chickenhead could fathom Latin he would cease to be a chickenhead. Mr Sloat, when this was pointed out to him, acknowledged its truth. And there existed chickenheads infinitely stupider than Isidore, who could hold no jobs at all,

death is certain,
life is uncertain.

who remained in custodial institutions quaintly called 'Institute of Special Trade Skills of America,' the word 'special' having to get in there somehow, as always.

'—your husband felt no protection,' the TV announcer was saying, 'in owning and continually wearing an expensive and clumsy radiation-proof lead codpiece, Mrs Klugman?'

'My husband,' Mrs Klugman began, but at that point, having finished shaving, Isidore strode into the living room and shut off the TV set.

Silence. It flashed from the woodwork and the walls; it smote him with an awful, total power, as if generated by a vast mill. It rose from the floor, up out of the tattered gray wall-to-wall carpeting. It unleashed itself from the broken and semi-broken appliances in the kitchen, the dead machines which hadn't worked in all the time Isidore had lived here. From the useless pole lamp in the living room it oozed out, meshing with the empty and wordless descent of itself from the fly-specked ceiling. It managed in fact to emerge from every object within his range of vision, as if it – the silence – meant to supplant all things tangible. Hence it assailed not only his ears but his eyes; as he stood by the inert TV set he experienced the silence as visible and, in its own way, alive. Alive! He had often felt its austere approach before; when it came it burst in without subtlety, evidently unable to wait. The silence of the world could not rein back its greed. Not any longer. Not when it had virtually won.

He wondered, then, if the others who had remained on Earth experienced the void this way. Or was it peculiar to his peculiar biological identity, a freak generated by his inept sensory apparatus? Interesting question, Isidore thought. But whom could he compare notes with? He lived alone in this deteriorating, blind building of a thousand uninhabited apartments, which like all its counterparts, fell, day by day, into greater entropic ruin. Eventually everything within the building would merge, would be faceless and identical, mere pudding-like kipple piled to the ceiling of each apartment. And, after that, the uncared-for building itself would settle into shapelessness, buried under the ubiquity of the dust. By then, naturally, he himself would be dead, another interesting event to anticipate as he stood here in his stricken living room alone with the lungless, all-penetrating, masterful world-silence.

Better, perhaps, to turn the TV back on. But the ads, directed at the remaining regulars, frightened him. They informed him in a countless procession of ways that he, a special, wasn't wanted. Had no use. Could not, even if he wanted to, emigrate. So why listen to that? he asked himself irritably. Fork them and their colonization; I hope a war gets started there – after all, it theoretically could – and they wind up like Earth. And everybody who emigrated turns out to be special.

Okay, he thought; I'm off to work. He reached for the doorknob that opened the way out into the unlit hall, then shrank back as he glimpsed the vacuity of the rest of the building. It lay in wait for him, out here, the force which he had felt busily penetrating his specific apartment. God, he thought, and reshut the door. He was not ready for the trip up those clanging stairs to the empty roof where he had no animal. The echo of himself ascending: the echo of nothing. Time to grasp the handles, he said to himself, and crossed the living room to the black empathy box.

When he turned it on the usual faint smell of negative ions surged from the power supply; he breathed in eagerly, already buoyed up. Then the cathode-ray tube glowed like an imitation, feeble TV image; a collage formed, made of apparently random colors, trails, and configurations which, until the handles were grasped, amounted to nothing. So, taking a deep breath to steady himself, he grasped the twin handles.

The visual image congealed; he saw at once a famous landscape, the old, brown, barren ascent, with tufts of dried-out bonelike weeds poking slantedly into a dim and sunless sky. One single figure, more or less human in form, toiled its way up the hillside: an elderly man wearing a dull, featureless robe, covering as meager as if it had been snatched from the hostile emptiness of the sky. The man, Wilbur Mercer, plodded ahead, and, as he clutched the handles, John Isidore gradually experienced a waning of the living room in which he stood; the dilapidated furniture and walls ebbed out and he ceased to experience them at all. He found himself, instead, as always before, entering into the landscape of drab hill, drab sky. And at the same time he no longer witnessed the climb of the elderly man. His own feet now scraped, sought purchase, among the familiar loose stones; he felt the same old painful, irregular roughness beneath his feet and once again smelled the acrid haze of the sky – not Earth's sky but that of some place alien, distant, and yet, by means of the empathy box, instantly available.

He had crossed over in the usual perplexing fashion; physical merging – accompanied by mental and spiritual identification – with Wilbur Mercer had reoccurred. As it did for everyone who at this moment clutched the handles, either here on Earth or on one of the colony planets. He experienced them, the others, incorporated the babble of their thoughts, heard in his own brain the noise of their many individual existences. They – and he – cared about one thing; this fusion of their mentalities oriented their attention on the hill, the climb, the need to ascend. Step by step it evolved, so slowly as to be nearly imperceptible. But it was there. Higher, he thought as stones rattled downward under his feet. Today we are higher than yesterday, and tomorrow – he, the compound figure of Wilbur Mercer, glanced up to view the ascent ahead. Impossible to make out the end. Too far. But it would come.

A rock, hurled at him, struck his arm. He felt the pain. He half turned and another rock sailed past him, missing him; it collided with the earth and the sound startled him. Who? he wondered, peering to see his tormentor. The old antagonists, manifesting themselves at the periphery of his vision; it, or they, had followed him all the way up the hill and they would remain until at the top—

He remembered the top, the sudden leveling of the hill, when the climb ceased and the other part of it began. How many times had he done this? The several times blurred; future and past blurred; what he had already experienced and what he would eventually experience blended so that nothing remained but the moment, the standing still and resting during which he rubbed the cut on his arm which the stone had left. God, he thought in weariness. In what way is this fair? Why am I up here alone like this, being tormented by something I can't even see? And then, within him, the mutual babble of everyone else in fusion broke the illusion of aloneness.

You felt it, too, he thought. Yes, the voices answered. We got hit, on the left arm; it hurts like hell. Okay, he said. We better get started moving again. He resumed walking, and all of them accompanied him immediately.

Once, he remembered, it had been different. Back before the curse had come, an earlier, happier part of life. They, his foster parents Frank and Cora Mercer, had found him floating on an inflated rubber air-rescue raft, off the coast of New England . . . or had it been Mexico, near the port of Tampico? He did not now remember the circumstances. Childhood had been nice; he had loved all life, especially the animals, had in fact been able for a time to bring dead animals back as they had been. He lived with rabbits and bugs, wherever it was, either on Earth or a colony world; now he had forgotten that, too. But he recalled the killers, because they had arrested him as a freak, more special than any of the other specials. And due to that everything had changed.

Local law prohibited the time-reversal faculty by which the dead returned to life; they had spelled it out to him during his sixteenth year. He continued for another year to do it secretly, in the still remaining woods, but an old woman whom he had never seen or heard of had told. Without his parents' consent they – the killers – had bombarded the unique nodule which had formed in his brain, had attacked it with radioactive cobalt, and this had plunged him into a different world, one whose existence he had never suspected. It had been a pit of corpses and dead bones and he had struggled for years to get up from it. The donkey and especially the toad, the creatures most important to him, had vanished, had become extinct; only rotting fragments, an eyeless head here, part of a hand there, remained. At last a bird which had come there to die told him where he was. He had sunk down into the tomb world. He could not get out until the bones strewn around him grew back into living creatures; he had become joined to the metabolism of other lives and until they rose he could not rise either.

How long that part of the cycle had lasted he did not now know; nothing had happened, generally, so it had been measureless. But at last the bones had regained flesh; the empty eyepits had filled up and the new eyes had seen, while meantime the restored beaks and mouths had cackled, barked, and caterwauled. Possibly he had done it; perhaps the extrasensory node of his brain had finally grown back. Or maybe he hadn't accomplished it; very likely it could have been a natural process. Anyhow he was no longer sinking; he had begun to ascend, along with the others. Long ago he had lost sight of them. He found himself evidently climbing alone. But they were there. They still accompanied him; he felt them, strangely, inside him.

Isidore stood holding the two handles, experiencing himself as encompassing every other living thing, and then, reluctantly, he let go. It had to end, as always, and anyhow his arm ached and bled where the rock had struck it.

Releasing the handles he examined his arm, then made his way unsteadily to the bathroom of his apartment to wash the cut off. This was not the first wound he had received while in fusion with Mercer and it probably would not be the last. People, especially elderly ones, had died, particularly later on at the top of the hill when the torment began in earnest. I wonder if I can go through that part again, he said to himself as he swabbed the injury. Chance of cardiac arrest; be better, he reflected, if I lived in town where those buildings have a doctor standing by with those electro-spark machines. Here, alone in this place, it's too risky.

But he knew he'd take the risk. He always had before. As did most people, even oldsters who were physically fragile.

Using a Kleenex he dried his damaged arm.

And heard, muffled and far off, a TV set.

It's someone else in this building, he thought wildly, unable to believe it. Not my TV; that's off, and I can feel the floor resonance. It's below, on another level entirely!

I'm not alone here any more, he realized. Another resident has moved in, taken one of the abandoned apartments, and close enough for me to hear him. Must be level two or level three, certainly no deeper. Let's see, he thought rapidly. What do you do when a new resident moves in? Drop by and borrow something, is that how it's done? He could not remember; this had never happened to him before, here or anywhere else:

people moved out, people emigrated, but nobody ever moved in. You take them something, he decided. Like a cup of water or rather milk; yes, it's milk or flour or maybe an egg – or, specifically, their ersatz substitutes.

Looking in his refrigerator – the compressor had long since ceased working – he found a dubious cube of margarine. And, with it, set off excitedly, his heart laboring, for the level below. I have to keep calm, he realized. Not let him know I'm a chickenhead. If he finds out I'm a chickenhead he won't talk to me; that's always the way it is for some reason. I wonder why?

He hurried down the hall.

Three

On his way to work Rick Deckard, as lord knew how many other people, stopped briefly to skulk about in front of one of San Francisco's larger pet shops, along animal row. In the center of the block-long display window an ostrich, in a heated clear-plastic cage, returned his stare. The bird, according to the info plaque attached to the cage, had just arrived from a zoo in Cleveland. It was the only ostrich on the West Coast. After staring at it, Rick spent a few more minutes staring grimly at the price tag. He then continued on to the Hall of Justice on Lombard Street and found himself a quarter of an hour late to work.

As he unlocked his office door his superior, Police Inspector Harry Bryant, jug-eared and redheaded, sloppily dressed but wise-eyed and conscious of nearly everything of any importance, hailed him. 'Meet me at nine-thirty in Dave Holden's office.' Inspector Bryant, as he spoke, flicked briefly through a clipboard of onionskin typed sheets. 'Holden,' he continued as he started off, 'is in Mount Zion Hospital with a laser track through his spine. He'll be there for a month at least. Until they can get one of those new organic plastic spinal sections to take hold.'

'What happened?' Rick asked, chilled. The department's chief bounty hunter had been all right yesterday; at the end of the day he had as usual zipped off in his hovercar to his apartment in the crowded high-prestige Nob Hill area of the city.

Bryant muttered over his shoulder something about

nine-thirty in Dave's office and departed, leaving Rick standing alone.

As he entered his own office Rick heard the voice of his secretary, Ann Marsten, behind him. 'Mr Deckard, you know what happened to Mr Holden? He got shot.' She followed after him into the stuffy, closed-up office and set the air-filtering unit into motion.

'Yeah,' he responded absently.

'It must have been one of those new, extra-clever andys the Rosen Association is turning out,' Miss Marsten said. 'Did you read over the company's brochure and the spec sheets? The Nexus-6 brain unit they're using now is capable of selecting within a field of two trillion constituents, or ten million separate neural pathways.' She lowered her voice. 'You missed the vidcall this morning. Miss Wild told me; it came through the switchboard exactly at nine.'

'A call in?' Rick asked.

Miss Marsten said, 'A call out by Mr Bryant to the WPO in Russia. Asking them if they would be willing to file a formal written complaint with the Rosen Association's factory representative East.'

'Harry still wants the Nexus-6 brain unit withdrawn from the market?' He felt no surprise. Since the initial release of its specifications and performance charts back in August of 1991 most police agencies which dealt with escaped andys had been protesting. 'The Soviet police can't do any more than we can,' he said. Legally, the manufacturers of the Nexus-6 brain unit operated under colonial law, their parent auto-factory being on Mars. 'We had better just accept the new unit as a fact of life,' he said. 'It's always been this way, with every improved brain unit that's come along. I remember the howls of pain when the Sudermann people showed their old T-14 back in '89. Every police agency in the Western Hemisphere clamored that no test would detect its presence, in an instance of illegal entry here. As a matter of fact, for a while they were right.' Over fifty of the T-14 android as he recalled had made their way by one means or another to Earth, and had not yet been detected for a period in some cases up to an entire year. But then the Voigt Empathy Test had been devised by the Pavlov Institute working in the Soviet Union. And no T-14 android – insofar, at least, as was known – had managed to pass that particular test.

'Want to know what the Russian police said?' Miss Marsten asked. 'I know that, too.' Her freckled, orange face glowed.

Rick said, 'I'll find out from Harry Bryant.' He felt irritable; office gossip annoyed him because it always proved better than the truth. Seating himself at his desk he pointedly fished about in a drawer until Miss Marsten, perceiving the hint, departed.

From the drawer he produced an ancient, creased manila envelope. Leaning back, tilting his important-style chair, he rummaged among the contents of the envelope until he came across what he wanted: the collected, extant data on the Nexus-6.

A moment's reading vindicated Miss Marsten's statement; the Nexus-6 did have two trillion constituents plus a choice within a range of ten million possible combinations of cerebral activity. In .45 of a second an android equipped with such a brain structure could assume any one of fourteen basic reaction-postures. Well, no intelligence test would trap such an andy. But then, intelligence tests hadn't trapped an andy in years, not since the primordial, crude varieties of the '70s.

The Nexus-6 android types, Rick reflected, surpassed several classes of human specials in terms of intelligence. In other words, androids equipped with the new Nexus-6 brain unit had from a sort of rough, pragmatic, no-nonsense standpoint evolved beyond a major – but inferior – segment of mankind. For better or worse. The servant had in some cases become more adroit than its master. But new scales of achievement, for example the Voigt-Kampff Empathy Test, had emerged as criteria by which to judge. An android, no matter how gifted as to pure intellectual capacity, could make no sense out of the fusion which took place routinely among the followers of Mercerism – an experience which he, and virtually everyone else, including subnormal chickenheads, managed with no difficulty.

He had wondered as had most people at one time or another precisely why an android bounced helplessly about when confronted by an empathy-measuring test. Empathy, evidently, existed only within the human community, whereas intelligence to some degree could be found throughout every phylum and order including the arachnida. For one thing, the emphatic faculty probably required an unimpaired group instinct; a solitary organism, such as a spider, would have no use for it; in fact it would tend to abort a spider's ability to survive. It would make him conscious of the desire to live on the part of his prey. Hence all predators, even highly developed mammals such as cats, would starve.

Empathy, he once had decided, must be limited to herbivores or anyhow omnivores who could depart from a meat diet. Because, ultimately, the emphatic gift blurred the boundaries between hunter and victim, between the successful and the defeated. As in the fusion with Mercer, everyone ascended together or, when the cycle had come to an end, fell together into the trough of the tomb world. Oddly, it resembled a sort of biological insurance, but double-edged. As long as some creature experienced joy, then the condition for all other creatures included a fragment of joy. However, if any living being suffered, then for all the rest the shadow could not be entirely cast off. A herd animal such as man would acquire a higher survival factor through this; an owl or a cobra would be destroyed.

Evidently the humanoid robot constituted a solitary predator.

Rick liked to think of them that way; it made his job palatable. In retiring – i.e. killing – an andy he did not violate the rule of life laid down by Mercer. *You shall kill only the killers*, Mercer had told them the year empathy boxes first appeared on Earth. And in Mercerism, as it evolved into a full theology, the concept of The Killers had grown insidiously. In Mercerism, an absolute evil plucked at the threadbare cloak of the tottering, ascending old man, but it was never clear who or what this evil presence was. A Mercerite *sensed* evil without understanding it. Put another way, a Mercerite was free to locate the nebulous presence of The Killers wherever he saw fit. For Rick Deckard an escaped humanoid robot, which had killed its master, which had been equipped with an intelligence greater than that of many human beings, which had no regard for animals, which possessed no ability to feel empathic joy for another life form's success or grief at its defeat – that, for him, epitomized The Killers.

Thinking about animals reminded him of the ostrich he had seen in the pet store. Temporarily he pushed away the specs on the Nexus-6 brain unit, took a pinch of Mrs Siddons' No 3 & 4 snuff and cogitated. Then he examined his watch, saw that he had time; he picked up his desk vidphone and said to Miss Marsten, 'Get me the Happy Dog Pet Shop on Sutter Street.'

'Yes sir,' Miss Marsten said, and opened her phone book.

They can't really want that much for the ostrich, Rick said to himself. They expect you to car-trade, like in the old days.

'Happy Dog Pet Shop,' a man's voice declared, and on

Rick's vidscreen a minute happy face appeared. Animals could be heard bawling.

'That ostrich you have in your display window,' Rick said; he toyed with a ceramic ashtray before him on the desk. 'What sort of a down payment would I need for that?'

'Let's see,' the animal salesman said, groping for a pen and pad of paper. 'One-third down.' He figured. 'May I ask, sir, if you're going to trade something in?'

Guardedly, Rick said, 'I – haven't decided.'

'Let's say we put the ostrich on a thirty-month contract,' the salesman said. 'At a low, low interest rate of six percent a month. That would make your monthly payment, after a reasonable down—'

'You'll have to lower the price you're asking,' Rick said. 'Knock off two thousand and I won't trade anything in; I'll come up with cash.' Dave Holden, he reflected, is out of action. That could mean a great deal . . . depending on how many assignments show up during the coming month.

'Sir,' the animal salesman said, 'our asking price is already a thousand dollars under book. Check your Sidney's; I'll hang on. I want you to see for yourself, sir, that our price is fair.'

Christ, Rick thought. They're standing firm. However, just for the heck of it, he wiggled his bent Sidney's out of his coat pocket, thumbed to ostrich comma male-female, old-young, sick-well, mint-used, and inspected the prices.

'Mint, male, young, well,' the salesman informed him. 'Thirty thousand dollars.' He, too, had his Sidney's out. 'We're exactly one thousand under book. Now, your down payment—'

'I'll think it over,' Rick said, 'and call you back.' He started to hang up.

'Your name, sir?' the salesman asked alertly.

'Frank Merriwell,' Rick said.

'And your address, Mr Merriwell? In case I'm not here when you call back.'

He made up an address and put the vidphone receiver back on its cradle. All that money, he thought. And yet, people buy them; some people have that kind of money. Picking up the receiver again he said harshly, 'Give me an outside line, Miss Marsten. And don't listen in on the conversation; it's confidential.' He glared at her.

'Yes, sir,' Miss Marsten said. 'Go ahead and dial.' She then cut herself out of the circuit, leaving him to face the outside world.

He dialed – by memory – the number of the false-animal shop at which he had gotten his ersatz sheep. On the small vidscreen a man dressed like a vet appeared. 'Dr McRae,' the man declared.

'This is Deckard. How much is an electric ostrich?'

'Oh, I'd say we could fix you up for less than eight hundred dollars. How soon did you want delivery? We would have to make it up for you; there's not that much call for—'

'I'll talk to you later,' Rick interrupted; glancing at his watch he saw that nine-thirty had arrived. 'Good-by.' He hurriedly hung up, rose, and shortly thereafter stood before Inspector Bryant's office door. He passed by Bryant's receptionist – attractive, with waist-length braided silver hair – and then the inspector's secretary, an ancient monster from the Jurassic swamp, frozen and sly, like some archaic apparition fixated in the tomb world. Neither woman spoke to him nor he to them. Opening the inner door he nodded to his superior, who was busy on the phone; seating himself he got out the specs on Nexus-6, which he had brought with him, and once more read them over as Inspector Bryant talked away.

He felt depressed. And yet, logically, because of Dave's sudden disappearance from the work scene, he should be at least guardedly pleased.

Four

Maybe I'm worried, Rick Deckard conjectured, that what happened to Dave will happen to me. An andy smart enough to laser him could probably take me, too. But that didn't seem to be it.

'I see you brought the poop sheet on that new brain unit,' Inspector Bryant said, hanging up the vidphone.

Rick said, 'Yeah, I heard about it on the grapevine. How many andys are involved and how far did Dave get?'

'Eight to start with,' Bryant said, consulting his clipboard. 'Dave got the first two.'

'And the remaining six are here in Northern California?'

'As far as we know. Dave thinks so. That was him I was talking to. I have his notes; they were in his desk. He says all he knows is here.' Bryant tapped the bundle of notepaper. So far he did not seem inclined to pass the notes on to Rick; for some reason he continued to leaf through them himself, frowning and working his tongue in and around the fringes of his mouth.

'I have nothing on my agenda,' Rick offered. 'I'm ready to take over in Dave's place.'

Bryant said thoughtfully, 'Dave used the Voigt-Kampff Altered Scale in testing out the individuals he suspected. You realize – you ought to, anyhow – that this test isn't specific for the new brain units. *No* test is; the Voigt scale, altered three years ago by Kampff, is all we have.' He paused, pondering. 'Dave considered it accurate. Maybe it is. But I would suggest this, before you take out after these six.' Again he tapped the pile of notes. 'Fly to Seattle and talk with the Rosen people. Have them supply you a representative sampling of types employing the new Nexus-6 unit.'

'And put them through the Voigt-Kampff,' Rick said.

'It sounds so easy,' Bryant said, half to himself.

'Pardon?'

Bryant said, 'I think I'll talk to the Rosen organization myself, while you're on your way.' He eyed Rick, then, silently. Finally he grunted, gnawed on a fingernail, and eventually decided on what he wanted to say. 'I'm going to discuss with them the possibility of including several humans, as well as their new androids. But you won't know. It'll be my decision, in conjunction with the manufacturers. It should be set up by the time you get there.' He abruptly pointed at Rick, his face severe. 'This is the first time you'll be acting as senior bounty hunter. Dave knows a lot; he's got years of experience behind him.'

'So have I,' Rick said tensely.

'You've handled assignments devolving to you from Dave's schedule; he's always decided exactly which ones to turn over to you and which not to. But now you've got six that he intended to retire himself – one of which managed to get him first. This one.' Bryant turned the notes around so that Rick could see. 'Max Polokov,' Bryant said. 'That's what it calls itself, anyhow. Assuming Dave was right. *Everything* is based on that assumption, this entire list. And yet the Voigt Kampff Altered Scale has only been administered to the first three, the two Dave retired and then Polokov. It was while Dave was administering the test; that's when Polokov lasered him.'

'Which proves that Dave was right,' Rick said. Otherwise he would not have been lasered; Polokov would have no motive.

'You get started for Seattle,' Bryant said. 'Don't tell them first: I'll handle it. Listen.' He rose to his feet, soberly confronted Rick. 'When you run the Voigt-Kampff scale up there, if one of the humans fails to pass it—'

'That can't happen,' Rick said.

'One day, a few weeks ago, I talked with Dave about exactly that. He had been thinking along the same lines. I had a memo from the Soviet police, WPO itself, circulated throughout Earth plus the colonies. A group of psychiatrists in Leningrad have approached WPO with the following proposition. They want the latest and most accurate personality profile analytical tools used in determining the presence of an android – in other words the Voigt-Kampff scale – applied to a carefully selected group of schizoid and schizophrenic human patients. Those, specifically, which reveal what's called a "flattening of affect." You've heard of that.'

Rick said, 'That's specifically what the scale measures.'

'Then you understand what they're worried about.'

'This problem has always existed. Since we first encountered androids posing as humans. The consensus of police opinion is known to you in Lurie Kampff's article, written eight years ago. *Role-taking Blockage in the Undeteriorated Schizophrenic.* Kampff compared the diminished empathic faculty found in human mental patients and a superficially similar but basically—'

'The Leningrad psychiatrists,' Bryant broke in brusquely, 'think that a small class of human beings could not pass the Voigt-Kampff scale. If you tested them in line with police work you'd assess them as humanoid robots. You'd be wrong, but by then they'd be dead.' He was silent, now, waiting for Rick's answer.

'But these individuals,' Rick said, 'would all be—'

'They'd be in institutions,' Bryant agreed. 'They couldn't

conceivably function in the outside world; they certainly couldn't go undetected as advanced psychotics – unless of course their breakdown had come recently and suddenly and no one had gotten around to noticing. *But this could happen.*'

'A million to one odds,' Rick said. But he saw the point.

'What worried Dave,' Bryant continued, 'is this appearance of the new Nexus-6 advance type. The Rosen organization assured us, as you know, that a Nexus-6 could be delineated by standard profile tests. We took their word for it. Now we're forced, as we knew we would be, to determine it on our own. That's what you'll be doing in Seattle. You understand, don't you, that this could go wrong either way. If you can't pick out all the humanoid robots, then we have no reliable analytical tool and we'll never find the ones who're already escaping. If your scale factors out a human subject, identifies him as android—' Bryant beamed at him icily. 'It would be awkward, although no one, absolutely not the Rosen people, will make the news public. Actually we'll be able to sit on it indefinitely, although of course we'll have to inform WPO and they in turn will notify Leningrad. Eventually it'll pop out of the 'papes at us. But by then we may have developed a better scale.' He picked the phone up. 'You want to get started? Use a department car and fuel yourself at our pumps.'

Standing, Rick said, 'Can I take Dave Holden's notes with me? I want to read them along the way.'

Bryant said, 'Let's wait until you've tried out your scale in Seattle.' His tone was interestingly merciless, and Rick Deckard noted it.

When he landed the police department hovercar on the roof of the Rosen Association Building in Seattle he found a young woman waiting for him. Black-haired and slender, wearing the new huge dust-filtering glasses, she approached his car, her hands deep in the pockets of her brightly striped long coat. She had, on her sharply defined small face, an expression of sullen distaste.

'What's the matter?' Rick said as he stepped from the parked car.

The girl said, obliquely, 'Oh, I don't know. Something about the way we got talked to on the phone. It doesn't matter.' Abruptly she held out her hand; he reflexively took it. 'I'm Rachael Rosen. I guess you're Mr Deckard.'

'This is not my idea,' he said.

'Yes, Inspector Bryant told us that. But you're officially the San Francisco Police Department, and it doesn't believe our unit is to the public benefit.' She eyed him from beneath long black lashes, probably artificial.

Rick said, 'A humanoid robot is like any other machine; it can fluctuate between being a benefit and a hazard very rapidly. As a benefit it's not our problem.'

'But as a hazard,' Rachael Rosen said, 'then you come in. Is it true, Mr Deckard, that you're a bounty hunter?'

He shrugged, with reluctance, nodded.

'You have no difficulty viewing an android as inert,' the girl said. 'So you can "retire" it, as they say.'

'Do you have the group selected out for me?' he said. 'I'd like to—' He broke off. Because, all at once, he had seen their animals.

A powerful corporation, he realized, would of course be able to afford this. In the back of his mind, evidently, he had anticipated such a collection; it was not surprise that he felt but more a sort of yearning. He quietly walked away from the girl, toward the closest pen. Already he could smell them, the several scents of the creatures standing or sitting, or, in the case of what appeared to be a raccoon, asleep.

Never in his life had he personally seen a raccoon. He knew

the animal only from 3-D films shown on television. For some reason the dust had struck that species almost as hard as it had the birds – of which almost none survived, now. In an automatic response he brought out his much-thumbed Sidney's and looked up raccoon with all the sublistings. The list prices, naturally, appeared in italics; like Percheron horses, none existed on the market for sale at any figure. Sidney's catalogue simply listed the price at which the last transaction involving a raccoon had taken place. It was astronomical.

'His name is Bill,' the girl said from behind him. 'Bill the raccoon. We acquired him just last year from a subsidiary corporation.' She pointed past him and he then perceived the armed company guards, standing with their machine guns, the rapid-fire little light Skoda issue; the eyes of the guards had been fastened on him since his car landed. And, he thought, my car is clearly marked as a police vehicle.

'A major manufacturer of androids,' he said thoughtfully, 'invests its surplus capital on living animals.'

'Look at the owl,' Rachael Rosen said. 'Here, I'll wake it up for you.' She started toward a small, distant cage, in the center of which jutted up a branching dead tree.

There are no owls, he started to say. Or so we've been told. Sidney's, he thought; they list it in their catalogue as extinct: the tiny, precise type, the *E*, again and again throughout the catalogue. As the girl walked ahead of him he checked to see, and he was right. Sidney's never makes a mistake, he said to himself. We know that, too. What else can we depend on?

'It's artificial,' he said, with sudden realization; his disappointment welled up keen and intense.

'No.' She smiled and he saw that she had small even teeth, as white as her eyes and hair were black.

'But Sidney's listing,' he said, trying to show her the catalogue. To prove it to her.

The girl said, 'We don't buy from Sidney's or from any animal dealer. All our purchases are from private parties and the prices we pay aren't reported.' She added, 'Also we have our own naturalists; they're now working up in Canada. There's still a good deal of forest left, comparatively speaking, anyhow. Enough for small animals and once in a while a bird.'

For a long time he stood gazing at the owl, who dozed on its perch. A thousand thoughts came into his mind, thoughts about the war, about the days when owls had fallen from the sky; he remembered how in his childhood it had been discovered that species upon species had become extinct and how the 'papes had reported it each day – foxes one morning, badgers the next, until people had stopped reading the perpetual animal obits.

He thought, too, about his need for a real animal; within him an actual hatred once more manifested itself toward his electric sheep, which he had to tend, had to care about, as if it lived. The tyranny of an object, he thought. It doesn't know I exist. Like the androids, it had no ability to appreciate the existence of another. He had never thought of this before, the similarity between an electric animal and an andy. The electric animal, he pondered, could be considered a subform of the other, a kind of vastly inferior robot. Or, conversely, the android could be regarded as a highly developed, evolved version of the ersatz animal. Both viewpoints repelled him.

'If you sold your owl,' he said to the girl Rachael Rosen, 'how much would you want for it, and how much of that down?'

'We would never sell our owl.' She scrutinized him with a mixture of pleasure and pity; or so he read her expression. 'And even if we sold it, you couldn't possibly pay the price. What kind of animal do you have at home?'

'A sheep,' he said. 'A black-faced Suffolk ewe.'

'Well, then you should be happy.'

'I'm happy,' he answered. 'It's just that I always wanted an owl, even back before they all dropped dead.' He corrected himself. 'All but yours.'

Rachael said, 'Our present crash program and overall planning call for us to obtain an additional owl which can mate with Scrappy.' She indicated the owl dozing on its perch; it had briefly opened both eyes, yellow slits which healed over as the owl settled back down to resume its slumber. Its chest rose conspicuously and fell, as if the owl, in its hypnagogic state, had sighed.

Breaking away from the sight – it made absolute bitterness blend throughout his prior reaction of awe and yearning – he said, 'I'd like to test out the selection, now. Can we go downstairs?'

'My uncle took the call from your superior and by now he probably has—'

'You're a family?' Rick broke in. 'A corporation this large is a *family* affair?'

Continuing her sentence, Rachael said, 'Uncle Eldon should have an android group and a control group set up by now. So let's go.' She strode toward the elevator, hands again thrust violently in the pockets of her coat; she did not look back, and he hesitated for a moment, feeling annoyance, before he at last trailed after her.

'What have you got against me?' he asked her as together they descended.

She reflected, as if up to now she hadn't known. 'Well,' she said, 'you, a little police department employee, are in a unique position. Know what I mean?' She gave him a malice-filled sidelong glance.

'How much of your current output,' he asked, 'consists of types equipped with the Nexus-6?'

'All,' Rachael said.

'I'm sure the Voigt-Kampff scale will work with them.'

'And if it doesn't we'll have to withdraw all Nexus-6 types from the market.' Her black eyes flamed up; she glowered at him as the elevator ceased descending and its doors slid back. 'Because you police departments can't do an adequate job in the simple matter of detecting the minuscule number of Nexus-6s who balk—'

A man, dapper and lean and elderly, approached them, hand extended; on his face a harried expression showed, as if everything recently had begun happening too fast. 'I'm Eldon Rosen,' he explained to Rick as they shook hands. 'Listen, Deckard; you realize we don't manufacture anything here on Earth, right? We can't just phone down to production and ask for a diverse flock of items; it's not that we don't want or intend to cooperate with you. Anyhow I've done the best I can.' His left hand, shakily, roved through his thinning hair.

Indicating his department briefcase, Rick said, 'I'm ready to start.' The senior Rosen's nervousness buoyed up his own confidence. They're afraid of me, he realized with a start. Rachael Rosen included. I *can* probably force them to abandon manufacture of their Nexus-6 types; what I do during the next hour will affect the structure of their operation. It could conceivably determine the future of the Rosen Association, here in the United States, in Russia, and on Mars.

The two members of the Rosen family studied him apprehensively and he felt the hollowness of their manner; by coming here he had brought the void to them, had ushered in emptiness and the hush of economic death. They control inordinate power, he thought. This enterprise is considered one of the system's industrial pivots; the manufacture of androids, in fact, has become so linked to the colonization effort that if one dropped into ruin, so would the other in time. The Rosen Association, naturally, understood this perfectly. Eldon Rosen had obviously been conscious of it since Harry Bryant's call.

'I wouldn't worry if I were you,' Rick said as the two Rosens led him down a highly illuminated wide corridor. He himself felt quietly content. This moment, more than any other which he could remember, pleased him. Well, they would all soon know what his testing apparatus could accomplish – and could not. 'If you have no confidence in the Voigt-Kampff scale,' he pointed out, 'possibly your organization should have researched an alternate test. It can be argued that the responsibility rests partly on you. Oh, thanks.' The Rosens had steered him from the corridor and into a chic, living roomish cubicle furnished with carpeting, lamps, couch, and modern little end-tables on which rested recent magazines . . . including, he noticed, the February supplement to the Sidney's catalogue, which he personally had not seen. In fact, the February supplement wouldn't be out for another three days. Obviously the Rosen Association had a special relationship with Sidney's.

Annoyed, he picked up the supplement. 'This is a violation of public trust. Nobody should get advance news of price changes.' As a matter of fact this might violate a federal statute; he tried to remember the relevant law, found he could not. 'I'm taking this with me,' he said, and, opening his briefcase, dropped the supplement within.

After an interval of silence, Eldon Rosen said wearily, 'Look, officer, it hasn't been our policy to solicit advance—'

'I'm not a peace officer,' Rick said. 'I'm a bounty hunter.' From his opened briefcase he fished out the Voigt-Kampff apparatus, seated himself at a nearby rosewood coffee table, and began to assemble the rather simple polygraphic instruments. 'You may send the first testee in,' he informed Eldon Rosen, who now looked more haggard than ever.

'I'd like to watch,' Rachael said, also seating herself. 'I've never seen an empathy test being administered. What do those things you have there measure?'

Rick said, 'This' – he held up the flat adhesive disk with its trailing wires – 'measures capillary dilation in the facial area. We know this to be a primary autonomic response, the so-called "shame" or "blushing" reaction to a morally shocking stimulus. It can't be controlled voluntarily, as can skin conductivity, respiration, and cardiac rate.' He showed her the other instrument, a pencil-beam light. 'This records fluctuations of tension within the eye muscles. Simultaneous with the blush phenomenon there generally can be found a small but detectable movement of—'

'And these can't be found in androids,' Rachael said.

'They're not engendered by the stimuli-questions; no. Although biologically they exist. Potentially.'

Rachael said, 'Give me the test.'

'Why?' Rick said, puzzled.

Speaking up, Eldon Rosen said hoarsely, 'We selected her as your first subject. She may be an android. We're hoping you can tell.' He seated himself in a series of clumsy motions, got out a cigarette, lit it and fixedly watched.

Five

The small beam of white light shone steadily into the left eye of Rachael Rosen, and against her cheek the wire-mesh disk adhered. She seemed calm.

Seated where he could catch the readings on the two gauges of the Voigt-Kampff testing apparatus, Rick Deckard said, 'I'm going to outline a number of social situations. You are to express your reaction to each as quickly as possible. You will be timed, of course.'

'And of course,' Rachael said distantly, 'my verbal responses won't count. It's solely the eye-muscle and capillary reaction that you'll use as indices. But I'll answer; I want to go through this and—' She broke off. 'Go ahead, Mr Deckard.'

Rick, selecting question three, said, 'You are given a calf-skin wallet on your birthday.' Both gauges immediately registered past the green and onto the red; the needles swung violently and then subsided.

'I wouldn't accept it,' Rachael said. 'Also I'd report the person who gave it to me to the police.'

After making a jot of notation Rick continued, turning to the eighth question of the Voigt-Kampff profile scale. 'You have a little boy and he shows you his butterfly collection, including his killing jar.'

'I'd take him to the doctor.' Rachael's voice was low but firm. Again the twin gauges registered, but this time not so far. He made a note of that, too.

'You're sitting watching TV,' he continued, 'and suddenly you discover a wasp crawling on your wrist.'

Rachael said, 'I'd kill it.' The gauges, this time, registered almost nothing: only a feeble and momentary tremor. He noted that and hunted cautiously for the next question.

'In a magazine you come across a full-page color picture of a nude girl.' He paused.

'Is this testing whether I'm an android,' Rachael asked tartly, 'or whether I'm homosexual?' The gauges did not register.

He continued, 'Your husband likes the picture.' Still the gauges failed to indicate a reaction. 'The girl,' he added, 'is lying face down on a large and beautiful bearskin rug.' The gauges remained inert, and he said to himself, An android response. Failing to detect the major element, the dead animal pelt. Her – its – mind is concentrating on other factors. 'Your husband hangs the picture up on the wall of his study,' he finishes, and this time the needles moved.

'I certainly wouldn't let him,' Rachael said.

'Okay,' he said, nodding. 'Now consider this. You're reading a novel written in the old days before the war. The characters are visiting Fisherman's Wharf in San Francisco. They become hungry and enter a seafood restaurant. One of them orders lobster, and the chef drops the lobster into the tub of boiling water while the characters watch.'

'Oh god,' Rachael said. 'That's awful! Did they really do that? It's depraved! You mean a *live* lobster?' The gauges, however, did not respond. Formally, a correct response. But simulated.

'You rent a mountain cabin,' he said, 'in an area still verdant. It's rustic knotty pine with a huge fireplace.'

'Yes,' Rachael said, nodding impatiently.

'On the walls someone has hung old maps, Currier and Ives

prints, and above the fireplace a deer's head has been mounted, a full stag with developed horns. The people with you admire the decor of the cabin and you all decide—'

'Not with the deer head,' Rachael said. The gauges, however, showed an amplitude within the green only.

'You become pregnant,' Rick continued, 'by a man who has promised to marry you. The man goes off with another woman, your best friend; you get an abortion and—'

'I would never get an abortion,' Rachael said. 'Anyhow you can't. It's a life sentence and the police are always watching.' This time both needles swung violently into the red.

'How do you know that?' Rick asked her, curiously. 'About the difficulty of obtaining an abortion?'

'Everybody knows that,' Rachael answered.

'It sounded like you spoke from personal experience.' He watched the needles intently; they still swept out a wide path across the dials. 'One more. You're dating a man and he asks you to visit his apartment. While you're there he offers you a drink. As you stand holding your glass you see into the bedroom; it's attractively decorated with bullfight posters, and you wander in to look closer. He follows after you, closing the door. Putting his arm around you, he says—'

Rachael interrupted, 'What's a bullfight poster?'

'Drawings, usually in color and very large, showing a matador with his cape, a bull trying to gore him.' He was puzzled. 'How old are you?' he asked; that might be a factor.

'I'm eighteen,' Rachael said. 'Okay; so this man closes the door and puts his arm around me. What does he say?'

Rick said, 'Do you know how bullfights ended?'

'I suppose somebody got hurt.'

'The bull, at the end, was always killed.' He waited, watching the two needles. They palpitated restlessly, nothing more. No real reading at all. 'A final question,' he said. 'Two-part.

You are watching an old movie on TV, a movie from before the war. It shows a banquet in progress; the guests are enjoying raw oysters.'

'Ugh,' Rachael said; the needles swung swiftly.

'The entrée,' he continued, 'consists of boiled dog, stuffed with rice.' The needles moved less this time, less than they had for the raw oysters. 'Are raw oysters more acceptable to you than a dish of boiled dog? Evidently not.' He put his pencil down, shut off the beam of light, removed the adhesive patch from her cheek. 'You're an android,' he said. 'That's the conclusion of the testing,' he informed her – or rather it – and Eldon Rosen, who regarded him with writhing worry; the elderly man's face contorted, shifted plastically with angry concern. 'I'm right, aren't I?' Rick said. There was no answer, from either of the Rosens. 'Look,' he said reasonably. 'We have no conflict of interest; it's important to me that the Voigt-Kampff test functions, almost as important as it is to you.'

The elder Rosen said, 'She's not an android.'

'I don't believe it,' Rick said.

'Why would he lie?' Rachael said to Rick fiercely. 'If anything, we'd lie the other way.'

'I want a bone marrow analysis made of you,' Rick said to her. 'It can eventually be organically determined whether you're android or not; it's slow and painful, admittedly, but—'

'Legally,' Rachael said, 'I can't be forced to undergo a bone marrow test. That's been established in the courts; self-incrimination. And anyhow on a live person – not the corpse of a retired android – it takes a long time. You can give that damn Voigt-Kampff profile test because of the specials; they have to be tested for constantly, and while the government was doing that you police agencies slipped the Voigt-Kampff through. But what you said is true; that's the end of the testing.' She rose to her feet, paced away from him, and stood with her hands on her hips, her back to him.

'The issue is not the legality of the bone marrow analysis,' Eldon Rosen said huskily. 'The issue is that your empathy delineation test failed in response to my niece. I can explain why she scored as an android might. Rachael grew up aboard *Salander 3*. She was born on it; she spent fourteen of her eighteen years living off its tape library and what the nine other crew members, all adults, knew about Earth. Then, as you know, the ship turned back a sixth of the way to Proxima. Otherwise Rachael would never have seen Earth – anyhow not until her later life.'

'You would have retired me,' Rachael said over her shoulder. 'In a police dragnet I would have been killed. I've known that since I got here four years ago; this isn't the first time the Voigt-Kampff test has been given to me. In fact I rarely leave this building; the risk is enormous, because of those roadblocks you police set up, those flying wedge spot checks to pick up unclassified specials.'

'And androids,' Eldon Rosen added. 'Although naturally the public isn't told that; they're not supposed to know that androids are on Earth, in our midst.'

'I don't think they are,' Rick said. 'I think the various police agencies here and in the Soviet Union have gotten them all. The population is small enough now; everyone, sooner or later, runs into a random checkpoint.' That, anyhow, was the idea.

'What were your instructions,' Eldon Rosen asked, 'if you wound up designating a human as android?'

'That's a departmental matter.' He began restoring his testing gear to his briefcase; the two Rosens watched silently. 'Obviously,' he added, 'I was told to cancel further testing, as

I'm now doing. If it failed once there's no point in going on.' He snapped the briefcase shut.

'We could have defrauded you,' Rachael said. 'Nothing forced us to admit you mistested me. And the same for the other nine subjects we've selected.' She gestured vigorously. 'All we had to do was simply go along with your test results, either way.'

Rick said, 'I would have insisted on a list in advance. A sealed-envelope breakdown. And compared my own test results for congruity. There would have had to be congruity.' And I can see now, he realized, that I wouldn't have gotten it. Bryant was right. Thank god I didn't go out bounty hunting on the basis of this test.

'Yes, I suppose you would have done that,' Eldon Rosen said. He glanced at Rachael, who nodded. 'We discussed that possibility,' Eldon said, then, with reluctance.

'This problem,' Rick said, 'stems entirely from your method of operation, Mr Rosen. Nobody forced your organization to evolve the production of humanoid robots to a point where—'

'We produced what the colonists wanted,' Eldon Rosen said. 'We followed the time-honored principle underlying every commercial venture. If our firm hadn't made these progressively more human types, other firms in the field would have. We knew the risk we were taking when we developed the Nexus-6 brain unit. *But your Voigt-Kampff test was a failure before we released that type of android.* If you had failed to classify a Nexus-6 android as an android, if you had checked it out as human – but that's not what happened.' His voice had become hard and bitingly penetrating. 'Your police department – others as well – may have retired, very probably have retired, authentic humans with underdeveloped empathic ability, such as my innocent niece here. Your position, Mr Deckard, is extremely bad morally. Ours isn't.'

'In other words,' Rick said with acuity, 'I'm not going to be given a chance to check out a single Nexus-6. You people dropped this schizoid girl on me beforehand.' And my test, he realized, is wiped out. I shouldn't have gone for it, he said to himself. However, it's too late now.

'We have you, Mr Deckard,' Rachael Rosen agreed in a quiet, reasonable voice; she turned toward him, then, and smiled.

He could not make out, even now, how the Rosen Association had managed to snare him, and so easily. Experts, he realized. A mammoth corporation like this – it embodies too much experience. It possesses in fact a sort of group mind. And Eldon and Rachael Rosen consisted of spokesmen for that corporate entity. His mistake, evidently, had been in viewing them as individuals. It was a mistake he would not make again.

'Your superior Mr Bryant,' Eldon Rosen said, 'will have difficulty understanding how you happened to let us void your testing apparatus before the test began.' He pointed toward the ceiling, and Rick saw the camera lens. His massive error in dealing with the Rosens had been recorded. 'I think the right thing for us all to do,' Eldon said, 'is sit down and—' He gestured affably. 'We can work something out, Mr Deckard. There's no need for anxiety. The Nexus-6 variety of android is a fact; we here at the Rosen Association recognize it and I think now you do, too.'

Rachael, leaning toward Rick, said, 'How would you like to own an owl?'

'I doubt if I'll ever own an owl.' But he knew what she meant; he understood the business the Rosen Association wanted to transact. Tension of a kind he had never felt before manifested itself inside him; it exploded, leisurely, in every part of his body. He felt the tension, the consciousness of what was happening, take over completely.

'But an owl,' Eldon Rosen said, 'is the thing you want.' He glanced at his niece inquiringly. 'I don't think he has any idea—'

'Of course he does,' Rachael contradicted. 'He knows exactly where this is heading. Don't you, Mr Deckard?' Again she leaned toward him, and this time closer; he could smell a mild perfume about her, almost a warmth. 'You're practically there, Mr Deckard. You practically have your owl.' To Eldon Rosen she said, 'He's a bounty hunter; remember? So he lives off the bounty he makes, not his salary. Isn't that so, Mr Deckard?'

He nodded.

'How many androids escaped this time?' Rachael inquired.

Presently he said, 'Eight. Originally. Two have already been retired, by someone else; not me.'

'You get how much for each android?' Rachael asked.

Shrugging, he said, 'It varies.'

Rachael said, 'If you have no test you can administer, then there is no way you can identify an android. And if there's no way you can identify an android there's no way you can collect your bounty. So if the Voigt-Kampff scale has to be abandoned—'

'A new scale,' Rick said, 'will replace it. This has happened before.' Three times, to be exact. But the new scale, the more modern analytical device, had been there already; no lag had existed. This time was different.

'Eventually, of course, the Voigt-Kampff scale will become obsolete,' Rachael agreed. 'But not now. We're satisfied ourselves that it will delineate the Nexus-6 types and we'd like you to proceed on that basis in your own particular, peculiar work.' Rocking back and forth, her arms tightly folded, she regarded him with intensity. Trying to fathom his reaction.

'Tell him he can have his owl,' Eldon Rosen grated.

'You can have the owl,' Rachael said, still eyeing him. 'The one up on the roof. Scrappy. But we will want to mate it if we can get our hands on a male. And any offspring will be ours; that has to be absolutely understood.'

Rick said, 'I'll divide the brood.'

'No,' Rachael said instantly; behind her Eldon Rosen shook his head, backing her up. 'That way you'd have claim to the sole bloodline of owls for the rest of eternity. And there's another condition. You can't will your owl to anybody; at your death it reverts back to the association.'

'That sounds,' Rick said, 'like an invitation for you to come in and kill me. To get your owl back immediately. I won't agree to that; it's too dangerous.'

'You're a bounty hunter,' Rachael said. 'You can handle a laser gun – in fact you're carrying one right now. If you can't protect yourself, how are you going to retire the six remaining Nexus-6 andys? They're a good deal smarter than the Grozzi Corporation's old W-4.'

'But I hunt *them*,' he said. 'This way, with a reversion clause on the owl, someone would be hunting me.' And he did not like the idea of being stalked; he had seen the effect on androids. It brought about certain notable changes, even in them.

Rachael said, 'All right; we'll yield on that. You can will the owl to your heirs. But we insist on getting the complete brood. If you can't agree to that, go on back to San Francisco and admit to your superiors in the department that the Voigt-Kampff scale, at least as administered by you, can't distinguish an andy from a human being. And then look for another job.'

'Give me some time,' Rick said.

'Okay,' Rachael said. 'We'll leave you in here, where it's comfortable.' She examined her wristwatch.

'Half an hour,' Eldon Rosen said. He and Rachael filed toward the door of the room, silently. They had said what they intended to say, he realized; the rest lay in his lap.

As Rachael started to close the door after herself and her uncle, Rick said starkly, 'You managed to set me up perfectly. You have it on tape that I missed on you; you know that my job depends on the use of the Voigt-Kampff scale; and you own that goddamn owl.'

'Your owl, dear,' Rachael said. 'Remember? We'll tie your home address around its leg and have it fly down to San Francisco; it'll meet you there when you get off work.'

It, he thought. *She keeps calling the owl it.* Not her. 'Just a second,' he said.

Pausing at the door, Rachael said, 'You've decided?'

'I want,' he said, opening his briefcase, 'to ask you one more question from the Voigt-Kampff scale. Sit down again.'

Rachael glanced at her uncle; he nodded and she grudgingly returned, seating herself as before. 'What's this for?' she demanded, her eyebrows lifted in distaste – and wariness. He perceived her skeletal tension, noted it professionally.

Presently he had the pencil of light trained on her right eye and the adhesive patch again in contact with her cheek. Rachael stared into the light rigidly, the expression of extreme distaste still manifest.

'My briefcase,' Rick said as he rummaged for the Voigt-Kampff forms. 'Nice, isn't it? Department issue.'

'Well, well,' Rachael said remotely.

'Babyhide,' Rick said. He stroked the black leather surface of the briefcase. 'One hundred percent genuine human babyhide.' He saw the two dial indicators gyrate frantically. But only after a pause. The reaction had come, but too late. He knew the reaction period down to a fraction of a second, the correct reaction period; there should have been none. 'Thanks, Miss Rosen,' he said, and gathered together the equipment again; he had concluded his retesting. 'That's all.'

'You're leaving?' Rachael asked.

'Yes,' he said. 'I'm satisfied.'

Cautiously, Rachael said, 'What about the other nine subjects?'

'The scale has been adequate in your case,' he answered. 'I can extrapolate from that; it's clearly still effective.' To Eldon Rosen, who slumped morosely by the door of the room, he said, 'Does she know?' Sometimes they didn't; false memories had been tried various times, generally in the mistaken idea that through them reactions to testing would be altered.

Eldon Rosen said, 'No. We programmed her completely. But I think toward the end she suspected.' To the girl he said, 'You guessed when he asked for one more try.'

Pale, Rachael nodded fixedly.

'Don't be afraid of him,' Eldon Rosen told her. 'You're not an escaped android on Earth illegally; you're the property of the Rosen Association, used as a sales device for prospective emigrants.' He walked to the girl, put his hand comfortingly on her shoulder; at the touch the girl flinched.

'He's right,' Rick said. 'I'm not going to retire you, Miss Rosen. Good day.' He started toward the door, then halted briefly. To the two of them he said, 'Is the owl genuine?'

Rachael glanced swiftly at the elder Rosen.

'He's leaving anyhow,' Eldon Rosen said. 'It doesn't matter; the owl is artificial. There are no owls.'

'Hmm,' Rick muttered, and stepped numbly out into the corridor. The two of them watched him go. Neither said anything. Nothing remained to say. So that's how the largest manufacturer of androids operates, Rick said to himself. Devious, and in a manner he had never encountered before. A weird and convoluted new personality type; no wonder law enforcement agencies were having trouble with the Nexus-6.

The Nexus-6. He had now come up against it. Rachael, he realized; *she must be a Nexus-6.* I'm seeing one of them for the first time. And they damn near did it; they came awfully damn close to undermining the Voigt-Kampff scale, the only method we have for detecting them. The Rosen Association does a good job – makes a good try, anyhow – at protecting its products.

And I have to face six more of them, he reflected. Before I'm finished.

He would earn the bounty money. Every cent.

Assuming he made it through alive.

Six

The TV set boomed; descending the great empty apartment building's dust-stricken stairs to the level below, John Isidore made out now the familiar voice of Buster Friendly, burbling happily to his system-wide vast audience.

'—ho ho, folks! Zip click zip! Time for a brief note on tomorrow's weather; first the Eastern seaboard of the USA. Mongoose satellite reports that fallout will be especially pronounced toward noon and then will taper off. So all you dear folks who'll be venturing out ought to wait until afternoon, eh? And speaking of waiting, it's now only ten hours 'til that big piece of news, my special exposé! Tell your friends to watch! I'm revealing something that'll amaze you. Now, you might guess that it's just the usual—'

As Isidore knocked on the apartment door the television died immediately into nonbeing. It had not merely become silent; it had stopped existing, scared into its grave by his knock.

He sensed, behind the closed door, the presence of life, beyond that of the TV. His straining faculties manufactured or else picked up a haunted, tongueless fear, by someone retreating from him, someone blown back to the farthest wall of the apartment in an attempt to evade him.

'Hey,' he called. 'I live upstairs. I heard your TV. Let's meet; okay?' He waited, listening. No sound and no motion; his words had not pried the person loose. 'I brought you a cube of margarine,' he said, standing close to the door in an effort to speak through its thickness. 'My name's J. R. Isidore and I work for the well-known animal vet Mr Hannibal Sloat; you've heard of him. I'm reputable; I have a job. I drive Mr Sloat's truck.'

The door, meagerly, opened and he saw within the apartment a fragmented and misaligned shrinking figure, a girl who cringed and slunk away and yet held onto the door, as if for physical support. Fear made her seem ill; it distorted her body lines, made her appear as if someone had broken her and then, with malice, patched her together badly. Her eyes, enormous, glazed over fixedly as she attempted to smile.

He said, with sudden understanding, 'You thought no one lived in this building. You thought it was abandoned.'

Nodding, the girl whispered, 'Yes.'

'But,' Isidore said, 'it's good to have neighbors. Heck, until you came along I didn't have any.' And that was no fun, god knew.

'You're the only one?' the girl asked. 'In this building besides me?' She seemed less timid, now; her body straightened and with her hand she smoothed her dark hair. Now he saw that she had a nice figure, although small, and nice eyes markedly established by long black lashes. Caught by surprise, the girl wore pajama bottoms and nothing more. And as he looked past her he perceived a room in disorder. Suitcases lay here and there, opened, their contents half spilled onto the littered floor. But this was natural; she had barely arrived.

'I'm the only one besides you,' Isidore said. 'And I won't bother you.' He felt glum; his offering, possessing the quality of an authentic old pre-war ritual, had not been accepted. In fact the girl did not even seem aware of it. Or maybe she did not understand what a cube of margarine was for. He had that intuition; the girl seemed more bewildered than anything else. Out of her depth and helplessly floating in now-receding circles of fear. 'Good old Buster,' he said, trying to reduce her rigid postural stance. 'You like him? I watch him every morning and then again at night when I get home; I watch him while I'm eating dinner and then his late late show until I go to bed. At least until my TV set broke.'

'Who—' the girl began and then broke off; she bit her lip as if savagely angry. Evidently at herself.

'Buster Friendly,' he explained. It seemed odd to him that this girl had never heard of Earth's most knee-slapping TV comic. 'Where did you come here from?' he asked curiously.

'I don't see that it matters.' She shot a swift glance upward at him. Something that she saw seemed to ease her concern; her body noticeably relaxed. 'I'll be glad to receive company,' she said, 'later on when I'm more moved in. Right now, of course, it's out of the question.'

'Why out of the question?' He was puzzled; everything about her puzzled him. Maybe, he thought, I've been living here alone too long. I've become strange. They say chickenheads are like that. The thought made him feel even more glum. 'I could help you unpack,' he ventured; the door, now, had virtually shut in his face. 'And your furniture.'

The girl said, 'I have no furniture. All these things' – she indicated the room behind her – 'they were here.'

'They won't do,' Isidore said. He could tell that at a glance. The chairs, the carpet, the tables – all had rotted away; they sagged in mutual ruin, victims of the despotic force of time. And of abandonment. No one had lived in this apartment for years; the ruin had become almost complete. He couldn't imagine how she figured on living in such surroundings. 'Listen,' he said earnestly. 'If we go all over the building looking we can probably find you things that aren't so tattered. A lamp from one apartment, a table from another.'

'I'll do it,' the girl said. 'Myself, thanks.'

'You'd go into those apartments *alone?*' He could not believe it.

'Why not?' Again she shuddered nervously, grimacing in awareness of saying something wrong.

Isidore said, 'I've tried it. Once. After that I just come home and go in my own place and I don't think about the rest. The apartments in which no one lives – hundreds of them and all full of the possessions people had, like family photographs and clothes. Those that died couldn't take anything and those who emigrated didn't want to. This building, except for my apartment, is completely kipple-ized.'

'Kipple-ized?' She did not comprehend.

'Kipple is useless objects, like junk mail or match folders after you use the last match or gum wrappers or yesterday's homeopape. When nobody's around, kipple reproduces itself. For instance, if you go to bed leaving any kipple around your apartment, when you wake up the next morning there's twice as much of it. It always gets more and more.'

'I see.' The girl regarded him uncertainly, not knowing whether to believe him. Not sure if he meant it seriously.

'There's the First Law of Kipple,' he said. ' "Kipple drives out nonkipple." Like Gresham's law about bad money. And in these apartments there's been nobody there to fight the kipple.'

'So it has taken over completely,' the girl finished. She nodded. 'Now I understand.'

'Your place, here,' he said, 'this apartment you've picked – it's too kipple-ized to live in. We can roll the kipple-factor back; we can do like I said, raid the other apts. But—' He broke off.

'But what?'

Isidore said, 'We can't win.'

'Why not?' The girl stepped into the hall, closing the door

behind her; arms folded self-consciously before her small high breasts she faced him, eager to understand. Or so it appeared to him, anyhow. She was at least listening.

'No one can win against kipple,' he said, 'except temporarily and maybe in one spot, like in my apartment I've sort of created a stasis between the pressure of kipple and nonkipple, for the time being. But eventually I'll die or go away, and then the kipple will again take over. It's a universal principle operating throughout the universe; the entire universe is moving toward a final state of total, absolute kipple-ization.' He added, 'Except of course for the upward climb of Wilbur Mercer.'

The girl eyed him. 'I don't see any relation.'

'That's what Mercerism is all about.' Again he found himself puzzled. 'Don't you participate in fusion? Don't you own an empathy box?'

After a pause the girl said carefully, 'I didn't bring mine with me. I assumed I'd find one here.'

'But an empathy box,' he said, stammering in his excitement, 'is the most personal possession you have! It's an extension of your body; it's the way you touch other humans, it's the way you stop being alone. But you know that. Everybody knows that. Mercer even lets people like me—' He broke off. But too late; he had already told her and he could see by her face, by the flicker of sudden aversion, that she knew. 'I almost passed the IQ test,' he said in a low, shaky voice. 'I'm not very special, only moderately; not like some you see. But that's what Mercer doesn't care about.'

'As far as I'm concerned,' the girl said, 'you can count that as a major objection to Mercerism.' Her voice was clean and neutral; she intended only to state a fact, he realized. The fact of her attitude towards chickenheads.

'I guess I'll go back upstairs,' he said, and started away from her, his cube of margarine clutched; it had become plastic and damp from the squeeze of his hand.

The girl watched him go, still with the neutral expression on her face. And then she called, 'Wait.'

Turning, he said, 'Why?'

'I'll need you. For getting myself adequate furniture. From other apartments, as you said.' She strolled toward him, her bare upper body sleek and trim, without an excess gram of fat. 'What time do you get home from work? You can help me then.'

Isidore said, 'Could you maybe fix dinner for us? If I brought home the ingredients?'

'No, I have too much to do.' The girl shook off the request effortlessly and he noticed that, perceived it without understanding it. Now that her initial fear had diminished, something else had begun to emerge from her. Something more strange. And, he thought, deplorable. A coldness. Like, he thought, a breath from the vacuum between inhabited worlds, in fact from nowhere: it was not what she did or said but what she did *not* do and say. 'Some other time,' the girl said, and moved back toward her apartment door.

'Did you get my name?' he said eagerly. 'John Isidore, and I work for—'

'You told me who you work for.' She had stopped briefly at her door; pushing it open she said, 'Some incredible person named Hannibal Sloat, who I'm sure doesn't exist outside your imagination. My name is—' She gave him one last warmthless glance as she returned to her apartment, hesitated, and said, 'I'm Rachael Rosen.'

'Of the Rosen Association?' he asked. 'The system's largest manufacturer of humanoid robots used in our colonization program?'

A complicated expression instantly crossed her face,

fleetingly, gone at once. 'No,' she said. 'I never heard of them; I don't know anything about it. More of your chickenhead imagination, I suppose. John Isidore and his personal, private empathy box. Poor Mr Isidore.'

'But your name suggests—'

'My name,' the girl said, 'is Pris Stratton. That's my married name; I always use it. I never use any other name but Pris. You can call me Pris.' She reflected, then said, 'No, you'd better address me as Miss Stratton. Because we don't really know each other. At least I don't know you.' The door shut after her and he found himself alone in the dust-strewn dim hall.

Seven

Well, so it goes, J. R. Isidore thought as he stood clutching his soft cube of margarine. Maybe she'll change her mind about letting me call her Pris. And possibly, if I can pick up a can of pre-war vegetables, about dinner, too.

But maybe she doesn't know how to cook, he thought suddenly. Okay, I can do it; I'll fix dinner for both of us. And I'll show her how so she can do it in the future if she wants. She'll probably want to, once I show her how; as near as I can make out, most women, even young ones like her, like to cook: it's an instinct.

Ascending the darkened stairs he returned to his own apartment.

She's really out of touch, he thought as he donned his white work uniform; even if he hurried he'd be late to work and Mr Sloat would be angry but so what? For instance, she's never heard of Buster Friendly. And that's impossible; Buster is the most important human being alive, except of course for Wilbur Mercer . . . but Mercer, he reflected, isn't a human being; he evidently is an archetypal entity from the stars, superimposed on our culture by a cosmic template. At least that's what I've heard people say; that's what Mr Sloat says, for instance. And Hannibal Sloat would know.

Odd that she isn't consistent about her own name, he pondered. She may need help. Can I give her any help? he asked himself. A special, a chickenhead; what do I know? I can't marry and I can't emigrate and the dust will eventually kill me. I have nothing to offer.

Dressed and ready to go he left his apartment, ascended to the roof where his battered used hovercar lay parked.

An hour later, in the company truck, he had picked up the first malfunctioning animal for the day. An electric cat: it lay in the plastic dust-proof carrying cage in the rear of the truck and panted erratically. You'd almost think it was real, Isidore observed as he headed back to the Van Ness Pet Hospital – that carefully misnamed little enterprise which barely existed in the tough, competitive field of false-animal repair.

The cat, in its travail, groaned.

Wow, Isidore said to himself. It really sounds as if it's dying. Maybe its ten-year battery has shorted, and all its circuits are systematically burning out. A major job; Milt Borogrove, Van Ness Pet Hospital's repairman, would have his hands full. And I didn't give the owner an estimate, Isidore realized gloomily. The guy simply thrust the cat at me, said it had begun failing during the night, and then I guess he took off for work. Anyhow all of a sudden the momentary verbal exchange had ceased; the cat's owner had gone roaring up into the sky in his custom new-model handsome hovercar. And the man constituted a new customer.

To the cat, Isidore said, 'Can you hang on until we reach the shop?' The cat continued to wheeze. 'I'll recharge you while we're en route,' Isidore decided; he dropped the truck toward the nearest available roof and there, temporarily parked with the motor running, crawled into the back of the truck and opened the plastic dust-proof carrying cage, which, in conjunction with his own white suit and the name on the truck, created a total impression of a true animal vet picking up a true animal.

The electric mechanism, within its compellingly authentic-style gray pelt, gurgled and blew bubbles, its vid-lenses glassy, its metal jaws locked together. This had always amazed him, these 'disease' circuits built into false animals; the construct which he now held on his lap had been put together in such a fashion that when a primary component misfired, the whole thing appeared – not broken – but organically ill. It would have fooled me, Isidore said to himself as he groped within the ersatz stomach fur for the concealed control panel (quite small on this variety of false animal) plus the quick-charge battery terminals. He could find neither. Nor could he search very long; the mechanism had almost failed. If it does consist of a short, he reflected, which is busy burning out circuits, then maybe I should try to detach one of the battery cables; the mechanism will shut down, but no more harm will be done. And then, in the shop, Milt can charge it back up.

Deftly, he ran his fingers along the pseudo bony spine. The cables should be about here. Damn expert workmanship; so absolutely perfect an imitation. Cables not apparent even under close scrutiny. Must be a Wheelright & Carpenter product – they cost more, but look what good work they do.

He gave up; the false cat had ceased functioning, so evidently the short – if that was what ailed the thing – had finished off the power supply and basic drive-train. That'll run into money, he thought pessimistically. Well, the guy evidently hadn't been getting the three-times-yearly preventive cleaning and lubricating, which made all the difference. Maybe this would teach the owner – the hard way.

Crawling back in the driver's seat he put the wheel into climb position, buzzed up into the air once more, and resumed his flight back to the repair shop.

Anyhow he no longer had to listen to the nerve-racking wheezing of the construct; he could relax. Funny, he thought;

even though I know rationally it's faked the sound of a false animal burning out its drive-train and power supply ties my stomach in knots. I wish, he thought painfully, that I could get another job. If I hadn't failed that IQ test I wouldn't be reduced to this ignominious task with its attendant emotional by-products. On the other hand, the synthetic sufferings of false animals didn't bother Milt Borogrove or their boss Hannibal Sloat. So maybe it's I, John Isidore said to himself. Maybe when you deteriorate back down the ladder of evolution as I have, when you sink into the tomb world slough of being a special – well, best to abandon that line of inquiry. Nothing depressed him more than the moments in which he contrasted his current mental powers with what he had formerly possessed. Every day he declined in sagacity and vigor. He and the thousands of other specials throughout Terra, all of them moving toward the ash heap. Turning into living kipple.

For company he clicked on the truck's radio and tuned for Buster Friendly's aud show, which, like the TV version, continued twenty-three unbroken warm hours a day . . . the additional one hour being a religious sign-off, ten minutes of silence, and then a religious sign-on.

'—glad to have you on the show again,' Buster Friendly was saying. 'Let's see, Amanda; it's been two whole days since we've visited with you. Starting on any new pics, dear?'

'Vell, I vuz goink to do a pic yestooday baht vell, dey vanted me to staht ad seven—'

'Seven A.M.?' Buster Friendly broke in.

'Yess, dot's *right*, Booster; it vuz seven hey hem!' Amanda Werner laughed her famous laugh, nearly as imitated as Buster's. Amanda Werner and several other beautiful, elegant, conically breasted foreign ladies, from unspecified vaguely defined countries, plus a few bucolic so-called humorists, comprised Buster's perpetual core of repeats. Women like Amanda Werner never made movies, never appeared in plays; they lived out their queer, beautiful lives as guests on Buster's unending show, appearing, Isidore had once calculated, as much as seventy hours a week.

How did Buster Friendly find the time to tape both his aud and vid shows? Isidore wondered. And how did Amanda Werner find time to be a guest every other day, month after month, year after year? How did they keep talking? They never repeated themselves – not so far as he could determine. Their remarks, always witty, always new, weren't rehearsed. Amanda's hair glowed, her eyes glinted, her teeth shone; she never ran down, never became tired, never found herself at a loss as to a clever retort to Buster's bang-bang string of quips, jokes, and sharp observations. The Buster Friendly Show, telecast and broadcast over all Earth via satellite, also poured down on the emigrants of the colony planets. Practice transmissions beamed to Proxima had been attempted, in case human colonization extended that far. Had the *Salander 3* reached its destination the travelers abroad would have found the Buster Friendly Show awaiting them. And they would have been glad.

But something about Buster Friendly irritated John Isidore, one specific thing. In subtle, almost inconspicuous ways, Buster ridiculed the empathy boxes. Not once but many times. He was, in fact, doing it right now.

'—no rock nicks on me,' Buster prattled away to Amanda Werner. 'And if I'm going up the side of a mountain I want a couple of bottles of Budweiser beer along!' The studio audience laughed, and Isidore heard a sprinkling of handclaps. 'And I'll reveal my carefully documented exposé from *up there* – that exposé coming exactly ten hours from now!'

'Ent me, too, dahlink!' Amanda gushed. 'Tek me wit you! I

go alonk en ven dey trow a rock et us I protek you!' Again the audience howled, and John Isidore felt baffled and impotent rage seep up into the back of his neck. Why did Buster Friendly always chip away at Mercerism? No one else seemed bothered by it; even the UN approved. And the American and Soviet police had publicly stated that Mercerism reduced crime by making citizens more concerned about the plight of their neighbors. Mankind needs more empathy, Titus Corning, the UN Secretary General, had declared several times. Maybe Buster is jealous, Isidore conjectured. Sure, that would explain it; he and Wilbur Mercer are in competition. But for what?

Our minds, Isidore decided. They're fighting for control of our psychic selves; the empathy box on one hand, Buster's guffaws and off-the-cuff jibes on the other. I'll have to tell Hannibal Sloat that, he decided. Ask him if it's true; he'll know.

When he had parked his truck on the roof of the Van Ness Pet Hospital he quickly carried the plastic cage containing the inert false cat downstairs to Hannibal Sloat's office. As he entered, Mr Sloat glanced up from a parts-inventory page, his gray, seamed face rippling like troubled water. Too old to emigrate, Hannibal Sloat, although not a special, was doomed to creep out his remaining life on Earth. The dust, over the years, had eroded him; it had left his features gray, his thoughts gray; it had shrunk him and made his legs spindly and his gait unsteady. He saw the world through glasses literally dense with dust. For some reason Sloat never cleaned his glasses. It was as if he had given up; he had accepted the radioactive dirt and it had begun its job, long ago, of burying him. Already it obscured his sight. In the few years he had remaining it would corrupt his other senses until at last only his bird-screech voice would remain, and then that would expire, too.

'What do you have there?' Mr Sloat asked.

'A cat with a short in its power supply.' Isidore set the cage down on the document-littered desk of his boss.

'Why show it to me?' Sloat demanded. 'Take it down in the shop to Milt.' However, reflexively, he opened the cage and tugged the false animal out. Once, he had been a repairman. A very good one.

Isidore said, 'I think Buster Friendly and Mercerism are fighting for control of our psychic souls.'

'If so,' Sloat said, examining the cat, 'Buster is winning.'

'He's winning now,' Isidore said, 'but ultimately he'll lose.'

Sloat lifted his head, peered at him. 'Why?'

'Because Wilbur Mercer is always renewed. He's eternal. At the top of the hill he's struck down; he sinks into the tomb world but then he rises inevitably. And us with him. So we're eternal, too.' He felt good, speaking so well; usually around Mr Sloat he stammered.

Sloat said, 'Buster is immortal, like Mercer. There's no difference.'

'How can he be? He's a man.'

'I don't know,' Sloat said. 'But it's true. They've never admitted it, of course.'

'Is that how come Buster Friendly can do forty-six hours of show a day?'

'That's right,' Sloat said.

'What about Amanda Werner and those other women?'

'They're immortal, too.'

'Are they a superior life form from another system?'

'I've never been able to determine that for sure,' Mr Sloat said, still examining the cat. He now removed his dust-filmed glasses, peered without them at the half-open mouth. 'As I have conclusively in the case of Wilbur Mercer,' he finished almost inaudibly. He cursed, then, a string of abuse lasting what seemed to Isidore a full minute. 'This cat,' Sloat said finally, 'isn't false. I knew sometime this would happen. And it's dead.' He stared down at the corpse of the cat. And cursed again.

Wearing his grimy blue sailcloth apron, burly pebble-skinned Milt Borogrove appeared at the office door. 'What's the matter?' he said. Seeing the cat he entered the office and picked up the animal.

'The chickenhead,' Sloat said, 'brought it in.' Never before had he used that term in front of Isidore.

'If it was still alive,' Milt said, 'we could take it to a real animal vet. I wonder what it's worth. Anybody got a copy of Sidney's?'

'D-doesn't y-y-your insurance c-c-cover this?' Isidore asked Mr Sloat. Under him his legs wavered and he felt the room begin to turn dark maroon cast over with specks of green.

'Yes,' Sloat said finally, half snarling. 'But it's the waste that gets me. The loss of one more living creature. Couldn't you tell, Isidore? Didn't you *notice* the difference?'

'I thought,' Isidore managed to say, 'it was a really good job. So good it fooled me; I mean, it seemed alive and a job that good—'

'I don't think Isidore can tell the difference,' Milt said mildly. 'To him they're all alive, false animals included. He probably tried to save it.' To Isidore he said, 'What did you do, try to recharge its battery? Or locate a short in it?'

'Y-yes,' Isidore admitted.

'It probably was so far gone it wouldn't have made it anyhow,' Milt said. 'Let the chickenhead off the hook, Han. He's got a point; the fakes are beginning to be darn near real, what with those disease circuits they're building into the new ones. And living animals do die; that's one of the risks in owning them. We're just not used to it because all we see are fakes.'

'The goddamn waste,' Sloat said.

'According to M-mercer,' Isidore pointed out, 'a-all life returns. The cycle is c-c-complete for a-a-animals, too. I mean, we all ascend with him, die—'

'Tell that to the guy that owned this cat,' Mr Sloat said.

Not sure if his boss was serious Isidore said, 'You mean I have to? But you always handle vidcalls.' He had a phobia about the vidphone and found making a call, especially to a stranger, virtually impossible. Mr Sloat, of course, knew this.

'Don't make him,' Milt said. 'I'll do it.' He reached for the receiver. 'What's his number?'

'I've got it here somewhere.' Isidore fumbled in his work smock pockets.

Sloat said, 'I want the chickenhead to do it.'

'I c-c-can't use the vidphone,' Isidore protested, his heart laboring. 'Because I'm hairy, ugly, dirty, stooped, snaggle-toothed, and gray. And also I feel sick from the radiation; I think I'm going to die.'

Milt smiled and said to Sloat, 'I guess if I felt that way I wouldn't use the vidphone either. Come on, Isidore; if you don't give me the owner's number I can't make the call and you'll have to.' He held out his hand amiably.

'The chickenhead makes it,' Sloat said, 'or he's fired.' He did not look either at Isidore or at Milt; he glared fixedly forward.

'Aw come on,' Milt protested.

Isidore said, 'I d-d-don't like to be c-c-called a chicken-head. I mean, the d-d-dust has d-d-done a lot to you, too, physically. Although maybe n-n-not your brain, as in m-my case.' I'm fired, he realized. I can't make the call. And then all at once he remembered that the owner of the cat had zipped off to work. There would be no one home. 'I g-guess I can call him,' he said, as he fished out the tag with the information on it.

'See?' Mr Sloat said to Milt. 'He can do it if he has to.'

Seated at the vidphone, receiver in hand, Isidore dialed.

'Yeah,' Milt said, 'but he shouldn't have to. And he's right; the dust has affected you; you're damn near blind and in a couple of years you won't be able to hear.'

Sloat said, 'It's got to you, too, Borogrove. Your skin is the color of dog manure.'

On the vidscreen a face appeared, a *mitteleuropäische* somewhat careful-looking woman who wore her hair in a tight bun. 'Yes?' she said.

'M-m-mrs Pilsen?' Isidore said, terror spewing through him; he had not thought of it naturally but the owner had a wife, who of course was home. 'I want to t-t-talk to you about your c-c-c-c-c-c—' He broke off, rubbed his chin tic-wise. 'Your cat.'

'Oh yes, you picked up Horace,' Mrs Pilsen said. 'Did it turn out to be pneumonitis? That's what Mr Pilsen thought.'

Isidore said, 'Your cat died.'

'Oh no god in heaven.'

'We'll replace it,' he said. 'We have insurance.' He glanced toward Mr Sloat; he seemed to concur. 'The owner of our firm, Mr Hannibal Sloat—' He floundered. 'Will personally—'

'No,' Sloat said, 'we'll give them a check. Sidney's list price.'

'—will personally pick the replacement cat out for you,' Isidore found himself saying. Having started a conversation which he could not endure he discovered himself unable to get back out. What he was saying possessed an intrinsic logic which he had no means of halting; it had to grind to its own conclusion. Both Mr Sloat and Milt Borogrove stared at him as he rattled on, 'Give us the specifications of the cat you desire. Color, sex, subtype, such as Manx, Persian, Abyssinian—'

'Horace is dead,' Mrs Pilsen said.

'He had pneumonitis,' Isidore said. 'He died on the trip to the hospital. Our senior staff physician, Dr Hannibal Sloat, expressed the belief that nothing at this point could have saved him. But isn't it fortunate, Mrs Pilsen, that we're going to replace him. Am I correct?'

Mrs Pilsen, tears appearing in her eyes, said, 'There is only one cat like Horace. He used to – when he was just a kitten – stand and stare up at us as if asking a question. We never understood what the question was. Maybe now he knows the answer.' Fresh tears appeared. 'I guess we all will eventually.'

An inspiration came to Isidore. 'What about an exact electric duplicate of your cat? We can have a superb hand-crafted job by Wheelright & Carpenter in which every detail of the old animal is faithfully repeated in permanent—'

'Oh that's dreadful!' Mrs Pilsen protested. 'What are you saying? Don't tell my husband that; don't suggest that to Ed or he'll go mad. He loved Horace more than any cat he ever had, and he's had a cat since he was a child.'

Taking the vidphone receiver from Isidore, Milt said to the woman, 'We can give you a check in the amount of Sidney's list, or as Mr Isidore suggested we can pick out a new cat for you. We're very sorry that your cat died, but as Mr Isidore pointed out, the cat had pneumonitis, which is almost always fatal.' His tone rolled out professionally; of the three of them at the Van Ness Pet Hospital, Milt performed the best in the matter of business phone calls.

'I can't tell my husband,' Mrs Pilsen said.

'All right, ma'am,' Milt said, and grimaced slightly. 'We'll call him. Would you give me his number at his place of employment?' He groped for a pen and pad of paper; Mr Sloat handed them to him.

'Listen,' Mrs Pilsen said; she seemed now to rally. 'Maybe the other gentleman is right. Maybe I ought to commission an electric replacement of Horace but without Ed ever knowing; could it be so faithful a reproduction that my husband wouldn't be able to tell?'

Dubiously, Milt said, 'If that's what you want. But it's been our experience that the owner of the animal is never fooled. It's only casual observers such as neighbors. You see, once you get real close to a false animal—'

'Ed never got physically close to Horace, even though he loved him; I was the one who took care of all Horace's personal needs such as his sandbox. I think I would like to try a false animal, and if it didn't work then you could find us a real cat to replace Horace. I just don't want my husband to know; I don't think he could live through it. That's why he never got close to Horace; he was afraid to. And when Horace got sick – with pneumonitis, as you tell me – Ed got panic-stricken and just wouldn't face it. That's why we waited so long to call you. Too long . . . as I knew before you called. I knew.' She nodded, her tears under control, now. 'How long will it take?'

Milt essayed, 'We can have it ready in ten days. We'll deliver it during the day while your husband is at work.' He wound up the call, said good-by, and hung up. 'He'll know,' he said to Mr Sloat. 'In five seconds. But that's what she wants.'

'Owners who get to love their animals,' Sloat said somberly, 'go to pieces. I'm glad we're not usually involved with real animals. You realize that actual animal vets have to make calls like that all the time?' He contemplated John Isidore. 'In some ways you're not so stupid after all, Isidore. You handled that reasonably well. Even though Milt had to come in and take over.'

'He was doing fine,' Milt said. 'God, that was tough.' He picked up the dead Horace. 'I'll take this down to the shop; Han, you phone Wheelright & Carpenter and get their builder over to measure and photograph it. I'm not going to let them take it to their shop; I want to compare the replica myself.'

'I think I'll have Isidore talk to them,' Mr Sloat decided. 'He got this started; he ought to be able to deal with Wheelright & Carpenter after handling Mrs Pilsen.'

Milt said to Isidore, 'Just don't let them take the original.' He held up Horace. 'They'll want to because it makes their work a hell of a lot easier. Be firm.'

'Um,' Isidore said, blinking. 'Okay. Maybe I ought to call them now before it starts to decay. Don't dead bodies decay or something?' He felt elated.

Eight

After parking the department's speedy beefed-up hovercar on the roof of the San Francisco Hall of Justice on Lombard Street, bounty hunter Rick Deckard, briefcase in hand, descended to Harry Bryant's office.

'You're back awfully soon,' his superior said, leaning back in his chair and taking a pinch of Specific No 1 snuff.

'I got what you sent me for.' Rick seated himself facing the desk. He set his briefcase down. I'm tired, he realized. It had begun to hit him, now that he had gotten back; he wondered if he would be able to recoup enough for the job ahead. 'How's Dave?' he asked. 'Well enough for me to go talk to him? I want to before I tackle the first of the andys.'

Bryant said, 'You'll be trying for Polokov first. The one that lasered Dave. Best to get him right out of it, since he knows we've got him listed.'

'Before I talk to Dave?'

Bryant reached for a sheet of onionskin paper, a blurred third or fourth carbon. 'Polokov has taken a job with the city as a trash collector, a scavenger.'

'Don't only specials do that kind of work?'

'Polokov is mimicking a special, an anthead. Very deteriorated – or so he pretends to be. That's what suckered Dave; Polokov apparently looks and acts so much like an anthead that Dave forgot. Are you sure about the Voigt-Kampff scale now? You're absolutely certain, from what happened up in Seattle, that—'

'I am,' Rick said shortly. He did not amplify.

Bryant said, 'I'll take your word for it. But there can't be even one slip-up.'

'There never could be in andy hunting. This is no different.'

'The Nexus-6 is different.'

'I already found my first one,' Rick said. 'And Dave found two. Three, if you count Polokov. Okay, I'll retire Polokov today, and then maybe tonight or tomorrow talk to Dave.' He reached for the blurred carbon, the poop sheet on the android Polokov.

'One more item,' Bryant said. 'A Soviet cop, from the WPO, is on his way here. While you were in Seattle I got a call from him; he's aboard an Aeroflot rocket that'll touch down at the public field, here, in about an hour. Sandor Kadalyi, his name is.'

'What's he want?' Rarely if ever did WPO cops show up in San Francisco.

'WPO is enough interested in the new Nexus-6 types that they want a man of theirs to be with you. An observer – and also, if he can, he'll assist you. It's for you to decide when and if he can be of value. But I've already given him permission to tag along.'

'What about the bounty?' Rick said.

'You won't have to split it,' Bryant said, and smiled creakily.

'I just wouldn't regard it as financially fair.' He had absolutely no intention of sharing his winnings with a thug from WPO. He studied the poop sheet on Polokov; it gave a description of the man – or rather the andy – and his current address and place of business: The Bay Area Scavengers Company with offices on Geary.

'Want to wait on the Polokov retirement until the Soviet cop gets here to help you?' Bryant asked.

Rick bristled. 'I've always worked alone. Of course, it's your decision – I'll do whatever you say. But I'd just as soon tackle Polokov right now, without waiting for Kadalyi to hit town.'

'You go ahead on your own,' Bryant declared. 'And then on the next one, which'll be a Miss Luba Luft – you have the sheet there on her, too – you can bring in Kadalyi.'

Having stuffed the onionskin carbons in his briefcase, Rick left his superior's office and ascended once more to the roof and his parked hovercar. And now let's visit Mr Polokov, he said to himself. He patted his laser tube.

For his first try at the android Polokov, Rick stopped off at the offices of the Bay Area Scavengers Company.

'I'm looking for an employee of yours,' he said to the severe, gray-haired switchboard woman. The scavengers' building impressed him; large and modern, it held a good number of high-class purely office employees. The deep-pile carpets, the expensive genuine wood desks, reminded him that garbage collecting and trash disposal had, since the war, become one of Earth's important industries. The entire planet had begun to disintegrate into junk, and to keep the planet habitable for the remaining population the junk had to be hauled away occasionally . . . or, as Buster Friendly liked to declare, Earth would die under a layer – not of radioactive dust – but of kipple.

'Mr Ackers,' the switchboard woman informed him. 'He's the personnel manager.' She pointed to an impressive but imitation oak desk at which sat a prissy, tiny, bespectacled individual, merged with his plethora of paperwork.

Rick presented his police ID. 'Where's your employee Polokov right now? At his job or at home?'

After reluctantly consulting his records Mr Ackers said, 'Polokov ought to be at work. Flattening hovercars at our Daly City plant and dumping them into the Bay. However—' The personnel manager consulted a further document, then picked up his vidphone and made an inside call to someone else in the building. 'He's not, then,' he said, terminating the call; hanging up he said to Rick, 'Polokov didn't show up for work today. No explanation. What's he done, officer?'

'If he should show up,' Rick said, 'don't tell him I was here asking about him. You understand?'

'Yes, I understand,' Ackers said sulkily, as if his deep schooling in police matters had been derided.

In the department's beefed-up hovercar Rick next flew to Polokov's apartment building in the Tenderloin. We'll never get him, he told himself. They – Bryant and Holden – waited too long. Instead of sending me to Seattle, Bryant should have sicced me on Polokov – better still last night, as soon as Dave Holden got his.

What a grimy place, he observed as he walked across the roof to the elevator. Abandoned animal pens, encrusted with months of dust. And, in one cage, a no longer functioning false animal, a chicken. By elevator he descended to Polokov's floor, found the hall unlit, like a subterranean cave. Using his police A-powered sealed-beam light he illuminated the hall and once again glanced over the onionskin carbon. The Voigt-Kampff test *had* been administered to Polokov; that part could be bypassed, and he could go directly to the task of destroying the android.

Best to get him from out here, he decided. Setting down his weapons kit he fumbled it open, got out a nondirectional Penfield wave transmitter; he punched the key for catalepsy, himself protected against the mood emanation by means of a counterwave broadcast through the transmitter's metal hull directed to him alone.

They're now all frozen stiff, he said to himself as he shut off the transmitter. Everyone, human and andy alike, in the vicinity. No risk to me; all I have to do is walk in and laser him. Assuming, of course, that he's in his apartment, which isn't likely.

Using an infinity key, which analysed and opened all forms of locks known, he entered Polokov's apartment, laser beam in hand.

No Polokov. Only semi-ruined furniture, a place of kipple and decay. In fact no personal articles: what greeted him consisted of unclaimed debris which Polokov had inherited when he took the apartment and which in leaving he had abandoned to the next – if any – tenant.

I knew it, he said to himself. Well, there goes the first thousand dollars bounty; probably skipped all the way to the Antarctic Circle. Out of my jurisdiction; another bounty hunter from another police department will retire Polokov and claim the money. On, I suppose, to the andys who haven't been warned, as was Polokov. On to Luba Luft.

Back again on the roof in his hovercar he reported by phone to Harry Bryant. 'No luck on Polokov. Left probably right after he lasered Dave.' He inspected his wristwatch. 'Want me to pick up Kadalyi at the field? It'll save time and I'm eager to get started on Miss Luft.' He already had the poop sheet on her laid out before him, had begun a thorough study of it.

'Good idea,' Bryant said, 'except that Mr Kadalyi is already here; his Aeroflot ship – as usual, he says – arrived early. Just a moment.' An invisible conference. 'He'll fly over and meet you where you are now,' Bryant said, returning to the screen. 'Meanwhile read up on Miss Luft.'

'An opera singer. Allegedly from Germany. At present attached to the San Francisco Opera Company.' He looked in reflexive agreement, his mind on the poop sheet. 'Must have a good voice to make connections so fast. Okay, I'll wait here for Kadalyi.' He gave Bryant his location and rang off.

I'll pose as an opera fan, Rick decided as he read further. I particularly would like to see her as Donna Anna in *Don Giovanni*. In my personal collection I have tapes by such old-time greats as Elisabeth Schwarzkopf and Lotte Lehmann and Lisa Della Casa; that'll give us something to discuss while I set up my Voigt-Kampff equipment.

His car phone buzzed. He picked up the receiver.

The police operator said, 'Mr Deckard, a call for you from Seattle; Mr Bryant said to put it through to you. From the Rosen Association.'

'Okay,' Rick said, and waited. What do they want? he wondered. As far as he could discern, the Rosens had already proven to be bad news. And undoubtedly would continue so, whatever they intended.

Rachael Rosen's face appeared on the tiny screen. 'Hello, Officer Deckard.' Her tone seemed placating; that caught his attention. 'Are you busy right now or can I talk to you?'

'Go ahead,' he said.

'We of the association have been discussing your situation regarding the escaped Nexus-6 types and knowing them as we do feel that you'll have better luck if one of us works in conjunction with you.'

'By doing what?'

'Well, by one of us coming along with you. When you go out looking for them.'

'Why? What would you add?'

Rachael said, 'The Nexus-6s would be wary at being

approached by a human. But if another Nexus-6 made the contact—'

'You specifically mean yourself.'

'Yes.' She nodded, her face sober.

'I've got too much help already.'

'But I really think you need me.'

'I doubt it. I'll think it over and call you back.' At some distant, unspecified future time, he said to himself. Or more likely never. That's all I need: Rachael Rosen popping up through the dust at every step.

'You don't really mean it,' Rachael said. 'You'll never call me. You don't realize how agile an illegal escaped Nexus-6 is, how impossible it'll be for you. We feel we owe you this because of – you know. What we did.'

'I'll take it under advisement.' He started to hang up.

'Without me,' Rachael said, 'one of them will get you before you can get it.'

'Good-by,' he said and hung up. What kind of world is it, he asked himself, when an android phones up a bounty hunter and offers him assistance? He rang the police operator back. 'Don't put any more calls through to me from Seattle,' he said.

'Yes, Mr Deckard. Has Mr Kadalyi reached you, yet?'

'I'm still waiting. And he had better hurry because I'm not going to be here long.' Again he hung up.

As he resumed reading the poop sheet on Luba Luft a hovercar taxi spun down to land on the roof a few yards off. From it a red-faced, cherubic-looking man, evidently in his mid-fifties, wearing a heavy and impressive Russian-style greatcoat, stepped and, smiling, his hand extended, approached Rick's car.

'Mr Deckard?' the man asked with a Slavic accent. 'The bounty hunter for the San Francisco Police Department?' The empty taxi rose, and the Russian watched it go, absently. 'I'm

Sandor Kadalyi,' the man said, and opened the car door to squeeze in beside Rick.

As he shook hands with Kadalyi, Rick noticed that the WPO representative carried an unusual type of laser tube, a subform which he had never seen before.

'Oh, this?' Kadalyi said. 'Interesting, isn't it?' He tugged it from his belt holster. 'I got this on Mars.'

'I thought I knew every handgun made,' Rick said. 'Even those manufactured at and for use in the colonies.'

'We made this ourselves,' Kadalyi said, beaming like a Slavic Santa, his ruddy face inscribed with pride. 'You like it? What is different about it, functionally, is – here, take it.' He passed the gun over to Rick, who inspected it expertly, by way of years of experience.

'How does it differ functionally?' Rick asked. He couldn't tell.

'Press the trigger.'

Aiming upward, out the window of the car, Rick squeezed the trigger of the weapon. Nothing happened; no beam emerged. Puzzled, he turned to Kadalyi.

'The triggering circuit,' Kadalyi said cheerfully, 'isn't attached. It remains with me. You see?' He opened his hand, revealed a tiny unit. 'And I can also direct it, within certain limits. Irrespective of where it's aimed.'

'You're not Polokov, you're Kadalyi,' Rick said.

'Don't you mean that the other way around? You're a bit confused.'

'I mean you're Polokov, the android; you're not from the Soviet police.' Rick, with his toe, pressed the emergency button on the floor of his car.

'Why won't my laser tube fire?' Kadalyi-Polokov said, switching on and off the miniaturized triggering and aiming device which he held in the palm of his hand.

'A sine wave,' Rick said. 'That phases out laser emanation and spreads the beam into ordinary light.'

'Then I'll have to break your pencil neck.' The android dropped the device and, with a snarl, grabbed with both hands for Rick's throat.

As the android's hands sank into his throat Rick fired his regulation issue old-style pistol from its shoulder holster; the .38 magnum slug struck the android in the head and its brain box burst. The Nexus-6 unit which operated it blew into pieces, a raging, mad wind which carried throughout the car. Bits of it, like the radioactive dust itself, whirled down on Rick. The retired remains of the android rocked back, collided with the car door, bounced off and struck heavily against him; he found himself struggling to shove the twitching remnants of the android away.

Shakily, he at last reached for the car phone, called in to the Hall of Justice. 'Shall I make my report?' he said. 'Tell Harry Bryant that I got Polokov.'

' "You got Polokov." He'll understand that, will he?'

'Yes,' Rick said, and hung up. Christ that came close, he said to himself. I must have overreacted to Rachael Rosen's warning; I went the other way and it almost finished me. But I got Polokov, he said to himself. His adrenal gland, by degrees, ceased pumping its several secretions into his bloodstream; his heart slowed to normal, his breathing became less frantic. But he still shook. Anyhow I made myself a thousand dollars just now, he informed himself. So it was worth it. And I'm faster to react than Dave Holden. Of course, however, Dave's experience evidently prepared me; that has to be admitted. Dave had not had such warning.

Again picking up the phone he placed a call home to his apt, to Iran. Meanwhile he managed to light a cigarette; the shaking had begun to depart.

His wife's face, sodden with the six-hour self-accusatory depression which she had prophesied, manifested itself on the vidscreen. 'Oh hello, Rick.'

'What happened to the 594 I dialed for you before I left? Pleased acknowledgment of—'

'I redialed. As soon as you left. What do you want?' Her voice sank into a dreary drone of despond. 'I'm so tired and I just have no hope left, of anything. Of our marriage and you possibly getting killed by one of those andys. Is that what you want to tell me, Rick? That an andy got you?' In the background the racket of Buster Friendly boomed and brayed, eradicating her words; he saw her mouth moving but heard only the TV.

'Listen,' he broke in. 'Can you hear me? I'm on to something. A new type of android that apparently nobody can handle but me. I've retired one already, so that's a grand to start with. You know what we're going to have before I'm through?'

Iran stared at him sightlessly. 'Oh,' she said, nodding.

'I haven't said yet!' He could tell, now; her depression this time had become too vast for her even to hear him. For all intents he spoke into a vacuum. 'I'll see you tonight,' he finished bitterly and slammed the receiver down. Damn her, he said to himself. What good does it do, my risking my life? She doesn't care whether we own an ostrich or not; nothing penetrates. I wish I had gotten rid of her two years ago when we were considering splitting up. I can still do it, he reminded himself.

Broodingly, he leaned down, gathered together on the car floor his crumpled papers, including the info on Luba Luft. No support, he informed himself. Most androids I've known have more vitality and desire to live than my wife. She has nothing to give me.

That made him think of Rachael Rosen again. Her advice to me as to the Nexus-6 mentality, he realized, turned out to be correct. Assuming she doesn't want any of the bounty money, maybe I could use her.

The encounter with Kadalyi-Polokov had changed his ideas rather massively.

Snapping on his hovercar's engine he whisked nippity-nip up into the sky, heading toward the old War Memorial Opera House, where, according to Dave Holden's notes, he would find Luba Luft this time of the day.

He wondered, now, about her, too. Some female androids seemed to him pretty; he had found himself physically attracted by several, and it was an odd sensation, knowing intellectually that they were machines but emotionally reacting anyhow.

For example Rachael Rosen. No, he decided; she's too thin. No real development, especially in the bust. A figure like a child's, flat and tame. He could do better. How old did the poop sheet say Luba Luft was? As he drove he hauled out the now wrinkled notes, found her so-called 'age.' Twenty-eight, the sheet read. Judged by appearance, which, with andys, was the only useful standard.

It's a good thing I know something about opera, Rick reflected. That's another advantage I have over Dave; I'm more culturally oriented.

I'll try one more andy before I ask Rachael for help, he decided. If Miss Luft proves exceptionally hard – but he had an intuition she wouldn't. Polokov had been the rough one; the others, unaware that anyone actively hunted them, would crumble in succession, plugged like a file of ducks.

As he descended toward the ornate, expansive roof of the opera house he loudly sang a potpourri of arias, with pseudo-Italian words made up on the spot by himself; even without the Penfield mood organ at hand his spirits brightened into optimism. And into hungry, gleeful anticipation.

Nine

In the enormous whale-belly of steel and stone carved out to form the long-enduring old opera house Rick Deckard found an echoing, noisy, slightly miscontrived rehearsal taking place. As he entered he recognized the music: Mozart's *The Magic Flute*, the first act in its final scenes. The moor's slaves – in other words the chorus – had taken up their song a bar too soon and this had nullified the simple rhythm of the magic bells.

What a pleasure; he loved *The Magic Flute*. He seated himself in a dress circle seat (no one appeared to notice him) and made himself comfortable. Now Papageno in his fantastic pelt of bird feathers had joined Pamina to sing words which always brought tears to Rick's eyes, when and if he happened to think about it.

Könnte jeder brave Mann
solche Glöckchen finden,
seine Feinde würden dann
ohne Mühe schwinden.

Well, Rick thought, in real life no such magic bells exist that make your enemy effortlessly disappear. Too bad. And Mozart, not long after writing *The Magic Flute*, had died – in his thirties – of kidney disease. And had been buried in an unmarked pauper's grave.

Thinking this he wondered if Mozart had had any intuition that the future did not exist, that he had already used up his little time. Maybe I have, too, Rick thought as he watched the rehearsal move along. This rehearsal will end, the performance will end, the singers will die, eventually the last score of the music will be destroyed in one way or another; finally the name 'Mozart' will vanish, the dust will have won. If not on this planet then another. We can evade it awhile. As the andys can evade me and exist a finite stretch longer. But I get them or some other bounty hunter gets them. In a way, he realized, I'm part of the form-destroying process of entropy. The Rosen Association creates and I unmake. Or anyhow so it must seem to them.

On the stage Papageno and Pamina engaged in a dialogue. He stopped his introspection to listen.

> Papageno: 'My child, what should we now say?'
> Pamina: 'The truth. That's what we will say.'

Leaning forward and peering, Rick studied Pamina in her heavy, convoluted robes, with her wimple trailing its veil about her shoulders and face. He re-examined the poop sheet, then leaned back, satisfied. I've now seen my third Nexus-6 android, he realized. This is Luba Luft. A little ironic, the sentiment her role calls for. However vital, active, and nice-looking, an escaped android could hardly tell the truth; about itself, anyhow.

On the stage Luba Luft sang, and he found himself surprised at the quality of her voice; it rated with that of the best, even that of notables in his collection of historic tapes. The Rosen Association built her well, he had to admit. And again he perceived himself *sub specie aeternitatis*, the form-destroyer called forth by what he heard and saw here. Perhaps the better she functions, the better a singer she is, the more I am needed. If the androids had remained substandard, like the ancient q-40s made by Derain Associates – there would be no problem and no need of my skill. I wonder when I should do it, he asked himself. As soon as possible, probably. At the end of the rehearsal when she goes to her dressing room.

At the end of the act the rehearsal ended temporarily. It would resume, the conductor said in English, French, and German, in an hour and a half. The conductor then departed; the musicians left their instruments and also left. Getting to his feet Rick made his way backstage to the dressing rooms; he followed the tail end of the cast, taking his time and thinking, It's better this way, getting it immediately over with. I'll spend as short a time talking to her and testing her as possible. As soon as I'm sure – but technically he could not be sure until after the test. Maybe Dave guessed wrong on her, he conjectured. I hope so. But he doubted it. Already, instinctively, his professional sense had responded. And he had yet to err . . . throughout years with the department.

Stopping a super he asked for Miss Luft's dressing room; the super, wearing makeup and the costume of an Egyptian spear carrier, pointed. Rick arrived at the indicated door, saw an ink-written note tacked to it reading MISS LUFT PRIVATE, and knocked.

'Come in.'

He entered. The girl sat at her dressing table, a much-handled clothbound score open on her knees, marking here and there with a ball-point pen. She still wore her costume and makeup, except for the wimple; that she had set down on its rack. 'Yes?' she said, looking up. The stage makeup enlarged her eyes; enormous and hazel they fixed on him and did not waver. 'I am busy, as you can see.' Her English contained no remnant of an accent.

Rick said, 'You compare favourably to Schwarzkopf.'

'Who are you?' Her tone held cold reserve – and that other cold, which he had encountered in so many androids. Always the same: great intellect, ability to accomplish much, but also this. He deplored it. And yet, without it, he could not track them down.

'I'm from the San Francisco Police Department,' he said.

'Oh?' The huge and intense eyes did not flicker, did not respond. 'What are you here about?' Her tone, oddly, seemed gracious.

Seating himself in a nearby chair he unzipped his briefcase. 'I have been sent here to administer a standard personality-profile test to you. It won't take more than a few minutes.'

'Is it necessary?' She gestured toward the big clothbound score. 'I have a good deal I must do.' Now she had begun to look apprehensive.

'It's necessary.' He got out the Voigt-Kampff instruments, began setting them up.

'An IQ test?'

'No. Empathy.'

'I'll have to put on my glasses.' She reached to open a drawer of her dressing table.

'If you can mark the score without your glasses you can take this test. I'll show you some pictures and ask you several questions. Meanwhile—' He got up and walked to her, and, bending, pressed the adhesive pad of sensitive grids against her deeply tinted cheek. 'And this light,' he said, adjusting the angle of the pencil beam, 'and that's it.'

'Do you think I'm an android? Is that it?' Her voice had faded almost to extinction. 'I'm not an android. I haven't even been on Mars; I've never even *seen* an android!' Her elongated lashes shuddered involuntarily; he saw her trying to appear calm. 'Do you have information that there's an android in the cast? I'd be glad to help you, and if I were an android would I be glad to help you?'

'An android,' he said, 'doesn't care what happens to another android. That's one of the indications we look for.'

'Then,' Miss Luft said, 'you must be an android.'

That stopped him; he stared at her.

'Because,' she continued, 'your job is to kill them, isn't it? You're what they call—' She tried to remember.

'A bounty hunter,' Rick said. 'But I'm not an android.'

'This test you want to give me.' Her voice, now, had begun to return. 'Have you taken it?'

'Yes.' He nodded. 'A long, long time ago; when I first started with the department.'

'Maybe that's a false memory. Don't androids sometimes go around with false memories?'

Rick said, 'My superiors know about the test. It's mandatory.'

'Maybe there was once a human who looked like you, and somewhere along the line you killed him and took his place. And your superiors don't know.' She smiled. As if inviting him to agree.

'Let's get on with the test,' he said, getting out the sheets of questions.

'I'll take the test,' Luba Luft said, 'if you'll take it first.'

Again he stared at her, stopped in his tracks.

'Wouldn't that be more fair?' she asked. 'Then I could be sure of you. I don't know; you seem so peculiar and hard and strange.' She shivered, then smiled again. Hopefully.

'You wouldn't be able to administer the Voigt-Kampff test. It takes considerable experience. Now please listen carefully. These questions will deal with social situations which you might find yourself in; what I want from you is a statement of response, what you'd do. And I want the response as quickly as you can give it. One of the factors I'll record is the time lag, if any.' He selected his initial question. 'You're sitting watching

TV and suddenly you discover a wasp crawling on your wrist.' He checked with his watch, counting the seconds. And checked, too, with the twin dials.

'What's a wasp?' Luba Luft asked.

'A stinging bug that flies.'

'Oh, how strange.' Her immense eyes widened with child-like acceptance, as if he had revealed the cardinal mystery of creation. 'Do they still exist? I've never seen one.'

'They died out because of the dust. Don't you really know what a wasp is? You must have been alive when there were wasps; that's only been—'

'Tell me the German word.'

He tried to think of the German word for wasp but couldn't. 'Your English is perfect,' he said angrily.

'My accent,' she corrected, 'is perfect. It has to be, for roles, for Purcell and Walton and Vaughn Williams. But my vocabulary isn't very large.' She glanced at him shyly.

'*Wespe*,' he said, remembering the German word.

'Ach yes; *eine Wespe*.' She laughed. 'And what was the question? I forget already.'

'Let's try another.' Impossible now to get a meaningful response. 'You are watching an old movie on TV, a movie from before the war. It shows a banquet in progress; the entrée' – he skipped over the first part of the question – 'consists of boiled dog, stuffed with rice.'

'Nobody would kill and eat a dog,' Luba Luft said. 'They're worth a fortune. But I guess it would be an imitation dog; ersatz. Right? But those are made of wires and motors; they can't be eaten.'

'Before the war,' he grated.

'I wasn't alive before the war.'

'But you've seen old movies on TV.'

'Was the movie made in the Philippines?'

'Why?'

'Because,' Luba Luft said, 'they used to eat boiled dog stuffed with rice in the Philippines. I remember reading that.'

'But your response,' he said. 'I want your social, emotional, moral reaction.'

'To the movie?' She pondered. 'I'd turn it off and watch Buster Friendly.'

'Why would you turn it off?'

'Well,' she said hotly, 'who the hell wants to watch an old movie set in the Philippines? What ever happened in the Philippines except the Bataan Death March, and would you want to watch that?' She glared at him indignantly. On his dials the needle swung in all directions.

After a pause he said carefully, 'You rent a mountain cabin.'

'*Ja.*' She nodded. 'Go on; I'm waiting.'

'In an area still verdant.'

'Pardon?' She cupped her ear. 'I don't ever hear that term.'

'Still trees and bushes growing. The cabin is rustic knotty pine with a huge fireplace. On the walls someone has hung old snaps, Currier and Ives prints, and above the fireplace a deer's head has been mounted, a full stag with developed horns. The people with you admire the decor of the cabin and—'

'I don't understand "Currier" or "Ives," or "decor," ' Luba Luft said; she seemed to be struggling, however, to make out the terms. 'Wait.' She held up her hand earnestly. 'With rice, like in the dog. Currier is what makes the rice currier rice. It's *Curry* in German.'

He could not fathom, for the life of him, if Luba Luft's semantic fog had purpose. After consultation with himself he decided to try another question; what else could he do? 'You're dating a man,' he said, 'and he asks you to visit his apartment. While you're there—'

'*O nein*,' Luba broke in. 'I wouldn't be there. That's easy to answer.'

'That's not the question!'

'Did you get the wrong question? But I understand that; why is a question I understand the wrong one? Aren't I *supposed* to understand?' Nervously fluttering she rubbed her cheek – and detached the adhesive disk. It dropped to the floor, skidded, and rolled under her dressing table. '*Ach Gott*,' she muttered, bending to retrieve it. A ripping sound, that of cloth tearing. Her elaborate costume.

'I'll get it,' he said, and lifted her aside; he knelt down, groped under the dressing table until his fingers located the disk.

When he stood up he found himself looking into a laser tube.

'Your questions,' Luba Luft said in a crisp, formal voice, 'began to do with sex. I thought they would finally. You're not from the police department; you're a sexual deviant.'

'You can look at my identification.' He reached toward his coat pocket. His hand, he saw, had again begun to shake, as it had with Polokov.

'If you reach in there,' Luba Luft said, 'I'll kill you.'

'You will anyhow.' He wondered how it would have worked out if he had waited until Rachael Rosen could join him. Well, no use dwelling on that.

'Let me see some more of your questions.' She held out her hand and, reluctantly, he passed her the sheets. ' "In a magazine you come across a full-page color picture of a nude girl." Well, that's one. "You became pregnant by a man who has promised to marry you. The man goes off with another woman, your best friend; you get an abortion." The pattern of your questioning is obvious. I'm going to call the police.' Still holding the laser tube in his direction she crossed the room, picked up the vidphone, dialed the operator. 'Connect me with the San Francisco Police Department,' she said. 'I need a policeman.'

'What you're doing,' Rick said, with relief, 'is the best idea possible.' Yet it seemed strange to him that Luba had decided to do this; why didn't she simply kill him? Once the patrolman arrived her chance would disappear and it all would go his way.

She must think she's human, he decided. Obviously she doesn't know.

A few minutes later, during which Luba carefully kept the laser tube on him, a large harness bull arrived in his archaic blue uniform with gun and star. 'All right,' he said at once to Luba. 'Put that thing away.' She set down the laser tube and he picked it up to examine it, to see if it carried a charge. 'Now what's been going on here?' he asked her. Before she could answer he turned to Rick. 'Who are you?' he demanded.

Luba Luft said, 'He came into my dressing room; I've never seen him before in my life. He pretended to be taking a poll or something and he wanted to ask me questions; I thought it was all right and I said okay, and then he began asking me obscene questions.'

'Let's see your identification,' the harness bull said to Rick, his hand extended.

As he got out his ID Rick said, 'I'm a bounty hunter with the department.'

'I know all the bounty hunters,' the harness bull said as he examined Rick's wallet. 'With the S. F. Police Department?'

'My supervisor is Inspector Harry Bryant,' Rick said. 'I've taken over Dave Holden's list, now that Dave's in the hospital.'

'As I say, I know all the bounty hunters,' the harness bull said, 'and I've never heard of you.' He handed Rick's ID back to him.

'Call Inspector Bryant,' Rick said.

'There isn't any Inspector Bryant,' the harness bull said.

It came to Rick what was going on. 'You're an android,' he said to the harness bull. 'Like Miss Luft.' Going to the vidphone he picked up the receiver himself. 'I'm going to call the department.' He wondered how far he would get before the two androids stopped him.

'The number,' the harness bull said, 'is—'

'I know the number.' Rick dialed, presently had the police switchboard operator. 'Let me talk to Inspector Bryant,' he said.

'Who is calling, please?'

'This is Rick Deckard.' He stood waiting; meanwhile, off to one side, the harness bull was getting a statement from Luba Luft; neither paid any attention to him.

A pause and then Harry Bryant's face appeared on the vidscreen. 'What's doing?' he asked Rick.

'Some trouble,' Rick said. 'One of those on Dave's list managed to call in and get a so-called patrolman out here. I can't seem to prove to him who I am; he says he knows all the bounty hunters in the department and he's never heard of me.' He added, 'He hasn't heard of you either.'

Bryant said, 'Let me talk to him.'

'Inspector Bryant wants to talk to you.' Rick held out the vidphone receiver. The harness bull ceased questioning Miss Luft and came over to take it.

'Officer Crams,' the harness bull said briskly. A pause. 'Hello?' He listened, said hello several times more, waited, then turned to Rick. 'There's nobody on the line. And nobody on the screen.' He pointed to the vidphone screen and Rick saw nothing on it.

Taking the receiver from the harness bull Rick said, 'Mr Bryant?' He listened, waited; nothing. 'I'll dial again.' He hung up, waited, then redialled the familiar number. The phone rang, but no one answered it; the phone rang on and on.

'Let me try,' Officer Crams said, taking the receiver away from Rick. 'You must have misdialed.' He dialed. 'The number is 842—'

'I know the number,' Rick said.

'Officer Crams calling in,' the harness bull said into the phone receiver. 'Is there an Inspector Bryant connected with the department?' A short pause. 'Well, what about a bounty hunter named Rick Deckard?' Again a pause. 'You're sure? Could he have recently – oh, I see; okay, thanks. No, I have it under control.' Officer Crams rang off, turned toward Rick.

'I had him on the line,' Rick said. 'I talked to him; he said he'd talk to you. It must be phone trouble; the connection must have been broken somewhere along the way. Didn't you see – Bryant's face showed on the screen and then it didn't.' He felt bewildered.

Officer Crams said, 'I have Miss Luft's statement, Deckard. So let's go down to the Hall of Justice so I can book you.'

'Okay,' Rick said. To Luba Luft he said, 'I'll be back in a short while. I'm still not finished testing you.'

'He's a deviant,' Luba Luft said to Officer Crams. 'He gives me the creeps.' She shivered.

'What opera are you practicing to give?' Officer Crams asked her.

'*The Magic Flute*,' Rick said.

'I didn't ask you; I asked her.' The harness bull gave him a glance of dislike.

'I'm anxious to get to the Hall of Justice,' Rick said. 'This matter should be straightened out.' He started toward the door of the dressing room, his briefcase gripped.

'I'll search you first.' Officer Crams deftly frisked him,

and came up with Rick's service pistol and laser tube. He appropriated both, after a moment of sniffing the muzzle of the pistol. 'This has been fired recently,' he said.

'I retired an andy just now,' Rick said. 'The remains are still in my car, up on the roof.'

'Okay,' Officer Crams said. 'We'll go up and have a look.'

As the two of them started from the dressing room, Miss Luft followed as far as the door. 'He won't come back again, will he, Officer? I'm really afraid of him; he's so strange.'

'If he's got the body of someone he killed upstairs in his car,' Crams said, 'he won't be coming back.' He nudged Rick forward and, together, the two of them ascended by elevator to the roof of the opera house.

Opening the door of Rick's car, Officer Crams silently inspected the body of Polokov.

'An android,' Rick said. 'I was sent after him. He almost got me by pretending to be—'

'They'll take your statement at the Hall of Justice,' Officer Crams interrupted. He nudged Rick over to his parked, plainly marked police car; there, by police radio, he put in a call for someone to come pick up Polokov. 'Okay, Deckard,' he said, then, ringing off. 'Let's get started.'

With the two of them aboard, the patrol car zummed up from the roof and headed south.

Something, Rick noticed, was not as it should be. Officer Crams had steered the car in the wrong direction.

'The Hall of Justice,' Rick said, 'is north, on Lombard.'

'That's the old Hall of Justice,' Officer Crams said. 'The new one is on Mission. That old building, it's disintegrating; it's a ruin. Nobody's used that for years. Has it been that long since you last got booked?'

'Take me there,' Rick said. 'To Lombard Street.' He understood it all, now; saw what the androids, working together, had achieved. He would not live beyond this ride; for him it was the end, as it had almost been for Dave – and probably eventually would be.

'That girl's quite a looker,' Officer Crams said. 'Of course, with that costume you can't tell about her figure. But I'd say it's damn okay.'

Rick said, 'Admit to me that you're an android.'

'Why? I'm not an android. What do you do, roam around killing people and telling yourself they're androids? I can see why Miss Luft was scared. It's a good thing for her that she called us.'

'Then take me to the Hall of Justice, on Lombard.'

'Like I said—'

'It'll take about three minutes,' Rick said. 'I want to see it. Every morning I check in for work, there; I want to see that it's been abandoned for years, as you say.'

'Maybe you're an android,' Officer Crams said. 'With a false memory, like they give them. Had you thought of that?' He grinned frigidly as he continued to drive south.

Conscious of his defeat and failure, Rick settled back, and, helplessly, waited for what came next. Whatever the androids had planned, now that they had physical possession of him.

But I did get one of them, he told himself; I got Polokov. And Dave got two.

Hovering over Mission, Officer Crams's police car prepared to descend for its landing.

Ten

The Mission Street Hall of Justice building, onto the roof of which the hovercar descended, jutted up in a series of baroque, ornamented spires; complicated and modern, the handsome structure struck Rick Deckard as attractive – except for one aspect. He had never seen it before.

The police hovercar landed. And, a few minutes later, he found himself being booked.

'304,' Officer Crams said to the sergeant at the high desk. 'And 612.4 and let's see. Representing himself to be a peace officer.'

'406.7,' the desk sergeant said, filling out the forms; he wrote leisurely, in a slightly bored manner. Routine business, his posture and expression declared. Nothing of importance.

'Over here,' Officer Crams said to Rick, leading him to a small white table at which a technician operated familiar equipment. 'For your cephalic pattern,' Crams said. 'Ident-purposes.'

Rick said brusquely, 'I know.' In the old days, when he had been a harness bull himself, he had brought many suspects to a table like this. *Like* this, but not this particular table.

His cephalic pattern taken, he found himself being led off to an equally familiar room; reflexively he began assembling his valuables for transfer. It makes no sense, he said to himself. Who are these people? If this place has always existed, *why didn't we know about it?* And why don't they know about us? Two parallel police agencies, he said to himself; ours and this one. But never coming in contact – as far as I know – until now. Or maybe they have, he thought. Maybe this isn't the first time. Hard to believe, he thought, that this wouldn't have happened long ago. If this really is a police apparatus, here; if it's what it asserts itself to be.

A man, not in uniform, detached himself from the spot at which he had been standing; he approached Rick Deckard at a measured, unruffled pace, gazing at him curiously. 'What's this one?' he asked Officer Crams.

'Suspected homicide,' Crams answered. 'We have a body – we found it in his car – but he claims it's an android. We're checking it out, giving it a bone marrow analysis at the lab. And posing as a police officer, a bounty hunter. To gain access to a woman's dressing room in order to ask her suggestive questions. She doubted he was what he said he was and called us in.' Stepping back, Crams said, 'Do you want to finish up with him, sir?'

'All right.' The senior police official, not in uniform, blue-eyed, with a narrow, flaring nose and inexpressive lips, eyed Rick, then reached for Rick's briefcase. 'What do you have in here, Mr Deckard?'

Rick said, 'Material pertaining to the Voigt-Kampff personality test. I was testing a suspect when Officer Crams arrested me.' He watched as the police official rummaged through the contents of the briefcase, examining each item. 'The questions I asked Miss Luft are standard V-K questions, printed on the—'

'Do you know George Gleason and Phil Resch?' the police official asked.

'No,' Rick said; neither name meant anything to him.

'They're the bounty hunters for Northern California. Both are attached to our department. Maybe you'll run into them while you're here. Are you an android, Mr Deckard? The reason I ask is that several times in the past we've had escaped andys turn up posing as out-of-state bounty hunters here in pursuit of a suspect.'

Rick said, 'I'm not an android. You can administer the Voigt-Kampff test to me; I've taken it before and I don't mind taking it again. But I know what the results will be. Can I phone my wife?'

'You're allowed one call. Would you rather phone her than a lawyer?'

'I'll phone my wife,' Rick said. 'She can get a lawyer for me.'

The plainclothes police officer handed him a fifty-cent piece and pointed. 'There's the vidphone over there.' He watched as Rick crossed the room to the phone. Then he returned to his examination of the contents of Rick's briefcase.

Inserting the coin, Rick dialed his home phone number. And stood for what seemed like an eternity, waiting.

A woman's face appeared on the vidscreen. 'Hello,' she said.

It was not Iran. He had never seen the woman before in his life.

He hung up, walked slowly back to the police officer.

'No luck?' the officer asked. 'Well, you can make another call; we have a liberal policy in that regard. I can't offer you the opportunity of calling a bondsman because your offense is unbailable, at present. When you're arraigned, however—'

'I know,' Rick said acridly. 'I'm familiar with police procedure.'

'Here's your briefcase,' the officer said; he handed it back to Rick. 'Come into my office . . . I'd like to talk with you further.' He started down a side hall, leading the way; Rick followed. Then, pausing and turning, the officer said, 'My name is Garland.' He held out his hand and they shook.

Briefly. 'Sit down,' Garland said as he opened his office door and pushed behind a large uncluttered desk.

Rick seated himself facing the desk.

'This Voigt-Kampff test,' Garland said, 'that you mentioned.' He indicated Rick's briefcase. 'All that material you carry.' He filled and lit a pipe, puffed for a moment. 'It's an analytical tool for detecting andys?'

'It's our basic test,' Rick said. 'The only one we currently employ. The only one capable of distinguishing the new Nexus-6 brain unit. You haven't heard of this test?'

'I've heard of several profile-analysis scales for use with androids. But not that one.' He continued to study Rick intently, his face turgid; Rick could not fathom what Garland was thinking. 'Those smudged carbon flimsies,' Garland continued, 'that you have there in your briefcase. Polokov, Miss Luft . . . your assignments. The next one is me.'

Rick stared at him, then grabbed for the briefcase.

In a moment the carbons lay spread out before him. Garland had told the truth; Rick examined the sheet. Neither man – or rather neither he nor Garland – spoke for a time and then Garland cleared his throat, coughed nervously.

'It's an unpleasant sensation,' he said. 'To find yourself a bounty hunter's assignment all of a sudden. Or whatever it is you are, Deckard.' He pressed a key on his desk intercom and said, 'Send one of the bounty hunters in here; I don't care which one. Okay; thank you.' He released the key. 'Phil Resch will be in here in a minute or so from now,' he said to Rick. 'I want to see his list before I proceed.'

'You think I might be on his list?' Rick said.

'It's possible. We'll know pretty soon. Best to be sure about these critical matters. Best not to leave it to chance. This info sheet about me.' He indicated the smudged carbon. 'It doesn't list me as a police inspector; it inaccurately gives my occupation as insurance underwriter. Otherwise it's correct, as to physical description, age, personal habits, home address. Yes, it's me, all right. Look for yourself.' He pushed the page to Rick, who picked it up and glanced over it.

The office door opened and a tall, fleshless man with hard-etched features, wearing horn-rim glasses and a fuzzy Van-dyke beard, appeared. Garland rose, indicating Rick.

'Phil Resch, Rick Deckard. You're both bounty hunters and it's probably time you met.'

As he shook hands with Rick, Phil Resch said, 'Which city are you attached to?'

Garland answered for Rick. 'San Francisco. Here; take a look at his schedule. This one comes up next.' He handed Phil Resch the sheet which Rick had been examining, that with his own description.

'Say, Gar,' Phil Resch said. 'This is you.'

'There's more,' Garland said. 'He's also got Luba Luft the opera singer there on his list of retirement-assignments, and Polokov. Remember Polokov? He's now dead; this bounty hunter or android or whatever he is got him, and we're running a bone marrow test at the lab. To see if there's any conceivable basis '

'Polokov I've talked to,' Phil Resch said. 'That big Santa Claus from the Soviet police?' He pondered, plucking at his disarrayed beard. 'I think it's a good idea to run a bone marrow test on him.'

'Why do you say that?' Garland asked, clearly annoyed. 'It's to remove any legal basis on which this man Deckard could claim he hadn't killed anyone; he only "retired an android."'

Phil Resch said, 'Polokov struck me as cold. Extremely cerebral and calculating; detached.'

'A lot of the Soviet police are that way,' Garland said, visibly nettled.

'Luba Luft I never met,' Phil Resch said. 'Although I've heard records she's made.' To Rick he said, 'Did you test her out?'

'I started to,' Rick said. 'But I couldn't get an accurate reading. And she called in a harness bull, which ended it.'

'And Polokov?' Phil Resch asked.

'I never got a chance to test him either.'

Phil Resch said, mostly to himself, 'And I assume you haven't had an opportunity to test out Inspector Garland, here.'

'Of course not,' Garland interjected, his face wrinkled with indignation; his words broke off, bitter and sharp.

'What test do you use?' Phil Resch asked.

'The Voigt-Kampff scale.'

'Don't know that particular one.' Both Resch and Garland seemed deep in rapid, professional thought – but not in unison. 'I've always said,' he continued, 'that the best place for an android would be with a big police organization such as WPO. Ever since I first met Polokov I've wanted to test him, but no pretext ever arose. It never would have, either . . . which is one of the values such a spot would have for an enterprising android.'

Getting slowly to his feet Inspector Garland faced Phil Resch and said, 'Have you wanted to test me, too?'

A discreet smile traveled across Phil Resch's face; he started to answer, then shrugged. And remained silent. He did not seem afraid of his superior, despite Garland's palpable wrath.

'I don't think you understand the situation,' Garland said. 'This man – or android – Rick Deckard comes to us from a phantom, hallucinatory, nonexistent police agency allegedly operating out of the old departmental headquarters on Lombard. He's never heard of us and we've never heard of him – yet ostensibly we're both working the same side of the street.

He employs a test we've never heard of. The list he carries around isn't of androids; it's a list of human beings. He's already killed once – at least once. And if Miss Luft hadn't gotten to a phone he probably would have killed her and then eventually he would have come sniffing around after me.'

'Hmm,' Phil Resch said.

'Hmm,' Garland mimicked, wrathfully. He looked, now, as if he bordered on apoplexy. 'Is that all you have to say?'

The intercom came on and a female voice said, 'Inspector Garland, the lab report on Mr Polokov's corpse is ready.'

'I think we should hear it,' Phil Resch said.

Garland glanced at him, seething. Then he bent, pressed the key of the intercom. 'Let's have it, Miss French.'

'The bone marrow test,' Miss French said, 'shows that Mr Polokov was a humanoid robot. Do you want a detailed—'

'No, that's enough.' Garland settled back in his seat, grimly contemplating the far wall; he said nothing to either Rick or Phil Resch.

Resch said, 'What is the basis of your Voigt-Kampff test, Mr Deckard?'

'Empathic response. In a variety of social situations. Mostly having to do with animals.'

'Ours is probably simpler,' Resch said. 'The reflex-arc response taking place in the upper ganglia of the spinal column requires several microseconds more in the humanoid robot than in a human nervous system.' Reaching across Inspector Garland's desk he plucked a pad of paper toward him; with a ball-point pen he drew a sketch. 'We use an audio signal or a light-flash. The subject presses a button and the elapsed time is measured. We try it a number of times, of course. Elapsed time varies in both the andy and the human. But by the time ten reactions have been measured, we believe we have a reliable clue. And, as in your case with Polokov, the bone marrow test backs us up.'

An interval of silence passed and then Rick said, 'You can test me out. I'm ready. Of course I'd like to test you, too. If you're willing.'

'Naturally,' Resch said. He was, however, studying Inspector Garland. 'I've said for years,' Resch murmured, 'that the Boneli Reflex-Arc Test should be applied routinely to police personnel, the higher up the chain of command the better. Haven't I, Inspector?'

'That's right you have,' Garland said. 'And I've always opposed it. On the grounds that it would lower department morale.'

'I think now,' Rick said, 'you're going to have to sit still for it. In view of your lab's report on Polokov.'

Eleven

Garland said, 'I guess so.' He jabbed a finger at the bounty hunter Phil Resch. 'But I'm warning you: you're not going to like the results of the tests.'

'Do you know what they'll be?' Resch asked, with visible surprise; he did not look pleased.

'I know almost to a hair,' Inspector Garland said.

'Okay.' Resch nodded. 'I'll go upstairs and get the Boneli gear.' He strode to the door of the office, opened it, and disappeared out into the hall. 'I'll be back in three or four minutes,' he said to Rick. The door shut after him.

Reaching into the right-hand top drawer of his desk, Inspector Garland fumbled about, then brought forth a laser tube; he swiveled it until it pointed at Rick.

'That's not going to make any difference,' Rick said. 'Resch will have a postmortem run on me, the same as your lab ran on Polokov. And he'll still insist on a – what did you call it – Boneli Reflex-Arc Test on you and on himself.'

The laser tube remained in its position, and then Inspector Garland said, 'It was a bad day all day. Especially when I saw Officer Crams bringing you in; I had an intuition – that's why I intervened.' By degrees he lowered the laser beam; he sat gripping it and then he shrugged and returned it to the desk drawer, locking the drawer and restoring the key to his pocket.

'What will tests on the three of us show?' Rick asked.

Garland said, 'That damn fool Resch.'

'He actually doesn't know?'

'He doesn't know; he doesn't suspect; he doesn't have the slightest idea. Otherwise he couldn't live out a life as a bounty hunter, a human occupation – hardly an android occupation.' Garland gestured toward Rick's briefcase. 'Those other carbons, the other suspects you're supposed to test and retire. I know them all.' He paused, then said, 'We all came here together on the same ship from Mars. Not Resch; he stayed behind another week, receiving the synthetic memory system.' He was silent, then.

Or rather it was silent.

Rick said, 'What'll he do when he finds out?'

'I don't have the foggiest idea,' Garland said remotely. 'It ought, from an abstract, intellectual viewpoint, to be interesting. He may kill me, kill himself; maybe you, too. He may kill everyone he can, human and android alike. I understand that such things happen, when there's been a synthetic memory system laid down. When one thinks it's human.'

'So when you do that, you're taking a chance.'

Garland said, 'It's a chance anyway, breaking free and coming here to Earth, where we're not even considered animals. Where every worm and wood louse is considered more desirable than all of us put together.' Irritably, Garland picked at his lower lip. 'Your position would be better if Phil Resch could pass the Boneli test, if it was just me. The results, that way, would be predictable; to Resch I'd just be another andy to retire as soon as possible. So you're not in a good position either, Deckard. Almost as bad, in fact, as I am. You know where I guessed wrong? I didn't know about Polokov. He must have come here earlier; *obviously* he came here earlier. In another group entirely – no contact with ours. He was already entrenched in the WPO when I arrived. I took a chance on the lab report, which I shouldn't have. Crams, of course, took the same chance.'

'Polokov was almost my finish, too,' Rick said.

'Yes, there was something about him. I don't think he could have been the same brain unit type as we; he must have been souped up or tinkered with – an altered structure, unfamiliar even to us. A good one, too. Almost good enough.'

'When I phoned my apartment,' Rick said, 'why didn't I get my wife?'

'All our vidphone lines here are trapped. They recirculate the call to other offices within the building. This is a homeostatic enterprise we're operating here, Deckard. We're a closed loop, cut off from the rest of San Francisco. We know about them but they don't know about us. Sometimes an isolated person such as yourself wanders in here or, as in your case, is brought here – for our protection.' He gestured convulsively toward the office door. 'Here comes eager-beaver Phil Resch back with his handy dandy portable little test. Isn't he clever? He's going to destroy his own life and mine and possibly yours.'

'You androids,' Rick said, 'don't exactly cover for each other in times of stress.'

Garland snapped, 'I think you're right; it would seem we lack a specific talent you humans possess. I believe it's called empathy.'

The office door opened; Phil Resch stood outlined, carrying a device which trailed wires. 'Here we are,' he said, closing the door after him; he seated himself, plugging the device into the electrical outlet.

Bringing out his right hand, Garland pointed at Resch. At once Resch – and also Rick Deckard – rolled from their chairs and onto the floor; at the same time, Resch yanked a laser tube and, as he fell, fired at Garland.

The laser beam, aimed with skill, based on years of training, bifurcated Inspector Garland's head. He slumped forward and, from his hand, his miniaturized laser beam rolled across the surface of his desk. The corpse teetered on its chair and then, like a sack of eggs, it slid to one side and crashed to the floor.

'It forgot,' Resch said, rising to his feet, 'that this is my job. I can almost foretell what an android is going to do. I suppose you can, too.' He put his laser beam away, bent, and, with curiosity, examined the body of his quondam superior. 'What did it say to you while I was gone?'

'That he – it – was an android. And you—' Rick broke off, the conduits of his brain humming, calculating, and selecting; he altered what he had started to say. '—would detect it,' he finished. 'In a few more minutes.'

'Anything else?'

'This building is android-infested.'

Resch said introspectively, 'That's going to make it hard for you and me to get out of here. Nominally I have the authority to leave any time I want, of course. And to take a prisoner with me.' He listened; no sound came from beyond the office. 'I guess they didn't hear anything. There's evidently no bug installed here, monitoring everything . . . as there should be.' Gingerly, he nudged the body of the android with the toe of his shoe. 'It certainly is remarkable, the psionic ability you develop in this business; I knew before I opened the office door that he would take a shot at me. Frankly I'm surprised he didn't kill you while I was upstairs.'

'He almost did,' Rick said. 'He had a big utility-model laser beam on me part of the time. He was considering it. But it was you he was worried about, not me.'

'The android flees,' Resch said humorlessly, 'where the bounty hunter pursues. You realize, don't you, that you're going to have to double back to the opera house and get Luba

Luft before anyone here has a chance to warn her as to how this came out. Warn it, I should say. Do you think of them as "it"?'

'I did at one time,' Rick said. 'When my conscience occasionally bothered me about the work I had to do; I protected myself by thinking of them that way but now I no longer find it necessary. All right, I'll head directly back to the opera house. Assuming you can get me out of here.'

'Suppose we sit Garland up at his desk,' Resch said; he dragged the corpse of the android back up into its chair, arranging its arms and legs so that its posture appeared reasonably natural – if no one looked closely. If no one came into the office. Pressing a key on the desk intercom, Phil Resch said, 'Inspector Garland has asked that no calls be put through to him for the next half hour. He's involved in work that can't be interrupted.'

'Yes, Mr Resch.'

Releasing the intercom key, Phil Resch said to Rick, 'I'm going to handcuff you to me during the time we're still here in the building. Once we're airborne I'll naturally let you go.' He produced a pair of cuffs, slapped one onto Rick's wrist and the other around his wrist. 'Come on; let's get it over with.' He squared his shoulders, took a deep breath, and pushed open the office door.

Uniformed police stood or sat on every side, conducting their routine business of the day; none of them glanced up or paid any attention as Phil Resch led Rick across the lobby to the elevator.

'What I'm afraid of,' Resch said as they waited for the elevator, 'is that the Garland one had a dead man's throttle warning component built into it. But—' He shrugged. 'I would have expected it to go off by now; otherwise it's not much good.'

The elevator arrived; several police-like nondescript men and women disemelevatored, clacked off across the lobby on their several errands. They paid no attention to Rick or Phil Resch.

'Do you think your department will take me on?' Resch asked, as the elevator doors shut, closing the two of them inside; he punched the roof button and the elevator silently rose. 'After all, as of now I'm out of a job. To say the least.'

Guardedly, Rick said, 'I – don't see why not. Except that we already have two bounty hunters.' I've got to tell him, he said to himself. It's unethical and cruel not to. Mr Resch, you're an android, he thought to himself. You got me out of this place and here's your reward; you're everything we jointly abominate. The essence of what we're committed to destroy.

'I can't get over it,' Phil Resch said. 'It doesn't seem possible. For three years I've been working under the direction of androids. Why didn't I suspect – I mean, enough to do something?'

'Maybe it isn't that long. Maybe they only recently infiltrated this building.'

'They've been here all the time. Garland has been my superior from the start, throughout my three years.'

'According to it,' Rick said, 'the bunch of them came to Earth together. And that wasn't as long ago as three years; it's only been a matter of months.'

'Then at one time an authentic Garland existed,' Phil Resch said. 'And somewhere along the way got replaced.' His sharklike lean face twisted and he struggled to understand. 'Or – I've been impregnated with a false memory system. Maybe I only remember Garland over the whole time. But—' His face, suffused now with growing torment, continued to twist and work spasmodically. 'Only androids show up with false memory systems; it's been found ineffective in humans.'

The elevator ceased rising; its doors slid back, and there, spread out ahead of them, deserted except for empty parked vehicles, lay the police station's roof field.

'Here's my car,' Phil Resch said, unlocking the door of a nearby hovercar and waving Rick rapidly inside; he himself got in behind the wheel and started up the motor. In a moment they had lifted into the sky and, turning north, headed back in the direction of the War Memorial Opera House. Preoccupied, Phil Resch drove by reflex; his progressively more gloomy train of thought continued to dominate his attention. 'Listen, Deckard,' he said suddenly. 'After we retire Luba Luft – I want you to—' His voice, husky and tormented, broke off. 'You know. Give me the Boneli test or that empathy scale you have. To see about me.'

'We can worry about that later,' Rick said evasively.

'You don't want me to take it, do you?' Phil Resch glanced at him with acute comprehension. 'I guess you know what the results will be; Garland must have told you something. Facts which I don't know.'

Rick said, 'It's going to be hard even for the two of us to take out Luba Luft; she's more than I could handle, anyhow. Let's keep our attention focused on that.'

'It's not just false memory structures,' Phil Resch said. 'I own an animal; not a false one but the real thing. A squirrel. I love the squirrel, Deckard; every goddamn morning I feed it and change its papers – you know, clean up its cage – and then in the evening when I get off work I let it loose in my apt and it runs all over the place. It has a wheel in its cage; ever seen a squirrel running inside a wheel? It runs and runs, the wheel spins, but the squirrel stays in the same spot. Buffy seems to like it, though.'

'I guess squirrels aren't too bright,' Rick said.

They flew on, then, in silence.

Twelve

At the opera house Rick Deckard and Phil Resch were informed that the rehearsal had ended. And Miss Luft had left.

'Did she say where she intended to go?' Phil Resch asked the stagehand, showing his police identification.

'Over to the museum.' The stagehand studied the ID card. 'She said she wanted to take in the exhibit of Edvard Munch that's there, now. It ends tomorrow.'

And Luba Luft, Rick thought to himself, ends today.

As the two of them walked down the sidewalk to the museum, Phil Resch said, 'What odds will you give? She's flown; we won't find her at the museum.'

'Maybe,' Rick said.

They arrived at the museum building, noted on which floor the Munch exhibit could be found, and ascended. Shortly, they wandered amid paintings and woodcuts. Many people had turned out for the exhibit, including a grammar school class; the shrill voice of the teacher penetrated all the rooms comprising the exhibit, and Rick thought, That's what you'd expect an andy to sound – and look – like. Instead of like Rachael Rosen and Luba Luft. And – the man beside him. Or rather the thing beside him.

'Did you ever hear of an andy having a pet of any sort?' Phil Resch asked him.

For some obscure reason he felt the need to be brutally honest; perhaps he had already begun preparing himself for what lay ahead. 'In two cases that I know of, andys owned and cared for animals. But it's rare. From what I've been able to learn, it generally fails; the andy is unable to keep the animal alive. Animals require an environment of warmth to flourish. Except for reptiles and insects.'

'Would a squirrel need that? An atmosphere of love? Because Buffy is doing fine, as sleek as an otter. I groom and comb him every other day.' At an oil painting Phil Resch halted, gazed intently. The painting showed a hairless, oppressed creature with a head like an inverted pear, its hands clapped in horror to its ears, its mouth open in a vast, soundless scream. Twisted ripples of the creature's torment, echoes of its cry, flooded out into the air surrounding it; the man or woman, whichever it was, had become contained by its own howl. It had covered its ears against its own sound. The creature stood on a bridge and no one else was present; the creature screamed in isolation. Cut off by – or despite – its outcry.

'He did a woodcut of this,' Rick said, reading the card tacked below the painting.

'I think,' Phil Resch said, 'that this is how an andy must feel.' He traced in the air the convolutions, visible in the picture, of the creature's cry. 'I don't feel like that, so maybe I'm not an—' He broke off, as several persons strolled up to inspect the picture.

'*There's Luba Luft.*' Rick pointed and Phil Resch halted his somber introspection and defense; the two of them walked at a measured pace toward her, taking their time as if nothing confronted them; as always it was vital to preserve the atmosphere of the commonplace. Other humans, having no knowledge of the presence of androids among them, had to be protected at all costs – even that of losing the quarry.

Holding a printed catalogue, Luba Luft, wearing shiny

tapered pants and an illuminated gold vestlike top, stood absorbed in the picture before her: a drawing of a young girl, hands clasped together, seated on the edge of a bed, an expression of bewildered wonder and new, groping awe imprinted on the face.

'Want me to buy it for you?' Rick said to Luba Luft; he stood beside her, holding laxly onto her upper arm, informing her by his loose grip that he knew he had possession of her – he did not have to strain in an effort to detain her. On the other side of her Phil Resch put his hand on her shoulder and Rick saw the bulge of the laser tube. Phil Resch did not intend to take chances, not after the near miss with Inspector Garland.

'It's not for sale.' Luba Luft glanced at him idly, then violently as she recognized him; her eyes faded and the color dimmed from her face, leaving it cadaverous, as if already starting to decay. As if life had in an instant retreated to some point far inside her, leaving the body to its automatic ruin. 'I thought they arrested you. Do you mean they let you *go*?'

'Miss Luft,' he said, 'this is Mr Resch. Phil Resch, this is the quite well-known opera singer Luba Luft.' To Luba he said, 'The harness bull that arrested me is an android. So was his superior. Do you know – did you know – an Inspector Garland? He told me that you all came here in one ship as a group.'

'The police department which you called,' Phil Resch said to her, 'operating out of a building on Mission, is the organizing agency by which it would appear your group keeps in touch. They even feel confident enough to hire a human bounty hunter; evidently—'

'You?' Luba Luft said. 'You're not human. No more than I am: you're an android, too.'

An interval of silence passed and then Phil Resch said in a

low but controlled voice, 'Well, we'll deal with that at the proper time.' To Rick he said, 'Let's take her to my car.'

One of them on each side of her they prodded her in the direction of the museum elevator. Luba Luft did not come willingly, but on the other hand she did not actively resist; seemingly she had become resigned. Rick had seen that before in androids, in crucial situations. The artificial life force animating them seemed to fail if pressed too far . . . at least in some of them. But not all.

And it could flare up again furiously.

Androids, however, had as he knew an innate desire to remain inconspicuous. In the museum, with so many people roaming around, Luba Luft would tend to do nothing. The real encounter – for her probably the final one – would take place in the car, where no one else could see. Alone, with appalling abruptness, she could shed her inhibitions. He prepared himself – and did not think about Phil Resch. As Resch had said, it would be dealt with at a proper time.

At the end of the corridor near the elevators, a little store-like affair had been set up; it sold prints and art books, and Luba halted there, tarrying. 'Listen,' she said to Rick. Some of the color had returned to her face; once more she looked – at least briefly – alive. 'Buy me a reproduction of that picture I was looking at when you found me. The one of the girl sitting on the bed.'

After a pause Rick said to the clerk, a heavy-jowled, middle-aged woman with netted gray hair, 'Do you have a print of Munch's *Puberty*?'

'Only in this book of his collected work,' the clerk said, lifting down a handsome glossy volume. 'Twenty-five dollars.'

'I'll take it.' He reached for his wallet.

Phil Resch said, 'My departmental budget could never in a million years be stretched—'

'My own money,' Rick said; he handed the woman the bills and Luba the book. 'Now let's get started down,' he said to her and Phil Resch.

'It's very nice of you,' Luba said as they entered the elevator. 'There's something very strange and touching about humans. An android would never have done that.' She glanced icily at Phil Resch. 'It wouldn't have occurred to him; as he said, never in a million years.' She continued to gaze at Resch, now with manifold hostility and aversion. 'I really don't like androids. Ever since I got here from Mars my life has consisted of imitating the human, doing what she would do, acting as if I had the thoughts and impulses a human would have. Imitating, as far as I'm concerned, a superior life form.' To Phil Resch she said, 'Isn't that how it's been with you, Resch? Trying to be—'

'I can't take this.' Phil Resch dug into his coat, groped.

'No,' Rick said; he grabbed at Phil Resch's hand; Resch retreated, eluding him. 'The Boneli test,' Rick said.

'It's admitted it's an android,' Phil Resch said. 'We don't have to wait.'

'But to retire it,' Rick said, 'because it's needling you – give me that.' He struggled to pry the laser tube away from Phil Resch. The tube remained in Phil Resch's possession; Resch circled back within the cramped elevator, evading him, his attention on Luba Luft only. 'Okay,' Rick said. 'Retire it; kill it now. Show it that it's right.' He saw, then, that Resch meant to. 'Wait—'

Phil Resch fired, and at the same instant Luba Luft, in a spasm of frantic hunted fear, twisted and spun away, dropping as she did so. The beam missed its mark but, as Resch lowered it, burrowed a narrow hole, silently, into her stomach. She began to scream; she lay crouched against the wall of the elevator, screaming. Like the picture, Rick thought to himself, and, with his own laser tube, killed her. Luba Luft's body fell forward, face down, in a heap. It did not even tremble.

With his laser tube, Rick systematically burned into blurred ash the book of pictures which he had just a few minutes ago bought Luba. He did the job thoroughly, saying nothing; Phil Resch watched without understanding, his face showing his perplexity.

'You could have kept the book yourself,' Resch said, when it had been done. 'That cost you—'

'Do you think androids have souls?' Rick interrupted.

Cocking his head on one side, Phil Resch gazed at him in even greater puzzlement.

'I could afford the book,' Rick said. 'I've made three thousand dollars so far today, and I'm not even half through.'

'You're claiming Garland?' Phil Resch asked. 'But I killed him, not you. You just lay there. And Luba, too. I got her.'

'You can't collect,' Rick said. 'Not from your own department and not from ours. When we get to your car I'll administer the Boneli test or the Voigt-Kampff to you and then we'll see. Even though you're not on my list.' His hands shaking, he opened his briefcase, rummaged among the crumpled onionskin carbons. 'No, you're not here. So legally I can't claim you; to make anything I'll have to claim Luba Luft and Garland.'

'You're sure I'm an android? Is that really what Garland said?'

'That's what Garland said.'

'Maybe he was lying,' Phil Resch said. 'To split us apart. As we are now. We're nuts, letting them split us; you were absolutely right about Luba Luft – I shouldn't have let her get my goat like that. I must be overly sensitive. That would be natural for a bounty hunter, I suppose; you're probably the same way. But look; we would have had to retire Luba Luft anyhow, half an hour from now – only one half hour more. She wouldn't even have had time to look through that book you got her. And I still think you shouldn't have destroyed it; that's a waste. I can't follow your reasoning; it isn't rational, that's why.'

Rick said, 'I'm getting out of this business.'

'And go into what?'

'Anything. Insurance underwriting, like Garland was supposed to be doing. Or I'll emigrate. Yes.' He nodded. 'I'll go to Mars.'

'But someone has to do this,' Phil Resch pointed out.

'They can use androids. Much better if andys do it. I can't any more; I've had enough. She was a wonderful singer. The planet could have used her. This is insane.'

'This is necessary. Remember: they killed humans in order to get away. And if I hadn't gotten you out of the Mission police station they would have killed you. That's what Garland wanted me for; that's why he had me come down to his office. Didn't Polokov almost kill you? Didn't Luba Luft almost? We're acting defensively; they're here on our planet – they're murderous illegal aliens masquerading as—'

'As police,' Rick said. 'As bounty hunters.'

'Okay; give me the Boneli test. Maybe Garland lied. I think he did – false memories just aren't that good. What about my squirrel?'

'Yes, your squirrel. I forgot about your squirrel.'

'If I'm an andy,' Phil Resch said, 'and you kill me, you can have my squirrel. Here; I'll write it out, willing it to you.'

'Andys can't will anything. They can't possess anything to will.'

'Then just take it,' Phil Resch said.

'Maybe so,' Rick said. The elevator had reached the first floor, now; its doors opened. 'You stay with Luba; I'll get a patrol car here to take her to the Hall of Justice. For her bone marrow test.' He saw a phone booth, entered it, dropped in a coin, and, his fingers shaking, dialed. Meanwhile a group of people, who had been waiting for the elevator, gathered around Phil Resch and the body of Luba Luft.

She was really a superb singer, he said to himself as he hung up the receiver, his call completed. I don't get it; how can a talent like that be a liability to our society? But it wasn't the talent, he told himself; it was she herself. As Phil Resch is, he thought. He's a menace in exactly the same way, for the same reasons. So I can't quit now. Emerging from the phone booth he pushed his way among the people, back to Resch and the prone figure of the android girl. Someone had put a coat over her. Not Resch's.

Going up to Phil Resch – who stood off to one side vigorously smoking a small gray cigar – he said to him, 'I hope to god you do test out as an android.'

'You really hate me,' Phil Resch said, marveling. 'All of a sudden; you didn't hate me back on Mission Street. Not while I was saving your life.'

'I see a pattern. The way you killed Garland and then the way you killed Luba. You don't kill the way I do; you don't try to— Hell,' he said, 'I know what it is. You like to kill. All you need is a pretext. If you had a pretext you'd kill me. That's why you picked up on the possibility of Garland being an android; it made him available for being killed. I wonder what you're going to do when you fail to pass the Boneli test. Will you kill yourself? Sometimes androids do that.' But the situation was rare.

'Yes, I'll take care of it,' Phil Resch said. 'You won't have to do anything, besides administering the test.'

A patrol car arrived; two policemen hopped out, strode up, saw the crowd of people and at once cleared themselves a passage through. One of them recognized Rick and nodded. So we can go now, Rick realized. Our business here is concluded. Finally.

As he and Resch walked back down the street to the opera house, on whose roof their hovercar lay parked, Resch said, 'I'll give you my laser tube now. So you won't have to worry about my reaction to the test. In terms of your own personal safety.' He held out the tube and Rick accepted it.

'How'll you kill yourself without it?' Rick asked. 'If you fail on the test?'

'I'll hold my breath.'

'Chrissake,' Rick said. 'It can't be done.'

'There's no automatic cut-in of the vagus nerve,' Phil Resch said, 'in an android. As there is in a human. Weren't you taught that when they trained you? I got taught that years ago.'

'But to die that way,' Rick protested.

'There's no pain. What's the matter with it?'

'It's—' He gestured. Unable to find the right words.

'I don't really think I'm going to have to,' Phil Resch said.

Together they ascended to the roof of the War Memorial Opera House and Phil Resch's parked hovercar.

Sliding behind the wheel and closing his door, Phil Resch said, 'I would prefer it if you used the Boneli test.'

'I can't. I don't know how to score it.' I would have to rely on you for an interpretation of the readings, he realized. And that's out of the question.

'You'll tell me the truth, won't you?' Phil Resch asked. 'If I'm an android you'll tell me?'

'Sure.'

'Because I really want to know. I *have* to know.' Phil Resch relit his cigar, shifted about on the bucket seat of the car, trying to make himself comfortable. Evidently he could not. 'Did you really like that Munch picture that Luba Luft was looking at?' he asked. 'I didn't care for it. Realism in art doesn't interest me; I like Picasso and—'

'*Puberty* dates from 1894,' Rick said shortly. 'Nothing but realism existed then; you have to take that into account.'

'But that other one, of the man holding his ears and yelling – that wasn't representational.'

Opening his briefcase, Rick fished out his test gear.

'Elaborate,' Phil Resch observed, watching. 'How many questions do you have to ask before you can make a determination?'

'Six or seven.' He handed the adhesive pad to Phil Resch. 'Attach that to your cheek. Firmly. And this light—' He aimed it. 'This stays focused on your eye. Don't move; keep your eyeball as steady as you can.'

'Reflex fluctuations,' Phil Resch said acutely. 'But not to the physical stimulus; you're not measuring dilation, for instance. It'll be to the verbal questions; what we call a flinch reaction.'

Rick said, 'Do you think you can control it?'

'Not really. Eventually, maybe. But not the initial amplitude; that's outside conscious control. If it weren't—' He broke off. 'Go ahead. I'm tense; excuse me if I talk too much.'

'Talk all you want,' Rick said. Talk all the way to the tomb, he said to himself. If you feel like it. It didn't matter to him.

'If I test out android,' Phil Resch prattled, 'you'll undergo renewed faith in the human race. But, since it's not going to work out that way, I suggest you begin framing an ideology which will account for—'

'Here's the first question,' Rick said; the gear had now been set up and the needles of the two dials quivered. 'Reaction time is a factor, so answer as rapidly as you can.' From memory he selected an initial question. The test had begun.

⋆

Afterward, Rick sat in silence for a time. Then he began gathering his gear together, stuffing it back in the briefcase.

'I can tell by your face,' Phil Resch said; he exhaled in absolute, weightless, almost convulsive relief. 'Okay; you can give me my gun back.' He reached out, his palm up, waiting.

'Evidently you were right,' Rick said. 'About Garland's motives. Wanting to split us up; what you said.' He felt both psychologically and physically weary.

'Do you have your ideology framed?' Phil Resch asked. 'That would explain me as part of the human race?'

Rick said, 'There is a defect in your empathic, role-taking ability. One which we don't test for. Your feelings toward androids.'

'Of course we don't test for that.'

'Maybe we should.' He had never thought of it before, had never felt any empathy on his own part toward the androids he killed. Always he had assumed that throughout his psyche he experienced the android as a clever machine – as in his conscious view. And yet, in contrast to Phil Resch, a difference had manifested itself. And he felt instinctively that he was right. Empathy toward an artificial construct? he asked himself. Something that only pretends to be alive? But Luba Luft had seemed *genuinely* alive; it had not worn the aspect of a simulation.

'You realize,' Phil Resch said quietly, 'what this would do. If we included androids in our range of empathic identification, as we do animals.'

'We couldn't protect ourselves.'

'Absolutely. These Nexus-6 types . . . they'd roll all over us and mash us flat. You and I, all the bounty hunters – we stand between the Nexus-6 and mankind, a barrier which keeps the two distinct. Furthermore—' He ceased, noticing that Rick was once again hauling out his test gear. 'I thought the test was over.'

'I want to ask myself a question,' Rick said. 'And I want you to tell me what the needles register. Just give me the calibration; I can compute it.' He plastered the adhesive disk against his cheek, arranged the beam of light until it fed directly into his eye. 'Are you ready? Watch the dials. We'll exclude time lapse in this; I just want magnitude.'

'Sure, Rick,' Phil Resch said obligingly.

Aloud, Rick said, 'I'm going down by elevator with an android I've captured. And suddenly someone kills it, without warning.'

'No particular response,' Phil Resch said.

'What'd the needles hit?'

'The left one 2.8. The right one 3.3.'

Rick said, 'A female android.'

'Now they're up to 4.0 and 6 respectively.'

'That's high enough,' Rick said; he removed the wired adhesive disk from his cheek and shut off the beam of light. 'That's an emphatically empathic response,' he said. 'About what a human subject shows for most questions. Except for the extreme ones, such as those dealing with human pelts used decoratively . . . the truly pathological ones.'

'Meaning?'

Rick said, 'I'm capable of feeling empathy for at least specific, certain androids. Not for all of them but – one or two.' For Luba Luft, as an example, he said to himself. So I was wrong. There's nothing unnatural or unhuman about Phil Resch's reactions; *it's me.*

I wonder, he wondered, if any human has ever felt this way before about an android.

Of course, he reflected, this may never come up again in my work; it could be an anomaly, something for instance to do with my feelings for *The Magic Flute*. And for Luba's voice, in fact her career as a whole. Certainly this had never come up before; or at least not that he had been aware of. Not, for example, with Polokov. Nor with Garland. And, he realized, if Phil Resch had proved out android I could have killed him without feeling anything, anyhow after Luba's death.

So much for the distinction between authentic living humans and humanoid constructs. In that elevator at the museum, he said to himself, I rode down with two creatures, one human, the other android . . . and my feelings were the reverse of those intended. Of those I'm accustomed to feel – am *required* to feel.

'You're in a spot, Deckard,' Phil Resch said; it seemed to amuse him.

Rick said, 'What – should I do?'

'It's sex,' Phil Resch said.

'Sex?'

'Because she – it – was physically attractive. Hasn't that ever happened to you before?' Phil Resch laughed. 'We were taught that it constitutes a prime problem in bounty hunting. Don't you know, Deckard, that in the colonies they have android mistresses?'

'It's illegal,' Rick said, knowing the law about that.

'Sure it's illegal. But most variations in sex are illegal. But people do it anyhow.'

'What about – not sex – but love?'

'Love is another name for sex.'

'Like love of country,' Rick said. 'Love of music.'

'If it's love toward a woman or an android imitation, it's sex. Wake up and face yourself, Deckard. You wanted to go to bed with a female type of android – nothing more, nothing less. I felt that way, on one occasion. When I had just started bounty hunting. Don't let it get you down; you'll heal. What's happened is that you've got your order reversed. Don't kill her – or be present when she's killed – and then feel physically attracted. Do it the other way.'

Rick stared at him. 'Go to bed with her first—'

'—and then kill her,' Phil Resch said succinctly. His grainy, hardened smile remained.

You're a good bounty hunter, Rick realized. Your attitude proves it. But am I?

Suddenly, for the first time in his life, he had begun to wonder.

Thirteen

Like an arc of pure fire, John R. Isidore soared across the late-afternoon sky on his way home from his job. I wonder if she's still there, he said to himself. Down in that kipple-infested old apt, watching Buster Friendly on her TV set and quaking with fear every time she imagines someone coming down the hall. Including, I suppose, me.

He had already stopped off at a blackmarket grocery store. On the seat beside him a bag of such delicacies as bean curd, ripe peaches, good soft evil-smelling cheese rocked back and forth as he alternately speeded up and slowed down his car; being tense, tonight, he drove somewhat erratically. And his allegedly repaired car coughed and floundered, as it had been doing for months prior to overhaul. Rats, Isidore said to himself.

The smell of peaches and cheese eddied about the car, filling his nose with pleasure. All rarities, for which he had squandered two weeks' salary – borrowed in advance from Mr Sloat. And, in addition, under the car seat where it could not roll and break, a bottle of Chablis wine knocked back and forth: the greatest rarity of all. He had been keeping it in a safety deposit box at the Bank of America, hanging onto it and not selling it no matter how much they offered, in case at some long, late, last moment a girl appeared. That had not happened, not until now.

The rubbish-littered, lifeless roof of his apartment building as always depressed him. Passing from his car to the elevator door he damped down his peripheral vision; he concentrated on the valuable bag and bottle which he carried, making certain that he tripped over no trash and took no ignominious pratfall to economic doom. When the elevator creakily arrived he rode it – not to his own floor – but to the lower level on which the new tenant, Pris Stratton, now lived. Presently he stood in front of her door, rapping with the edge of the wine bottle, his heart going to pieces inside his chest.

'Who's there?' Her voice, muffled by the door and yet clear. A frightened, but blade-sharp tone.

'This is J. R. Isidore speaking,' he said briskly, adopting the new authority which he had so recently acquired via Mr Sloat's vidphone. 'I have a few desirable items here and I think we can put together a more than reasonable dinner.'

The door, to a limited extent, opened; Pris, no lights on in the room behind her, peered out into the dim hall. 'You sound different,' she said. 'More grown up.'

'I had a few routine matters to deal with during business hours today. The usual. If you c-c-could let me in—'

'You'd talk about them.' However, she held the door open wide enough for him to enter. And then, seeing what he carried, she exclaimed, her face ignited with elfin, exuberant glee. But almost at once, without warning, a lethal bitterness crossed her features, set concrete-like in place. The glee had gone.

'What is it?' he said; he carried the packages and bottle to the kitchen, set them down and hurried back.

Tonelessly, Pris said, 'They're wasted on me.'

'Why?'

'Oh . . .' She shrugged, walking aimlessly away, her hands in the pockets of her heavy, rather old-fashioned skirt. 'Sometime I'll tell you.' She raised her eyes, then. 'It was nice of you anyhow. Now I wish you'd leave. I don't feel like seeing anyone.' In a vague fashion she moved toward the door to the hall; her steps dragged and she seemed depleted, her store of energy fading almost out.

'I know what's the matter with you,' he said.

'Oh?' Her voice, as she reopened the hall door, dropped even further into uselessness, listless and barren.

'You don't have any friends. You're a lot worse than when I saw you this morning; it's because—'

'I have friends.' Sudden authority stiffened her voice; she palpably regained vigor. 'Or I had. Seven of them. That was to start with but now the bounty hunters have had time to get to work. So some of them – maybe all of them – are dead.' She wandered toward the window, gazed out at the blackness and the few lights here and there. 'I may be the only one of the eight of us left. So maybe you're right.'

'What's a bounty hunter?'

'That's right. You people aren't supposed to know. A bounty hunter is a professional murderer who's given a list of those he's supposed to kill. He's paid a sum – a thousand dollars is the going rate, I understand – for each he gets. Usually he has a contract with a city so he draws a salary as well. But they keep that low so he'll have incentive.'

'Are you sure?' Isidore asked.

'Yes.' She nodded. 'You mean am I sure he has incentive? Yes, he has incentive. He *enjoys* it.'

'I think,' Isidore said, 'you're mistaken.' Never in his life had he heard of such a thing. Buster Friendly, for instance, had never mentioned it. 'It's not in accord with present-day Mercerian ethics,' he pointed out. 'All life is one; "no man is an island," as Shakespeare said in olden times.'

'John Donne.'

Isidore gestured in agitation. 'That's worse than anything I ever heard of. Can't you call the police?'

'No.'

'And they're after *you*? They're apt to come here and kill *you*?' He understood, now, why the girl acted in so secretive a fashion. 'No wonder you're scared and don't want to see anybody.' But he thought, it must be a delusion. She must be psychotic. With delusions of persecution. Maybe from brain damage due to the dust; maybe she's a special. 'I'll get them first,' he said.

'With what?' Faintly, she smiled; she showed her small, even, white teeth.

'I'll get a license to carry a laser beam. It's easy to get, out here where there's hardly anybody; the police don't patrol – you're expected to watch out for yourself.'

'How about when you're at work?'

'I'll take a leave of absence!'

Pris said, 'That's very nice of you, J. R. Isidore. But if bounty hunters got the others, got Max Polokov and Garland and Luba and Hasking and Roy Baty—' She broke off. 'Roy and Irmgard Baty. If they're dead then it really doesn't matter. They're my best friends. Why the hell don't I hear from them, I wonder?' She cursed, angrily.

Making his way into the kitchen he got down dusty, long unused plates and bowls and glasses; he began washing them in the sink, running the rusty hot water until it cleared at last. Presently Pris appeared, seated herself at the table. He uncorked the bottle of Chablis, divided the peaches and the cheese and the bean curd.

'What's that white stuff? Not the cheese.' She pointed.

'Made from soy bean whey. I wish I had some—' He broke off, flushing. 'It used to be eaten with beef gravy.'

'An android,' Pris murmured. 'That's the sort of slip an android makes. That's what gives it away.' She came over, stood beside him, and then to his stunned surprise put her arm around his waist and for an instant pressed against him. 'I'll try a slice of peach,' she said, and gingerly picked out a slippery pink-orange furry slice with her long fingers. And then, as she ate the slice of peach, she began to cry. Cold tears descended her cheeks, splashed on the bosom of her dress. He did not know what to do, so he continued dividing the food. 'God-damn it,' she said, furiously. 'Well—' She moved away from him, paced slowly, with measured steps, about the room. '—see, we lived on Mars. That's how come I know androids.' Her voice shook but she managed to continue; obviously it meant a great deal to her to have someone to talk to.

'And the only people on Earth that you know,' Isidore said, 'are your fellow ex-emigrants.'

'We knew each other before the trip. A settlement near New New York. Roy Baty and Irmgard ran a drugstore; he was a pharmacist and she handled the beauty aids, the creams and ointments; on Mars they use a lot of skin conditioners. I—' She hesitated. 'I got various drugs from Roy – I needed them at first because – well, anyhow, it's an awful place. This' – she swept in the room, the apartment, in one violent gesture – 'this is nothing. You think I'm suffering because I'm lonely. Hell, all Mars is lonely. Much worse than this.'

'Don't the androids keep you company? I heard a commercial on—' Seating himself he ate, and presently she too picked up the glass of wine; she sipped expressionlessly. 'I understood that the androids helped.'

'The androids,' she said, 'are lonely, too.'

'Do you like the wine?'

She set down her glass. 'It's fine.'

'It's the only bottle I've seen in three years.'

'We came back,' Pris said, 'because nobody should have to live there. It wasn't conceived for habitation, at least not within the last billion years. It's so *old*. You feel it in the stones, the terrible old age. Anyhow, at first I got drugs from Roy; I lived for that new synthetic pain-killer, that silenizine. And then I met Horst Hartman, who at that time ran a stamp store, rare postage stamps; there's so much time on your hands that you've got to have a hobby, something you can pore over endlessly. And Horst got me interested in pre-colonial fiction.'

'You mean old books?'

'Stories written before space travel but about space travel.'

'How could there have been stories about space travel before—'

'The writers,' Pris said, 'made it up.'

'Based on what?'

'On imagination. A lot of times they turned out wrong. For example they wrote about Venus being a jungle paradise with huge monsters and women in breastplates that glistened.' She eyed him. 'Does that interest you? Big women with long braided blond hair and gleaming breastplates the size of melons?'

'No,' he said.

'Irmgard is blond,' Pris said. 'But small. Anyhow, there's a fortune to be made in smuggling pre-colonial fiction, the old magazines and books and films, to Mars. Nothing is as exciting. To read about cities and huge industrial enterprises, and really successful colonization. You can imagine what it might have been like. What Mars *ought* to be like. Canals.'

'Canals?' Dimly, he remembered reading about that; in the olden days they had believed in canals on Mars.

'Crisscrossing the planet,' Pris said. 'And beings from other stars. With infinite wisdom. And stories about Earth, set in our time and even later. Where there's no radioactive dust.'

'I would think,' Isidore said, 'it would make you feel worse.'

'It doesn't,' Pris said curtly.

'Did you bring any of that pre-colonial reading material back with you?' It occurred to him that he ought to try some.

'It's worthless, here, because here on Earth the craze never caught on. Anyhow there's plenty here, in the libraries; that's where we get all of ours – stolen from libraries here on Earth and shot by autorocket to Mars. You're out at night bumbling across the open space, and all of a sudden you see a flare, and there's a rocket, cracked open, with old pre-colonial fiction magazines spilling out everywhere. A fortune. But of course you read them before you sell them.' She warmed to her topic. 'Of all—'

A knock sounded on the hall door.

Ashen, Pris whispered, 'I can't go. Don't make any noise; just sit.' She strained, listening. 'I wonder if the door's locked,' she said almost inaudibly. 'God, I hope so.' Her eyes, wild and powerful, fixed themselves beseechingly on him, as if praying to him to make it true.

A far-off voice from the hall called, 'Pris, are you in there?' A man's voice. 'It's Roy and Irmgard. We got your card.'

Rising and going into the bedroom, Pris reappeared carrying a pen and scrap of paper; she reseated herself, scratched out a hasty message.

YOU GO TO THE DOOR.

Isidore, nervously, took the pen from her and wrote:

AND SAY WHAT?

With anger, Pris scratched out:

SEE IF IT'S REALLY THEM.

Getting up, he walked glumly into the living room. How would I know if it was them? he inquired of himself. He opened the door.

Two people stood in the dim hall, a small woman, lovely in the manner of Greta Garbo, with blue eyes and yellow-blond hair; the man larger, with intelligent eyes but flat, Mongolian features which gave him a brutal look. The woman wore a fashionable wrap, high shiny boots, and tapered pants; the man lounged in a rumpled shirt and stained trousers, giving an air of almost deliberate vulgarity. He smiled at Isidore but his bright, small eyes remained oblique.

'We're looking—' the small blond woman began, but then she saw past Isidore; her face dissolved in rapture and she whisked past him, calling. 'Pris! How are you?' Isidore turned. The two women were embracing. He stepped aside, and Roy Baty entered, somber and large, smiling his crooked, tuneless smile.

Fourteen

'Can we talk?' Roy said, indicating Isidore.

Pris, vibrant with bliss, said, 'It's okay up to a point.' To Isidore she said, 'Excuse us.' She led the Batys off to one side and muttered at them; then the three of them returned to confront J. R. Isidore, who felt uncomfortable and out of place. 'This is Mr Isidore,' Pris said. 'He's taking care of me.' The words came out tinged with an almost malicious sarcasm; Isidore blinked. 'See? He brought me some natural food.'

'Food,' Irmgard Baty echoed, and trotted lithely into the kitchen to see. 'Peaches,' she said, immediately picking up a bowl and spoon; smiling at Isidore she ate with brisk little animal bites. Her smile, different from Pris's, provided simple warmth; it had no veiled overtones.

Going after her – he felt attracted to her – Isidore said, 'You're from Mars.'

'Yes, we gave up.' Her voice bobbed, as, with birdish acumen, her blue eyes sparkled at him. 'What an awful building you live in. Nobody else lives here, do they? We didn't see any other lights.'

'I live upstairs,' Isidore said.

'Oh, I thought you and Pris were maybe living together.' Irmgard Baty did not sound disapproving; she meant it, obviously, as merely a statement.

Dourly – but still smiling his smile – Roy Baty said, 'Well, they got Polokov.'

The joy which had appeared on Pris's face at seeing her friends at once melted away. 'Who else?'

'They got Garland,' Roy Baty said. 'They got Anders and Gitchel and then just a little earlier today they got Luba.' He delivered the news as if, perversely, it pleased him to be telling this. As if he derived pleasure from Pris's shock. 'I didn't think they'd get Luba; remember I kept saying that during the trip?'

'So that leaves—' Pris said.

'The three of us,' Irmgard said with apprehensive urgency.

'That's why we're here.' Roy Baty's voice boomed out with new, unexpected warmth; the worse the situation the more he seemed to enjoy it. Isidore could not fathom him in the slightest.

'Oh god,' Pris said, stricken.

'Well, they had this investigator, this bounty hunter,' Irmgard said in agitation, 'named Dave Holden.' Her lips dripped venom at the name. 'And then Polokov almost got him.'

'*Almost* got him,' Roy echoed, his smile now immense.

'So he's in this hospital, this Holden,' Irmgard continued. 'And evidently they gave his list to another bounty hunter, and Polokov almost got him, too. But it wound up with him retiring Polokov. And then he went after Luba; we know that because she managed to get hold of Garland and he sent out someone to capture the bounty hunter and take him to the Mission Street building. See, Luba called us after Garland's agent picked up the bounty hunter. She was sure it would be okay; she was sure that Garland would kill him.' She added, 'But evidently something went wrong on Mission. We don't know what. Maybe we never will.'

Pris asked, 'Does this bounty hunter have our names?'

'Oh yes, dear, I suppose he does,' Irmgard said. 'But he doesn't know where we are. Roy and I aren't going back to our apartment; we have as much stuff in our car as we could cram in, and we've decided to take one of these abandoned apartments in this ratty old building.'

'Is that wise?' Isidore spoke up, summoning courage. 'T-t-to all be in one place?'

'Well, they got everybody else,' Irmgard said, matter-of-factly; she, too, like her husband, seemed strangely resigned, despite her superficial agitation. All of them, Isidore thought; they're all strange. He sensed it without being able to finger it. As if a peculiar and malign *abstractness* pervaded their mental processes. Except, perhaps, for Pris; certainly she was radically frightened. Pris seemed almost right, almost natural. But—

'Why don't you move in with him?' Roy said to Pris, indicating Isidore. 'He could give you a certain amount of protection.'

'A chickenhead?' Pris said. 'I'm not going to live with a chickenhead.' Her nostrils flared.

Irmgard said rapidly, 'I think you're foolish to be a snob at a time like this. Bounty hunters move fast; he may try to tie it up this evening. There may be a bonus in it for him if he got it done by—'

'Keerist, close the hall door,' Roy said, going over to it; he slammed it with one blow of his hand, thereupon summarily locking it. 'I think you should move in with Isidore, Pris, and I think Irm and I should be here in the same building; that way we can help each other. I've got some electronic components in my car, junk I ripped off the ship. I'll install a two-way bug so Pris you can hear us and we can hear you, and I'll ring up an alarm system that any of the four of us can set off. It's obvious that the synthetic identities didn't work out, even Garland's. Of course, Garland put his head in the noose by bringing the bounty hunter to the Mission Street building; that was a mistake. And Polokov, instead of staying as far away as possible from the hunter, chose to approach him. We won't do that; we'll stay put.' He did not sound worried in the slightest; the situation seemed to rouse him to crackling near-manic energy. 'I think—' He sucked in his breath noisily, holding the attention of everyone else in the room, including Isidore. '*I* think that there's a reason why the three of us are still alive. I think if he had any clue as to where we are he'd have shown up here by now. The whole idea in bounty hunting is to work as fast as hell. That's where the profit comes.'

'And if he waits,' Irmgard said in agreement, 'we slip away, like we've done. I bet Roy is right; I bet he has our names but no location. Poor Luba; stuck in the War Memorial Opera House, right out in the open. No difficulty finding her.'

'Well,' Roy said stiltedly, 'she wanted it that way; she believed she'd be safer as a public figure.'

'You told her otherwise,' Irmgard said.

'Yes,' Roy agreed, 'I told her, and I told Polokov not to try to pass himself off as a WPO man. And I told Garland that one of his own bounty hunters would get him, which is very possibly, just conceivably, exactly what did happen.' He rocked back and forth on his heavy heels, his face wise with profundity.

Isidore spoke up. 'I-I-I gather from l-l-listening to Mr Baty that he's your n-n-natural leader.'

'Oh yes, Roy's a leader,' Irmgard said.

Pris said, 'He organized our – trip. From Mars to here.'

'Then,' Isidore said, 'you better do what h-h-he suggests.' His voice broke with hope and tension. 'I think it would be t-t-terrific, Pris, if you l-l-lived with me. I'll stay home a couple of days from my job – I have a vacation coming. To make sure you're okay.' And maybe Milt, who was very inventive, could design a weapon for him to use. Something imaginative, which would slay bounty hunters . . . whatever they were. He had an indistinct, glimpsed darkly impression: of something merciless that carried a printed list and a gun, that moved machine-like through the flat, bureaucratic job of killing. A thing without emotions, or even a face; a thing that if killed got replaced immediately by another resembling it. And so on, until everyone real and alive had been shot.

Incredible, he thought, that the police can't do anything. I can't believe that. *These people must have done something.* Perhaps they emigrated back to Earth illegally. We're told – the TV tells us – to report any landing of a ship outside the approved pads. The police must be watching for this.

But even so, no one got killed deliberately any more. It ran contrary to Mercerism.

'The chickenhead,' Pris said, 'likes me.'

'Don't call him that, Pris,' Irmgard said; she gave Isidore a look of compassion. 'Think what he could call *you.*'

Pris said nothing. Her expression became enigmatic.

'I'll go start rigging up the bug,' Roy said. 'Irmgard and I'll stay in this apartment; Pris you go with – Mr Isidore.' He started toward the door, striding with amazing speed for a man so heavy. In a blur he disappeared out the door, which banged back as he flung it open. Isidore, then, had a momentary, strange hallucination; he saw briefly a frame of metal, a platform of pullies and circuits and batteries and turrets and gears – and then the slovenly shape of Roy Baty faded back into view. Isidore felt a laugh rise up inside him; he nervously choked it off. And felt bewildered.

'A man,' Pris said distantly, 'of action. Too bad he's so poor with his hands, doing mechanical things.'

'If we get saved,' Irmgard said in a scolding, severe tone, as if chiding her, 'it'll be because of Roy.'

'But is it worth it,' Pris said, mostly to herself. She

shrugged, then nodded to Isidore. 'Okay, J. R. I'll move in with you and you can protect me.'

'A-a-all of you,' Isidore said immediately.

Solemnly, in a formal little voice, Irmgard Baty said to him, 'I want you to know we appreciate it very much, Mr Isidore. You're the first friend I think any of us have found here on Earth. It's very nice of you and maybe sometime we can repay you.' She glided over to pat him on the arm.

'Do you have any pre-colonial fiction I could read?' he asked her.

'Pardon?' Irmgard Baty glanced inquiringly at Pris.

'Those old magazines,' Pris said; she had gathered a few things together to take with her, and Isidore lifted the bundle from her arms, feeling the glow that comes only from satisfaction at a goal achieved. 'No, J. R. We didn't bring any back with us, for reasons I explained.'

'I'll g-g-go to a library tomorrow,' he said, going out into the hall. 'And g-g-get you and me too some to read, so you'll have something to do besides just waiting.'

He led Pris upstairs to his own apartment, dark and empty and stuffy and lukewarm as it was; carrying her possessions into the bedroom, he at once turned on the heater, lights, and the TV to its sole channel.

'I like this,' Pris said, but in the same detached and remote tone as before. She meandered about, hands thrust in her skirt pockets; on her face a sour expression, almost righteous in the degree of its displeasure, appeared. In contrast to her stated reaction.

'What's the matter?' he asked as he laid her possessions out on the couch.

'Nothing.' She halted at the picture window, drew the drapes back, and gazed morosely out.

'If you think they're looking for you—' he began.

'It's a dream,' Pris said. 'Induced by drugs that Roy gave me.'

'P-pardon?'

'You really think that bounty hunters exist?'

'Mr Baty said they killed your friends.'

'Roy Baty is as crazy as I am,' Pris said. 'Our trip was between a mental hospital on the East Coast and here. We're all schizophrenic, with defective emotional lives – flattening of affect, it's called. And we have group hallucinations.'

'I didn't think it was true,' he said full of relief.

'Why didn't you?' She swiveled to stare intently at him; her scrutiny was so strict that he felt himself flushing.

'B-b-because things like that don't happen. The g-g-government never kills anyone, for any crime. And Mercerism—'

'But you see,' Pris said, 'if you're not human, then it's all different.'

'That's not true. Even animals – even eels and gophers and snakes and spiders – are sacred.'

Pris, still regarding him fixedly, said, 'So it can't be, can it? As you say, even animals are protected by law. All life. Everything organic that wriggles or squirms or burrows or flies or swarms or lays eggs or—' She broke off, because Roy Baty had appeared, abruptly throwing the door of the apartment open and entering; a trail of wire rustled after him.

'Insects,' he said, showing no embarrassment at overhearing them, 'are especially sacrosanct.' Lifting a picture from the wall of the living room he attached a small electronic device to the nail, stepped back, viewed it, then replaced the picture. 'Now the alarm.' He gathered up the trailing wire, which led to a complex assembly. Smiling his discordant smile, he showed the assembly to Pris and John Isidore. 'The alarm. These wires go under the carpet; they're antennae. It picks up the presence of a—' He hesitated. 'A mentational entity,' he said obscurely, 'which isn't one of us four.'

'So it rings,' Pris said, 'and then what? He'll have a gun. We can't fall on him and bite him to death.'

'This assembly,' Roy continued, 'has a Penfield unit built into it. When the alarm has been triggered it radiates a mood of panic to the – intruder. Unless he acts very fast, which he may. Enormous panic; I have the gain turned all the way up. No human being can remain in the vicinity more than a matter of seconds. That's the nature of panic: it leads to random circus-motions, purposeless flight, and muscle and neural spasms.' He concluded, 'Which will give us an opportunity to get him. Possibly. Depending on how good he is.'

Isidore said, 'Won't the alarm affect us?'

'That's right,' Pris said to Roy Baty. 'It'll affect Isidore.'

'Well, so what,' Roy said. And resumed his task of installation. 'So they both go racing out of here panic-stricken. It'll still give us time to react. And they won't kill Isidore; he's not on their list. That's why he's usable as a cover.'

Pris said brusquely, 'You can't do any better, Roy?'

'No,' he answered, 'I can't.'

'I'll be able to g-g-get a weapon tomorrow,' Isidore spoke up.

'You're sure Isidore's presence here won't set off the alarm?' Pris said. 'After all, he's – you know.'

'I've compensated for his cephalic emanations,' Roy explained. 'Their sum won't trip anything; it'll take an additional human. Person.' Scowling, he glanced at Isidore, aware of what he had said.

'You're androids,' Isidore said. But he didn't care; it made no difference to him. 'I see why they want to kill you,' he said. 'Actually you're not alive.' Everything made sense to him, now. The bounty hunter, the killing of their friends, the trip to Earth, all these precautions.

'When I used the word "human," ' Roy Baty said to Pris, 'I used the wrong word.'

'That's right, Mr Baty,' Isidore said. 'But what does it matter to me? I mean, I'm a special; they don't treat me very well either, like for instance I can't emigrate.' He found himself yabbering away like a folletto. 'You can't come here; I can't—' He calmed himself.

After a pause Roy Baty said laconically, 'You wouldn't enjoy Mars. You're missing nothing.'

'I wondered how long it would be,' Pris said to Isidore, 'before you realized. We are different, aren't we?'

'That's what probably tripped up Garland and Max Polokov,' Roy Baty said. 'They were so goddamn sure they could pass. Luba, too.'

'You're intellectual,' Isidore said; he felt excited again at having understood. Excitement and pride. 'You think abstractly, and you don't—' He gesticulated, his words tangling up with one another. As usual. 'I wish I had an IQ like you have; then I could pass the test, I wouldn't be a chickenhead. I think you're very superior; I could learn a lot from you.'

After an interval Roy Baty said, 'I'll finish wiring up the alarm.' He resumed work.

'He doesn't understand yet,' Pris said in a sharp, brittle, stentorian voice, 'how we got off Mars. What we did there.'

'What we couldn't help doing,' Roy Baty grunted.

At the open door to the hall Irmgard Baty had been standing; they noticed her as she spoke up. 'I don't think we have to worry about Mr Isidore,' she said earnestly; she walked swiftly toward him, looked up into his face. 'They don't treat him very well either, as he said. And what we did on Mars he isn't interested in; he knows us and he likes us and an emotional acceptance like that – it's everything to him. It's hard for us to grasp that, but it's true.' To Isidore she said, standing very close to him once again and peering up at him, 'You could get a lot of money by turning us in; do you realize that?' Twisting, she said to her husband, 'See, he realizes that but still he wouldn't say anything.'

'You're a great man, Isidore,' Pris said. 'You're a credit to your race.'

'If he was an android,' Roy said heartily, 'he'd turn us in about ten tomorrow morning. He'd take off for his job and that would be it. I'm overwhelmed with admiration.' His tone could not be deciphered; at least Isidore could not crack it. 'And we imagined this would be a friendless world, a planet of hostile faces, all turned against us.' He barked out a laugh.

'I'm not at all worried,' Irmgard said.

'You ought to be scared to the soles of your feet,' Roy said.

'Let's vote,' Pris said. 'As we did on the ship, when we had a disagreement.'

'Well,' Irmgard said, 'I won't say anything more. But if we turn this down I don't think we'll find any other human being who'll take us in and help us. Mr Isidore is—' She searched for the word.

'Special,' Pris said.

Fifteen

Solemnly, and with ceremony, the vote was taken.

'We stay here,' Irmgard said, with firmness. 'In this apartment, in this building.'

Roy Baty said, 'I vote we kill Mr Isidore and hide somewhere else.' He and his wife – and John Isidore – now turned tautly toward Pris.

In a low voice Pris said, 'I vote we make our stand here.' She added, more loudly, 'I think J.R.'s value to us outweighs his danger, that of his knowing. Obviously we can't live among humans without being discovered; that's what killed Polokov and Garland and Luba and Anders. That's what killed all of them.'

'Maybe they did just what we're doing,' Roy Baty said. 'Confided in, trusted, one given human being who they believed was different. As you said, special.'

'We don't know that,' Irmgard said. 'That's only a conjecture. I think they, they—' She gestured. 'Walked around. Sang from a stage like Luba. We trust— I'll tell you what we trust that fouls us up, Roy; it's our goddamn superior intelligence!' She glared at her husband, her small, high breasts rising and falling rapidly. 'We're so *smart* – Roy, you're doing it right now; goddamn you, you're doing it *now!*'

Pris said, 'I think Irm's right.'

'So we hang our lives on a substandard, blighted—' Roy

began, then gave up. 'I'm tired,' he said simply. 'It's been a long trip, Isidore. But not very long here. Unfortunately.'

'I hope,' Isidore said happily, 'I can help make your stay here on Earth pleasant.' He felt sure he could. It seemed to him a cinch, the culmination of his whole life – and of the new authority which he had manifested on the vidphone today at work.

As soon as he officially quit work that evening, Rick Deckard flew across town to animal row: the several blocks of big-time animal dealers with their huge glass windows and lurid signs. The new and horribly unique depression which had floored him earlier in the day had not left. This, his activity here with animals and animal dealers, seemed the only weak spot in the shroud of depression, a flaw by which he might be able to grab it and exorcise it. In the past, anyhow, the sight of animals, the scent of money deals with expensive stakes, had done much for him. Maybe it would accomplish as much now.

'Yes, sir,' a nattily dressed new animal salesman said to him chattily as he stood gaping with a sort of glazed, meek need at the displays. 'See anything you like?'

Rick said, 'I see a lot I like. It's the cost that bothers me.'

'You tell us the deal you want to make,' the salesman said. 'What you want to take home with you and how you want to pay for it. We'll take the package to our sales manager and get his big okay.'

'I've got three thou cash.' The department, at the end of the day, had paid him his bounty. 'How much,' he asked, 'is that family of rabbits over there?'

'Sir, if you have a down payment of three thou, I can make you owner of something a lot better than a pair of rabbits. What about a goat?'

'I haven't thought much about goats,' Rick said.

'May I ask if this represents a new price bracket for you?'

'Well, I don't usually carry around three thou,' Rick conceded.

'I thought as much, sir, when you mentioned rabbits. The thing about rabbits, sir, is that everybody has one. I'd like to see you step up to the goat-class where I feel you belong. Frankly you look more like a goat man to me.'

'What are the advantages to goats?'

The animal salesman said, 'The distinct advantage of a goat is that it can be taught to butt anyone who tries to steal it.'

'Not if they shoot it with a hypno-dart and descend by rope ladder from a hovering hovercar,' Rick said.

The salesman, undaunted, continued, 'A goat is loyal. And it has a free, natural soul which no cage can chain up. And there is one exceptional additional feature about goats, one which you may not be aware of. Often times when you invest in an animal and take it home you find, some morning, that it's eaten something radioactive and died. A goat isn't bothered by contaminated quasi-foodstuffs; it can eat eclectically, even items that would fell a cow or a horse or most especially a cat. As a long term investment we feel that the goat – especially the female – offers unbeatable advantages to the serious animal-owner.'

'Is this goat a female?' He had noticed a big black goat standing squarely in the center of its cage; he moved that way and the salesman accompanied him. The goat, it seemed to Rick, was beautiful.

'Yes, this goat is a female. A black Nubian goat, very large, as you can see. This is a superb contender in this year's market, sir. And we're offering her at an attractive, unusually low, low price.'

Getting out his creased Sidney's, Rick looked up the listings on goats, black Nubian.

'Will this be a cash deal?' the salesman asked. 'Or are you trading in a used animal?'

'All cash,' Rick said.

On a slip of paper the salesman scribbled a price and then briefly, almost furtively, showed it to Rick.

'Too much,' Rick said. He took the slip of paper and wrote down a more modest figure.

'We couldn't let a goat go for that,' the salesman protested. He wrote another figure. 'This goat is less than a year old; she has a very long life expectancy.' He showed the figure to Rick.

'It's a deal,' Rick said.

He signed the time-payment contract, paid over his three thousand dollars – his entire bounty money – as down payment, and shortly found himself standing by his hovercar, rather dazed, as employees of the animal dealer loaded the crate of goat into the car. I own an animal now, he said to himself. A living animal, not electric. For the second time in my life.

The expense, the contractual indebtedness, appalled him; he found himself shaking. But I had to do it, he said to himself. The experience with Phil Resch – I have to get my confidence, my faith in myself and my abilities, back. Or I won't keep my job.

His hands numb he guided the hovercar up into the sky and headed for his apartment and Iran. She'll be angry, he said to himself. Because it'll worry her, the responsibility. And since she's home all day a lot of the maintenance will fall to her. Again he felt dismal.

When he had landed on the roof of his building he sat for a time, weaving together in his mind a story thick with verisimilitude. My job requires it, he thought, scraping bottom. Prestige. We couldn't go on with the electric sheep any longer; it sapped my morale. Maybe I can tell her that, he decided.

Climbing from the car he maneuvered the goat cage from the back seat, with wheezing effort managed to set it down on the roof. The goat, which had slid about during the transfer, regarded him with bright-eyed perspicacity, but made no sound.

He descended to his floor, followed a familiar path down the hall to his own door.

'Hi,' Iran greeted him, busy in the kitchen with dinner. 'Why so late tonight?'

'Come up on the roof,' he said. 'I want to show you something.'

'*You bought an animal.*' She removed her apron, smoothed back her hair reflexively, and followed him out of the apartment; they progressed down the hall with huge, eager strides. 'You shouldn't have gotten it without me,' Iran gasped. 'I have a right to participate in the decision, the most important acquisition we'll ever—'

'I wanted it to be a surprise,' he said.

'You made some bounty money today,' Iran said, accusingly.

Rick said, 'Yes. I retired three andys.' He entered the elevator and together they moved nearer to god. 'I had to buy this,' he said. 'Something went wrong, today; something about retiring them. It wouldn't have been possible for me to go on without getting an animal.' The elevator had reached the roof; he led his wife out into the evening darkness, to the cage; switching on the spotlights – maintained for the use of all building residents – he pointed to the goat, silent. Waiting for her reaction.

'Oh my god,' Iran said softly. She walked to the cage, peered in; then she circled around it, viewing the goat from every angle. 'Is it really real?' she asked. 'It's not false?'

'Absolutely real,' he said. 'Unless they swindled me.' But that rarely happened; the fine for counterfeiting would be enormous: two and a half times the full market value of the genuine animal. 'No, they didn't swindle me.'

'It's a goat,' Iran said. 'A black Nubian goat.'

'Female,' Rick said. 'So maybe later on we can mate her. And we'll get milk out of which we can make cheese.'

'Can we let her out? Put her where the sheep is?'

'She ought to be tethered,' he said. 'For a few days at least.'

Iran said in an odd little voice, '"My life is love and pleasure." An old, old song by Josef Strauss. Remember? When we first met.' She put her hand gently on his shoulder, leaned toward him, and kissed him. 'Much love. And very much pleasure.'

'Thanks,' he said, and hugged her.

'Let's run downstairs and give thanks to Mercer. Then we can come up here again and right away name her; she needs a name. And maybe you can find some rope to tether her.' She started off.

Standing by his horse Judy, grooming and currying her, their neighbor Bill Barbour called to them, 'Hey, that's a nice-looking goat you have, Deckards. Congratulations. Evening, Mrs Deckard. Maybe you'll have kids; I'll maybe trade you my colt for a couple of kids.'

'Thanks,' Rick said. He followed after Iran, in the direction of the elevator. 'Does this cure your depression?' he asked her. 'It cures mine.'

Iran said, 'It certainly does cure my depression. Now we can admit to everybody that the sheep's false.'

'No need to do that,' he said cautiously.

'But we *can*,' Iran persisted. 'See, now we have nothing to hide; what we've always wanted has come true. It's a dream!' Once more she stood on tiptoe, leaning and nimbly kissing him; her breath, eager and erratic, tickled his neck. She reached, then, to stab at the elevator button.

Something warned him. Something made him say, 'Let's not go down to the apartment yet. Let's stay up here with the goat. Let's just sit and look at her and maybe feed the goat something. They gave me a bag of oats to start us out. And we can read the manual on goat maintenance; they included that, too, at no extra charge. We can call her Euphemia.' The elevator, however, had come and already Iran was trotting inside. 'Iran, wait,' he said.

'It would be immoral not to fuse with Mercer in gratitude,' Iran said. 'I had hold of the handles of the box today and it overcame my depression a little – just a little, not like this. But anyhow I got hit by a rock, here.' She held up her wrist; on it he made out a small dark bruise. 'And I remember thinking how much better we are, how much better off, when we're with Mercer. Despite the pain. Physical pain but spiritually together; I felt everyone else, all over the world, all who had fused at the same time.' She held the elevator door from sliding shut. 'Get in, Rick. This'll be just for a moment. You hardly ever undergo fusion; I want you to transmit the mood you're in now to everyone else; you owe it to them. It would be immoral to keep it for ourselves.'

She was, of course, right. So he entered the elevator and once again descended.

In their living room, at the empathy box, Iran swiftly snapped the switch, her face animated with growing gladness; it lit her up like a rising new crescent of moon. 'I want everyone to know,' she told him. 'Once that happened to me; I fused and picked up someone who had just acquired an animal. And then one day—' Her features momentarily darkened; the pleasure fled. 'One day I found myself receiving from someone whose animal had died. But others of us shared our different joys with them – I didn't have any, as you might know – and that cheered the person up. We might even reach a potential suicide; what we have, what we're feeling, might—'

'They'll have our joy,' Rick said, 'but we'll lose. We'll exchange what we feel for what they feel. Our joy will be lost.'

The screen of the empathy box now showed rushing streams of bright formless color; taking a breath his wife hung on tightly to the two handles. 'We won't really lose what we feel, not if we keep it clearly in mind. You never really have gotten the hang of fusion, have you, Rick?'

'Guess not,' he said. But now he had begun to sense, for the first time, the value that people such as Iran obtained from Mercerism. Possibly his experience with the bounty hunter Phil Resch had altered some minute synapsis in him, had closed one neurological switch and opened another. And this perhaps had started a chain reaction. 'Iran,' he said urgently; he drew her away from the empathy box. 'Listen; I want to talk about what happened to me today.' He led her over to the couch, sat her down facing him. 'I met another bounty hunter,' he said. 'One I never saw before. A predatory one who seemed to like to destroy them. For the first time, after being with him, I looked at them differently. I mean, in my own way I had been viewing them as he did.'

'Won't this wait?' Iran said.

Rick said, 'I took a test, one question, and verified it; I've begun to empathize with androids, and look what that means. You said it this morning yourself. "Those poor andys." So you know what I'm talking about. That's why I bought the goat. I never felt like that before. Maybe it could be a depression, like you get. I can understand now how you suffer when you're depressed; I always thought you liked it and I thought you could have snapped yourself out any time, if not alone then by means of the mood organ. But when you get that depressed you don't care. Apathy, because you've lost a sense of worth. It doesn't matter whether you feel better because if you have no worth—'

'What about your job?' Her tone jabbed at him; he blinked. 'Your *job*,' Iran repeated. 'What are the monthly payments on the goat?' She held out her hand; reflexively he got out the contract which he had signed, passed it to her. 'That much,' she said in a thin voice. 'The interest; good god – the interest alone. And you did this because you were depressed. Not as a surprise for me, as you originally said.' She handed the contract back to him. 'Well, it doesn't matter. I'm still glad you got the goat; I love the goat. But it's such an economic burden.' She looked gray.

Rick said, 'I can get switched to some other desk. The department does ten or eleven separate jobs. Animal theft; I could transfer to that.'

'But the bounty money. We need it or they'll repossess the goat!'

'I'll get the contract extended from thirty-six months to forty-eight.' He whipped out a ball-point pen, scribbled rapidly on the back of the contract. 'That way it'll be fifty-two fifty less a month.'

The vidphone rang.

'If we hadn't come back down here,' Rick said, 'if we'd stayed up on the roof, with the goat, we wouldn't have gotten this call.'

Going to the vidphone, Iran said, 'Why are you afraid? They're not repossessing the goat, not yet.' She started to lift the receiver.

'It's the department,' he said. 'Say I'm not here.' He headed for the bedroom.

'Hello,' Iran said, into the receiver.

Three more andys, Rick thought to himself, that I should have followed up on today, instead of coming home. On the vidscreen Harry Bryant's face had formed, so it was too late to get away. He walked, with stiff leg muscles, back toward the phone.

'Yes, he's here,' Iran was saying. 'We bought a goat. Come over and see it, Mr Bryant.' A pause as she listened and then she held the receiver up to Rick. 'He has something he wants to say to you,' she said. Going over to the empathy box she quickly seated herself and once more gripped the twin handles. She became involved almost at once. Rick stood holding the phone receiver, conscious of her mental departure. Conscious of his own aloneness.

'Hello,' he said into the receiver.

'We have a tail on two of the remaining androids,' Harry Bryant said. He was calling from his office; Rick saw the familiar desk, the litter of documents and papers and kipple. 'Obviously they've become alerted – they've left the address Dave gave you and now they can be found at . . . wait.' Bryant groped about on his desk, at last located the material he wanted.

Automatically Rick searched for his pen; he held the goat-payment contract on his knee and prepared to write.

'Conapt Building 3967-C,' Inspector Bryant said. 'Get over there as soon as you can. We have to assume they know about the ones you picked off, Garland and Luft and Polokov; that's why they've taken unlawful flight.'

'Unlawful,' Rick repeated. To save their lives.

'Iran says you bought a goat,' Bryant said. 'Just today? After you left work?'

'On my way home.'

'I'll come and look at your goat after you retire the

remaining androids. By the way – I talked to Dave just now. I told him the trouble they gave you; he says congratulations and be more careful. He says the Nexus-6 types are smarter than he thought. In fact he couldn't believe you got three in one day.'

'Three is enough,' Rick said. 'I can't do anything more. I have to rest.'

'By tomorrow they'll be gone,' Inspector Bryant said. 'Out of our jurisdiction.'

'Not that soon. They'll still be around.'

Bryant said, 'You get over there tonight. Before they get dug in. They won't expect you to move in so fast.'

'Sure they will,' Rick said. 'They'll be waiting for me.'

'Got the shakes? Because of what Polokov—'

'I haven't got the shakes,' Rick said.

'Then what's wrong?'

'Okay,' Rick said. 'I'll get over there.' He started to hang up the phone.

'Let me know as soon as you get results. I'll be here in my office.'

Rick said, 'If I get them I'm going to buy a sheep.'

'You have a sheep. You've had one as long as I've known you.'

'It's electric,' Rick said. He hung up. A real sheep this time, he said to himself. I have to get one. In compensation.

At the black empathy box his wife crouched, her face rapt. He stood beside her for a time, his hand resting on her breast; he felt it rise and fall, the life in her, the activity. Iran did not notice him; the experience with Mercer had, as always, become complete.

On the screen the faint, old, robed figure of Mercer toiled upward, and all at once a rock sailed past him. Watching, Rick thought, My god; there's something worse about my situation than his. Mercer doesn't have to do anything alien to him. He suffers but at least he isn't required to violate his own identity.

Bending, he gently removed his wife's fingers from the twin handles. He then himself took her place. For the first time in weeks. An impulse: he hadn't planned it; all at once it had happened.

A landscape of weeds confronted him, a desolation. The air smelled of harsh blossoms; this was the desert, and there was no rain.

A man stood before him, a sorrowful light in his weary, pain-drenched eyes.

'Mercer,' Rick said.

'I am your friend,' the old man said. 'But you must go on as if I did not exist. Can you understand that?' He spread empty hands.

'No,' Rick said. 'I can't understand that. I need help.'

'How can I save you,' the old man said, 'if I can't save myself?' He smiled. 'Don't you see? *There is no salvation.*'

'Then what's this for?' Rick demanded. 'What are you for?'

'To show you,' Wilbur Mercer said, 'that you aren't alone. I am here with you and always will be. Go and do your task, even though you know it's wrong.'

'Why?' Rick said. 'Why should I do it? I'll quit my job and emigrate.'

The old man said, 'You will be required to do wrong no matter where you go. It is the basic condition of life, to be required to violate your own identity. At some time, every creature which lives must do so. It is the ultimate shadow, the defeat of creation; this is the curse at work, the curse that feeds on all life. Everywhere in the universe.'

'That's all you can tell me?' Rick said.

A rock whizzed at him; he ducked and the rock struck him on the ear. At once he let go of the handles and again he stood in his own living room, beside his wife and the empathy box. His head ached wildly from the blow; reaching, he found fresh blood collecting, spilling in huge bright drops down the side of his face.

Iran, with a handkerchief, patted his ear. 'I guess I'm glad you pried me loose. I really can't stand it, being hit. Thanks for taking the rock in my place.'

'I'm going,' Rick said.

'The job?'

'Three jobs.' He took the handkerchief from her and went to the hall door, still dizzy and, now, feeling nausea.

'Good luck,' Iran said.

'I didn't get anything from holding onto those handles,' Rick said. 'Mercer talked to me but it didn't help. He doesn't know any more than I do. He's just an old man climbing a hill to his death.'

'Isn't that the revelation?'

Rick said, 'I have that revelation already.' He opened the hall door. 'I'll see you later.' Stepping out into the hall he shut the door after him. Conapt 3967-C, he reflected, reading it off the back of the contract. That's out in the suburbs; it's mostly abandoned, there. A good place to hide. Except for the lights at night. That's what I'll be going by, he thought. The lights. Phototropic, like the death's head moth. And then after this, he thought, there won't be any more. I'll do something else, earn my living another way. These three are the last. Mercer is right; I have to get this over with. But, he thought, I don't think I can. Two andys together – this isn't a moral question, it's a practical question.

I probably *can't* retire them, he realized. Even if I try; I'm too tired and too much has happened today. Maybe Mercer knew this, he reflected. Maybe he foresaw everything that will happen.

But I know where I can get help, offered to me before but declined.

He reached the roof and a moment later sat in the darkness of his hovercar, dialing.

'Rosen Association,' the answering-service girl said.

'Rachael Rosen,' he said.

'Pardon, sir?'

Rick grated, 'Get me Rachael Rosen.'

'Is Miss Rosen expecting—'

'I'm sure she is,' he said. He waited.

Ten minutes later Rachael Rosen's small dark face appeared on the vidscreen. 'Hello, Mr Deckard.'

'Are you busy right now or can I talk to you?' he said. 'As you said earlier today.' It did not seem like today; a generation had risen and declined since he had talked to her last. And all the weight, all the weariness of it, had recapitulated itself in his body; he felt the physical burden. Perhaps, he thought, because of the rock. With the handkerchief he dabbed at his still-bleeding ear.

'Your ear is cut,' Rachael said. 'What a shame.'

Rick said, 'Did you really think I wouldn't call you? As you said?'

'I told you,' Rachael said, 'that without me one of the Nexus-6s would get you before you got it.'

'You were wrong.'

'But you are calling. Anyhow. Do you want me to come down there to San Francisco?'

'Tonight,' he said.

'Oh, it's too late. I'll come tomorrow; it's an hour trip.'

'I have been told I have to get them tonight.' He paused and then said, 'Out of the original eight, three are left.'

'You sound like you've had a just awful time.'

'If you don't fly down here tonight,' he said, 'I'll go after them alone and I won't be able to retire them. I just bought a goat,' he added. 'With the bounty money from the three I did get.'

'You humans.' Rachael laughed. 'Goats smell terrible.'

'Only male goats. I read it in the book of instructions that came with it.'

'You really are tired,' Rachael said. 'You look dazed. Are you sure you know what you're doing, trying for three more Nexus-6s the same day? No one has ever retired six androids in one day.'

'Franklin Powers,' Rick said. 'About a year ago, in Chicago. He retired seven.'

'The obsolete McMillan Y-4 variety,' Rachael said. 'This is something else.' She pondered. 'Rick, I can't do it. I haven't even had dinner.'

'I need you,' he said. Otherwise I'm going to die, he said to himself. I know it; Mercer knew it; I think you know it, too. And I'm wasting my time appealing to you, he reflected. An android can't be appealed to; there's nothing in there to reach.

Rachael said, 'I'm sorry, Rick, but I can't do it tonight. It'll have to be tomorrow.'

'Android vengeance,' Rick said.

'What?'

'Because I tripped you up on the Voigt-Kampff scale.'

'Do you think that?' Wide-eyed, she said, '*Really?*'

'Good-by,' he said, and started to hang up.

'Listen,' Rachael said rapidly. 'You're not using your head.'

'It seems that way to you because you Nexus-6 types are cleverer than humans.'

'No, I really don't understand,' Rachael sighed. 'I can tell that you don't want to do this job tonight – maybe not at all. Are you sure you want me to make it possible for you to retire the three remaining androids? Or do you want me to persuade you not to try?'

'Come down here,' he said, 'and we'll rent a hotel room.'

'Why?'

'Something I heard today,' he said hoarsely. 'About situations involving human men and android women. Come down here to San Francisco tonight and I'll give up on the remaining andys. We'll do something else.'

She eyed him, then abruptly said, 'Okay, I'll fly down. Where should I meet you?'

'At the St Francis. It's the only halfway decent hotel still in operation in the Bay Area.'

'And you won't do anything until I get there.'

'I'll sit in the hotel room,' he said, 'and watch Buster Friendly on TV. His guest for the last three days has been Amanda Werner. I like her; I could watch her the rest of my life. She has breasts that smile.' He hung up, then, and sat for a time, his mind vacant. At last the cold of the car roused him; he switched on the ignition key and a moment later headed in the direction of downtown San Francisco. And the St Francis Hotel.

Sixteen

In the sumptuous and enormous hotel room Rick Deckard sat reading the typed carbon sheets on the two androids Roy and Irmgard Baty. In these two cases telescopic snapshots had been included, fuzzy 3-D color prints which he could barely make out. The woman, he decided, looks attractive. Roy Baty, however, is something different. Something worse.

A pharmacist on Mars, he read. Or at least the android had made use of that cover. In actuality it had probably been a manual laborer, a field hand, with aspirations for something better. Do androids dream? Rick asked himself. Evidently; that's why they occasionally kill their employers and flee here. A better life, without servitude. Like Luba Luft; singing *Don Giovanni* and *Le Nozze* instead of toiling across the face of a barren rock-strewn field. On a fundamentally uninhabitable colony world.

> Roy Baty (the poop sheet informed him) has an aggressive, assertive air of ersatz authority. Given to mystical preoccupations, this android proposed the group escape attempt, underwriting it ideologically with a pretentious fiction as to the sacredness of so-called android 'life.' In addition, this android stole, and experimented with, various mind-fusing drugs, claiming when caught that it hoped to promote in androids a group experience similar to that of Mercerism, which it pointed out remains unavailable to androids.

The account had a pathetic quality. A rough, cold android, hoping to undergo an experience from which, due to a deliberately built-in defect, it remained excluded. But he could not work up much concern for Roy Baty; he caught, from Dave's jottings, a repellent quality hanging about this particular android. Baty had tried to force the fusion experience into existence for itself – and then, when that fell through, it had engineered the killing of a variety of human beings . . . followed by the flight to Earth. And now, especially as of today, the chipping away of the original eight androids until only the three remained. And they, the outstanding members of the illegal group, were also doomed, since if he failed to get them someone else would. Time and tide, he thought. The cycle of life. Ending in this, the last twilight. Before the silence of death. He perceived in this a micro-universe, complete.

The door of the hotel room banged open. 'What a flight,' Rachael Rosen said breathlessly, entering in a long fish-scale coat with matching bra and shorts; she carried, besides her big, ornate, mail-pouch purse, a paper bag. 'This is a *nice* room.' She examined her wristwatch. 'Less than an hour; I made good time. Here.' She held out the paper bag. 'I bought a bottle. Bourbon.'

Rick said, 'The worst of the eight is still alive. The one who organized them.' He held the poop sheet on Roy Baty toward her; Rachael set down the paper bag and accepted the carbon sheet.

'You've located this one?' she asked, after reading.

'I have a conapt number. Out in the suburbs where possibly a couple of deteriorated specials, antheads and chickenheads, hang out and go through their versions of living.'

Rachael held out her hand. 'Let's see about the others.'

'Both females.' He passed her the sheets, one dealing with Irmgard Baty, the other an android calling itself Pris Stratton.

Glancing at the final sheet Rachael said, 'Oh—' She tossed the sheets down, moved over to the window of the room to look out at downtown San Francisco. 'I think you're going to get thrown by the last one. Maybe not; maybe you don't care.' She had turned pale and her voice shook. All at once she had become exceptionally unsteady.

'Exactly what are you muttering about?' He retrieved the sheets, studied them, wondering which part had upset Rachael.

'Let's open the bourbon.' Rachael carried the paper bag into the bathroom, got two glasses, returned; she still seemed distracted and uncertain – and preoccupied. He sensed the rapid flight of her hidden thoughts: the transitions showed on her frowning, tense face. 'Can you get this open?' she asked. 'It's worth a fortune, you realize. It's not synthetic; it's from before the war, made from genuine mash.'

Taking the bottle he opened it, poured bourbon in the two tumblers. 'Tell me what's the matter,' he said.

Rachael said, 'On the phone you told me if I flew down here tonight you'd give up on the remaining three andys. "We'll do something else," you said. But here we are—'

'Tell me what upset you,' he said.

Facing him defiantly, Rachael said, 'Tell me what we're going to do instead of fussing and fretting around about those last three Nexus-6 andys.' She unbuttoned her coat, carried it to the closet, and hung it up. This gave him his first chance to have a good long look at her.

Rachael's proportions, he noticed once again, were odd; with her heavy mass of dark hair her head seemed large, and because of her diminutive breasts her body assumed a lank, almost childlike stance. But her great eyes, with their elaborate lashes, could only be those of a grown woman; there the resemblance to adolescence ended. Rachael rested very slightly on the fore-part of her feet, and her arms, as they hung, bent at the joint: the stance, he reflected, of a wary hunter of perhaps the Cro-Magnon persuasion. The race of tall hunters, he said to himself. No excess flesh, a flat belly, small behind and smaller bosom – Rachael had been modeled on the Celtic type of build, anachronistic and attractive. Below the brief shorts her legs, slender, had a neutral, nonsexual quality, not much rounded off in nubile curves. The total impression was good, however. Although definitely that of a girl, not a woman. Except for the restless, shrewd eyes.

He sipped the bourbon; the power of it, the authoritative strong taste and scent, had become almost unfamiliar to him and he had trouble swallowing. Rachael, in contrast, had no difficulty with hers.

Setting herself on the bed Rachael smoothed absently at the spread; her expression had now become one of moodiness. He set his glass down on the bedside table and arranged himself beside her. Under his gross weight the bed gave, and Rachael shifted her position.

'What is it?' he said. Reaching, he took hold of her hand; it felt cold, bony, slightly moist. 'What upset you?'

'That last goddamn Nexus-6 type,' Rachael said, enunciating with effort, 'is the same type as I am.' She stared down at the bedspread, found a thread, and began rolling it into a pellet. 'Didn't you notice the description? It's of me, too. She may wear her hair differently and dress differently – she may even have bought a wig. But when you see her you'll know what I mean.' She laughed sardonically. 'It's a good thing the association admitted I'm an andy; otherwise you'd probably have gone mad when you caught sight of Pris Stratton. Or thought she was me.'

'Why does that bother you so much?'

'Hell, I'll be along when you *retire* her.'

'Maybe not. Maybe I won't find her.'

Rachael said, 'I know Nexus-6 psychology. That's why I'm here; that's why I can help you. They're all holed up together, the last three of them. Clustered around the deranged one calling himself Roy Baty. He'll be masterminding their crucial, all-out, final defense.' Her lips twisted. 'Jesus,' she said.

'Cheer up,' he said; he cupped her sharp, small chin in the palm of his hand, lifted her head so that she had to face him. I wonder what it's like to kiss an android, he said to himself. Leaning forward an inch he kissed her dry lips. No reaction followed; Rachael remained impassive. As if unaffected. And yet he sensed otherwise. Or perhaps it was wishful thinking.

'I wish,' Rachael said, 'that I had known that before I came. I never would have flown down here. I think you're asking too much. You know what I have? Toward this Pris android?'

'Empathy,' he said.

'Something like that. Identification; there goes I. My god; maybe that's what'll happen. In the confusion you'll retire me, not her. And she can go back to Seattle and live my life. I never felt this way before. We *are* machines, stamped out like bottle caps. It's an illusion that I – I personally – really exist; I'm just representative of a type.' She shuddered.

He could not help being amused; Rachael had become so mawkishly morose. 'Ants don't feel like that,' he said, 'and they're physically identical.'

'Ants. They don't feel period.'

'Identical human twins. They don't—'

'But they identify with each other; I understand they have an empathic, special bond.' Rising, she got to the bourbon bottle, a little unsteadily; she refilled her glass and again drank swiftly. For a time she slouched about the room, brows knitted darkly, and then, as if sliding his way by chance, she settled back onto the bed; she swung her legs up and stretched out, leaning against the fat pillows. And sighed. 'Forget the three andys.' Her voice filled with weariness. 'I'm so worn out, from the trip I guess. And from all I learned today. I just want to sleep.' She shut her eyes. 'If I die,' she murmured, 'maybe I'll be born again when the Rosen Association stamps out its next unit of my subtype.' She opened her eyes and glared at him ferociously. 'Do you know,' she said, 'why I really came here? Why Eldon and the other Rosens – the human ones – wanted me to go along with you?'

'To observe,' he said. 'To detail exactly what the Nexus-6 does that gives it away on the Voigt-Kampff test.'

'On the test or otherwise. Everything that gives it a different quality. And then I report back and the association makes modifications of its zygote-bath DNS factors. And we then have the Nexus-7. And when that gets caught we modify again and eventually the association has a type that can't be distinguished.'

'Do you know of the Boneli Reflex-Arc Test?' he asked.

'We're working on the spinal ganglia, too. Someday the Boneli test will fade into yesterday's hoary shroud of spiritual oblivion.' She smiled innocuously – at variance with her words. At this point he could not discern her degree of seriousness. A topic of world shaking importance, yet dealt with facetiously; an android trait, possibly, he thought. No emotional awareness, no feeling-sense of the actual *meaning* of what she said. Only the hollow, formal, intellectual definitions of the separate terms.

And, more, Rachael had begun to tease him. Imperceptibly she had passed from lamenting her condition to taunting him about his.

'Damn you,' he said.

Rachael laughed. 'I'm drunk. I can't go with you. If you leave here—' She gestured in dismissal. 'I'll stay behind and sleep and you can tell me later what happened.'

'Except,' he said, 'there won't be a later because Roy Baty will nail me.'

'But I can't help you anyhow now because I'm drunk. Anyhow, you know the truth, the brick-hard, irregular, slithery surface of truth. I'm just an observer and I won't intervene to save you; I don't care if Roy Baty nails you or not. I care whether *I* get nailed.' She opened her eyes round and wide. 'Christ, I'm empathic about myself. And, see, if I go to that suburban broken-down conapt building—' She reached out, toyed with a button of his shirt; in slow, facile twists she began unbuttoning it. 'I don't dare go because androids have no loyalty to one another and I know that that goddamn Pris Stratton will destroy me and occupy my place. See? Take off your coat.'

'Why?'

'So we can go to bed,' Rachael said.

'I bought a black Nubian goat,' he said. 'I have to retire the three more andys. I have to finish up my job and go home to my wife.' He got up, walked around the bed to the bottle of bourbon. Standing there he carefully poured himself a second drink; his hands, he observed, shook only very slightly. Probably from fatigue. Both of us, he realized, are tired. Too tired to hunt down three andys, with the worst of the eight calling the shots.

Standing there he realized, all at once, that he had acquired an overt, incontestable fear directed toward the principal android. It all hung on Baty – had hung on it from the start. Up to now he had encountered and retired progressively more ominous manifestations of Baty. Now came Baty itself. Thinking that he felt the fear grow; it snared him completely, now that he had let it approach his conscious mind. 'I can't go without you now,' he said to Rachael. 'I can't even leave here. Polokov came after me; Garland virtually came after me.'

'You think Roy Baty will look you up?' Setting down her empty glass she bent forward, reached back, and unfastened her bra. With agility she slid it from her, then stood, swaying, and grinning because she swayed. 'In my purse,' she said, 'I have a mechanism which our autofac on Mars builds as an emer—' She grimaced. 'An emergency safety thingamajing, -jig, while they're putting a newly made andy through its routine inspection checks. Get it out. It resembles an oyster. You'll see it.'

He began hunting through the purse. Like a human woman, Rachael had every class of object conceivable filched and hidden away in her purse; he found himself rooting interminably.

Meanwhile, Rachael kicked off her boots and unzipped her shorts; balancing on one foot she caught the discarded fabric with her toe and tossed it across the room. She then dropped onto the bed, rolled over to fumble for her glass, accidentally pushed the glass to the carpeted floor. 'Damn,' she said, and once again got shakily to her feet; in her underpants she stood watching him at work on her purse, and then, with careful deliberation and attention she drew the bedcovers back, got in, drew the covers over her.

'Is this it?' He held up a metallic sphere with a button-stem projecting.

'That cancels an android into catalepsy,' Rachael said, her eyes shut. 'For a few seconds. Suspends its respiration; yours, too, but humans can function without respiring – perspiring? – for a couple of minutes, but the vagus nerve of an andy—'

'I know.' He staightened up. 'The android autonomic nervous system isn't as flexible at cutting in and out as ours. But as you say, this wouldn't work for more than five or six seconds.'

'Long enough,' Rachael murmured, 'to save your life. So,

see—' She roused herself, sat up in the bed. 'If Roy Baty shows up here you can be holding that in your hand and you can press the stem on that thing. And while Roy Baty is frozen stiff with no air supply to his blood and his brain cells deteriorating you can kill Roy Baty with your laser.'

'You have a laser tube,' he said. 'In your purse.'

'A fake. Androids' – she yawned, eyes again shut – 'aren't permitted to carry lasers.'

He walked over to the bed.

Squirming about, Rachael managed to roll over at last onto her stomach, face buried in the white lower sheet. 'This is a clean, noble, virgin type of bed,' she stated. 'Only clean, noble girls who—' She pondered. 'Androids can't bear children,' she said, then. 'Is that a loss?'

He finished undressing her. Exposed her pale, cold loins.

'Is it a loss?' Rachael repeated. 'I don't really know; I have no way to tell. How does it feel to have a child? How does it feel to be born, for that matter? We're not born; we don't grow up; instead of dying from illness or old age we wear out like ants. Ants again; that's what we are. Not you; I mean me. Chitinous reflex-machines who aren't really alive.' She twisted her head to one side, said loudly, '*I'm not alive!* You're not going to bed with a woman. Don't be disappointed; okay? Have you ever made love to an android before?'

'No,' he said, taking off his shirt and tie.

'I understand – they tell me – it's convincing if you don't think too much about it. But if you think too much, if you reflect on what you're doing – then you can't go on. For ahem physiological reasons.'

Bending, he kissed her bare shoulder.

'Thanks, Rick,' she said wanly. 'Remember, though: don't think about it, just do it. Don't pause and be philosophical, because from a philosophical standpoint it's dreary. For us both.'

He said, 'Afterward I still intend to look for Roy Baty. I still need you to be there. I know that laser tube you have in your purse is—'

'You think I'll retire one of your andys for you?'

'I think in spite of what you said you'll help me all you can. Otherwise you wouldn't be lying there in that bed.'

'I love you,' Rachael said. 'If I entered a room and found a sofa covered with your hide I'd score very high on the Voigt-Kampff test.'

Tonight sometime, he thought as he clicked off the bedside light, I will retire a Nexus-6 which looks exactly like this naked girl. My good god, he thought; I've wound up where Phil Resch said. Go to bed with her first, he remembered. Then kill her. 'I can't do it,' he said, and backed away from the bed.

'I wish you could,' Rachael said. Her voice wavered.

'Not because of you. Because of Pris Stratton; what I have to do to her.'

'We're not the same. *I* don't care about Pris Stratton. Listen.' Rachael thrashed about in the bed, sitting up; in the gloom he could dimly make out her almost breastless, trim shape. '*Go to bed with me and I'll retire Stratton.* Okay? Because I can't stand getting this close and then—'

'Thank you,' he said; gratitude – undoubtedly because of the bourbon – rose up inside him, constricting his throat. Two, he thought. I now have only two to retire; just the Batys. Would Rachael really do it? Evidently. Androids thought and functioned that way. Yet he had never come across anything quite like this.

'Goddamn it, get into bed,' Rachael said.

He got into bed.

Seventeen

Afterward they enjoyed a great luxury: Rick had room service bring up coffee. He sat for a long time within the arms of a green, black, and gold leaf lounge chair, sipping coffee and meditating about the next few hours. Rachael, in the bathroom, squeaked and hummed and splashed in the midst of a hot shower.

'You made a good deal when you made that deal,' she called when she had shut off the water; dripping, her hair tied up with a rubber band, she appeared bare and pink at the bathroom door. 'We androids can't control our physical, sensual passions. You probably knew that; in my opinion you took advantage of me.' She did not, however, appear genuinely angry. If anything she had become cheerful and certainly as human as any girl he had known. 'Do we really have to go track down those three andys tonight?'

'Yes,' he said. Two for me to retire, he thought; one for you. As Rachael put it, the deal had been made.

Gathering a giant white bath towel about her, Rachael said, 'Did you enjoy that?'

'Yes.'

'Would you ever go to bed with an android again?'

'If it was a girl. If she resembled you.'

Rachael said, 'Do you know what the lifespan of a humanoid robot such as myself is? I've been in existence two years. How long do you calculate I have?'

After a hesitation he said, 'About two more years.'

'They never could solve that problem. I mean cell replacement. Perpetual or anyhow semi-perpetual renewal. Well, so it goes.' Vigorously she began drying herself. Her face had become expressionless.

'I'm sorry,' Rick said.

'Hell,' Rachael said, 'I'm sorry I mentioned it. Anyhow it keeps humans from running off and living with an android.'

'And this is true with you Nexus-6 types too?'

'It's the metabolism. Not the brain unit.' She trotted out, swept up her underpants, and began to dress.

He, too, dressed. Then together, saying little, the two of them journeyed to the roof field, where his hovercar had been parked by the pleasant white-clad human attendant.

As they headed toward the suburbs of San Francisco, Rachael said, 'It's a nice night.'

'My goat is probably asleep by now,' he said. 'Or maybe goats are nocturnal. Some animals never sleep. Sheep never do, not that I could detect; whenever you look at them they're looking back. Expecting to be fed.'

'What sort of wife do you have?'

He did not answer.

'Do you—'

'If you weren't an android,' Rick interrupted, 'if I could legally marry you, I would.'

Rachael said, 'Or we could live in sin, except that I'm not alive.'

'Legally you're not. But really you are. Biologically. You're not made out of transistorized circuits like a false animal; you're an organic entity.' And in two years, he thought, you'll wear out and die. Because we never solved the problem of cell replacement, as you pointed out. So I guess it doesn't matter anyhow.

This is my end, he said to himself. As a bounty hunter.

After the Batys there won't be any more. Not after this, tonight.

'You look so sad,' Rachael said.

Putting his hand out he touched her cheek.

'You're not going to be able to hunt androids any longer,' she said calmly. 'So don't look sad. Please.'

He stared at her.

'No bounty hunter ever has gone on,' Rachael said. 'After being with me. Except one. A very cynical man. Phil Resch. And he's nutty; he works out in left field on his own.'

'I see,' Rick said. He felt numb. Completely. Throughout his entire body.

'But this trip we're taking,' Rachael said, 'won't be wasted, because you're going to meet a wonderful, spiritual man.'

'Roy Baty,' he said. 'Do you know all of them?'

'I knew all of them, when they still existed. I know three, now. We tried to stop you this morning, before you started out with Dave Holden's list. I tried again, just before Polokov reached you. But then after that I had to wait.'

'Until I broke down,' he said. 'And had to call you.'

'Luba Luft and I had been close, very close friends for almost two years. What did you think of her? Did you like her?'

'I liked her.'

'But you killed her.'

'Phil Resch killed her.'

'Oh, so Phil accompanied you back to the opera house. We didn't know that; our communications broke down about then. We knew just that she had been killed; we naturally assumed by you.'

'From Dave's notes,' he said, 'I think I can still go ahead and retire Roy Baty. But maybe not Irmgard Baty.' And not Pris Stratton, he thought. Even now; even knowing this. 'So all that took place at the hotel,' he said, 'consisted of a—'

'The association,' Rachael said, 'wanted to reach the bounty hunters here and in the Soviet Union. This seemed to work . . . for reasons which we do not fully understand. Our limitation again, I guess.'

'I doubt if it works as often or as well as you say,' he said thickly.

'But it has with you.'

'We'll see.'

'I already know,' Rachael said. 'When I saw that expression on your face, that grief. I look for that.'

'How many times have you done this?'

'I don't remember. Seven, eight. No, I believe it's nine.' She – or rather it – nodded. 'Yes, nine times.'

'The idea is old-fashioned,' Rick said.

Startled, Rachael said, 'W-what?'

Pushing the steering wheel away from him he put the car into a gliding decline. 'Or anyhow that's how it strikes me. I'm going to kill you,' he said. 'And go on to Roy and Irmgard Baty and Pris Stratton alone.'

'That's why you're landing?' Apprehensively, she said, 'There's a fine; I'm the property, the legal property, of the association. I'm not an escaped android who fled here from Mars; I'm not in the same class as the others.'

'But,' he said, 'if I can kill you then I can kill them.'

Her hands dived for her bulging, overstuffed, kipple-filled purse; she searched frantically, then gave up. 'Goddamn this purse,' she said with ferocity. 'I never can lay my hands on anything in it. Will you kill me in a way that won't hurt? I mean, do it carefully. If I don't fight; okay? I promise not to fight. Do you agree?'

Rick said, 'I understand now why Phil Resch said what he

said. He wasn't being cynical; he had just learned too much. Going through this – I can't blame him. It warped him.'

'But the wrong way.' She seemed more externally composed, now. But still fundamentally frantic and tense. Yet, the dark fire waned; the life force oozed out of her, as he had so often witnessed before with other androids. The classic resignation. Mechanical, intellectual acceptance of that which a genuine organism – with two billion years of the pressure to live and evolve hagriding it – could never have reconciled itself to.

'I can't stand the way you androids give up,' he said savagely. The car now swooped almost to the ground; he had to jerk the wheel toward him to avoid a crash. Braking, he managed to bring the car to a staggering, careening halt; he slammed off the motor and got out his laser tube.

'At the occipital bone, the posterior base of my skull,' Rachael said. 'Please.' She twisted about so that she did not have to look at the laser tube; the beam would enter unperceived.

Putting his laser tube away Rick said, 'I can't do what Phil Resch said.' He snapped the motor back on, and a moment later they had taken off again.

'If you're ever going to do it,' Rachael said, 'do it now. Don't make me wait.'

'I'm not going to kill you.' He steered the car in the direction of downtown San Francisco once again. 'Your car's at the St Francis, isn't it? I'll let you off there and you can head for Seattle.' That ended what he had to say; he drove in silence.

'Thanks for not killing me,' Rachael said presently.

'Hell, as you said you've only got two years of life left, anyhow. And I've got fifty. I'll live twenty-five times as long as you.'

'But you really look down on me,' Rachael said. 'For what I did.' Assurance had returned to her; the litany of her voice picked up pace. 'You've gone the way of the others. The bounty hunters before you. Each time they get furious and talk wildly about killing me, but when the time comes they can't do it. Just like you, just now.' She lit a cigarette, inhaled with relish. 'You realize what this means, don't you? It means I was right; you won't be able to retire any more androids; it won't be just me, it'll be the Batys and Stratton, too. So go on home to your goat. And get some rest.' Suddenly she brushed at her coat, violently. 'Yife! I got a burning ash from my cigarette – there, it's gone.' She sank back against the seat, relaxing.

He said nothing.

'That goat,' Rachael said. 'You love the goat more than me. More than you love your wife, probably. First the goat, then your wife, then last of all—' She laughed merrily. 'What can you do but laugh?'

He did not answer. They continued in silence for a while and then Rachael poked about, found the car's radio, and switched it on.

'Turn it off,' Rick said.

'Turn off Buster Friendly and his Friendly Friends? Turn off Amanda Werner and Oscar Scruggs? It's time to hear Buster's big sensational exposé, which is finally almost arrived.' She stooped to read the dial of her watch by the radio's light. 'Very soon now. Did you already know about it? He's been talking about it, building up to it, for—'

The radio said, '—ah jes wan ta tell ya, folks, that ahm sitten hih with my pal Bustuh, an we're tawkin en havin a real mighty fine time, waitin expectantly as we ah with each tick uh the clock foh what ah understan is the mos *im*portant *a*nnouncement of—'

Rick shut the radio off. 'Oscar Scruggs,' he said. 'The voice of intelligent man.'

Instantly reaching, Rachael clicked the radio back on. 'I want to listen. I *intend* to listen. This is important, what Buster Friendly has to say on his show tonight.' The idiotic voice babbled once more from the speaker, and Rachael Rosen settled back and made herself comfortable. Beside him in the darkness the coal of her cigarette glowed like the rump of a complacent lightning bug: a steady, unwavering index of Rachael Rosen's achievement. Her victory over him.

Eighteen

'Bring the rest of my property up here,' Pris ordered J. R. Isidore. 'In particular I want the TV set. So we can hear Buster's announcement.'

'Yes,' Irmgard Baty agreed, bright-eyed, like a darting, plumed swift. 'We *need* the TV; we've been waiting a long time for tonight and now it'll be starting soon.'

Isidore said, 'My own set gets the government channel.'

Off in a corner of the living room, seated in a deep chair as if he intended to remain permanently, as if he had taken up lodgings in the chair, Roy Baty belched and said patiently, 'It's Buster Friendly and his Friendly Friends that we want to watch, Iz. Or do you want me to call you J. R.? Anyhow, do you understand? So will you go get the set?'

Alone, Isidore made his way down the echoing, empty hall to the stairs. The potent, strong fragrance of happiness still bloomed in him, the sense of being – for the first time in his dull life – useful. Others depend on me now, he exulted as he trudged down the dust-impacted steps to the level beneath.

And, he thought, it'll be nice to see Buster Friendly on TV again, instead of just listening on the radio in the store truck. And that's right, he realized; Buster Friendly is going to reveal his carefully documented sensational exposé tonight. So because of Pris and Roy and Irmgard I get to watch what will probably be the most important piece of news to be released in many years. How about that, he said to himself.

Life, for J. R. Isidore, had definitely taken an upswing.

He entered Pris's former apartment, unplugged the TV set, and detached the antenna. The silence, all at once, penetrated; he felt his arms grow vague. In the absence of the Batys and Pris he found himself fading out, becoming strangely like the inert television set which he had just unplugged. You have to be with other people, he thought. In order to live at all. I mean, before they came here I could stand it, being alone in the building. But now it's changed. You can't go back, he thought. You can't go from people to nonpeople. In panic he thought, I'm dependent on them. Thank god they stayed.

It would require two trips to transfer Pris's possessions to the apartment above. Hoisting the TV set he decided to take it first, then the suitcases and remaining clothes.

A few minutes later he had gotten the TV set upstairs; his fingers groaning he placed it on a coffee table in his living room. The Batys and Pris watched impassively.

'We get a good signal in this building,' he panted as he plugged in the cord and attached the antenna. 'When I used to get Buster Friendly and his—'

'Just turn the set on,' Roy Baty said. 'And stop talking.'

He did so, then hurried to the door. 'One more trip,' he said, 'will do it.' He lingered, warming himself at the hearth of their presence.

'Fine,' Pris said remotely.

Isidore started off once more. I think, he thought, they're exploiting me sort of. But he did not care. They're still good friends to have, he said to himself.

Downstairs again, he gathered the girl's clothing together, stuffed every piece into the suitcases, then labored back down the hall once again and up the stairs.

On a step ahead of him something small moved in the dust.

Instantly he dropped the suitcases; he whipped out a plastic medicine bottle, which, like everyone else, he carried for just this. A spider, undistinguished but alive. Shakily he eased it into the bottle and snapped the cap – perforated by means of a needle – shut tight.

Upstairs, at the door of his apartment, he paused to get his breath.

'—yes sir, folks; the time is *now*. This is Buster Friendly, who hopes and trusts you're as eager as I am to share the discovery which I've made and by the way had verified by top trained research workers working extra hours over the past weeks. Ho ho, folks; *this is it!*'

John Isidore said, 'I found a spider.'

The three androids glanced up, momentarily moving their attention from the TV screen to him.

'Let's see it,' Pris said. She held out her hand.

Roy Baty said, 'Don't talk while Buster is on.'

'I've never seen a spider,' Pris said. She cupped the medicine bottle in her palms, surveying the creature within. 'All those legs. Why's it need so many legs, J. R.?'

'That's the way spiders are,' Isidore said, his heart pounding; he had difficulty breathing. 'Eight legs.'

Rising to her feet, Pris said, 'You know what I think, J. R.? I think it doesn't need all those legs.'

'Eight?' Irmgard Baty said. 'Why couldn't it get by on four? Cut four off and see.' Impulsively opening her purse she produced a pair of clean, sharp cuticle scissors, which she passed to Pris.

A weird terror struck at J. R. Isidore.

Carrying the medicine bottle into the kitchen Pris seated herself at J. R. Isidore's breakfast table. She removed the lid from the bottle and dumped the spider out. 'It probably won't be able to run as fast,' she said, 'but there's nothing for it to catch around here anyhow. It'll die anyway.' She reached for the scissors.

'Please,' Isidore said.

Pris glanced up inquiringly. 'Is it worth something?'

'Don't mutilate it,' he said wheezingly. Imploringly.

With the scissors Pris snipped off one of the spider's legs.

In the living room Buster Friendly on the TV screen said, 'Take a look at this enlargement of a section of background. This is the sky you usually see. Wait, I'll have Earl Parameter, head of my research staff, explain their virtually world-shaking discovery to you.'

Pris clipped off another leg, restraining the spider with the edge of her hand. She was smiling.

'Blowups of the video pictures,' a new voice from the TV said, 'when subjected to rigorous laboratory scrutiny, reveal that the gray backdrop of sky and daytime moon against which Mercer moves is not only not Terran – *it is artificial*.'

'You're missing it!' Irmgard called anxiously to Pris; she rushed to the kitchen door, saw what Pris had begun doing. 'Oh, do that afterward,' she said coaxingly. 'This is so important, what they're saying; it proves that everything we believed—'

'Be quiet,' Roy Baty said.

'—is true,' Irmgard finished.

The TV set continued, 'The "moon" is painted; in the enlargements, one of which you see now on your screen, brushstrokes show. And there is even some evidence that the scraggly weeds and dismal, sterile soil – perhaps even the stones hurled at Mercer by unseen alleged parties – are equally faked. It is quite possible in fact that the "stones" are made of soft plastic, causing no authentic wounds.'

'In other words,' Buster Friendly broke in, 'Wilbur Mercer is not suffering at all.'

The research chief said, 'We at last managed, Mr Friendly, to track down a former Hollywood special-effects man, a Mr

Wade Cortot, who flatly states, from his years of experience, that the figure of "Mercer" could well be merely some bit player marching across a sound stage. Cortot has gone so far as to declare that he recognizes the stage as one used by a now out-of-business minor moviemaker with whom Cortot had various dealings several decades ago.'

'So according to Cortot,' Buster Friendly said, 'there can be virtually no doubt.'

Pris had now cut three legs from the spider, which crept about miserably on the kitchen table, seeking a way out, a path to freedom. It found none.

'Quite frankly we believed Cortot,' the research chief said in his dry, pedantic voice, 'and we spent a good deal of time examining publicity pictures of bit players once employed by the now defunct Hollywood movie industry.'

'And you found—'

'Listen to this,' Roy Baty said. Irmgard gazed fixedly at the TV screen and Pris had ceased her mutilation of the spider.

'We located, by means of thousands upon thousands of photographs, a very old man now, named Al Jarry, who played a number of bit parts in pre-war films. From our lab we sent a team to Jarry's home in East Harmony, Indiana. I'll let one of the members of that team describe what he found.' Silence, then a new voice, equally pedestrian. 'The house on Lark Avenue in East Harmony is tottering and shabby and at the edge of town, where no one, except Al Jarry, still lives. Invited amiably in, and seated in the stale-smelling, moldering, kipple-filled living room, I scanned by telepathic means the blurred, debris-cluttered, and hazy mind of Al Jarry seated across from me.'

'Listen,' Roy Baty said, on the edge of his seat, poised as if to pounce.

'I found,' the technician continued, 'that the old man did in actuality make a series of short fifteen minute video films, for an employer whom he never met. And, as we had theorized, the "rocks" did consist of rubber-like plastic. The "blood" shed was catsup, and' – the technician chuckled – 'the only suffering Mr Jarry underwent was having to go an entire day without a shot of whisky.'

'Al Jarry,' Buster Friendly said, his face returning to the screen. 'Well, well. An old man who even in his prime never amounted to anything which either he or ourselves could respect. Al Jarry made a repetitious and dull film, a series of them in fact, for whom he knew not – and does not to this day. It has often been said by adherents of the experience of Mercerism that Wilbur Mercer is not a human being, that he is in fact an archetypal superior entity perhaps from another star. Well, in a sense this contention has proven correct. Wilbur Mercer is not human, does not in fact exist. The world in which he climbs is a cheap, Hollywood, commonplace sound stage which vanished into kipple years ago. And who, then, has spawned this hoax on the Sol System? Think about that for a time, folks.'

'We may never know,' Irmgard murmured.

Buster Friendly said, 'We may never know. Nor can we fathom the peculiar purpose behind this swindle. Yes, folks, swindle. *Mercerism is a swindle!*'

'I think we know,' Roy Baty said. 'It's obvious. Mercerism came into existence—'

'But ponder this,' Buster Friendly continued. 'Ask yourselves what is it that Mercerism does. Well, if we're to believe its many practitioners, the experience fuses—'

'It's that empathy that humans have,' Irmgard said.

'—men and women throughout the Sol System into a single entity. But an entity which is manageable by the so-called telepathic voice of "Mercer." Mark that. An ambitious politically minded would-be Hitler could—'

'No, it's that empathy,' Irmgard said vigorously. Fists clenched, she roved into the kitchen, up to Isidore. 'Isn't it a way of proving that humans can do something we can't do? Because without the Mercer experience we just have your *word* that you feel this empathy business, this shared, group thing. How's the spider?' She bent over Pris's shoulder.

With the scissors Pris snipped off another of the spider's legs. 'Four now,' she said. She nudged the spider. 'He won't go. But he can.'

Roy Baty appeared at the doorway, inhaling deeply, an expression of accomplishment on his face. 'It's done. Buster said it out loud, and nearly every human in the system heard him say it. "Mercerism is a swindle." The whole experience of empathy is a swindle.' He came over to look curiously at the spider.

'It won't try to walk,' Irmgard said.

'I can make it walk.' Roy Baty got out a book of matches, lit a match; he held it near the spider, closer and closer, until at last it crept feebly away.

'I was right,' Irmgard said. 'Didn't I say it could walk with only four legs?' She peered up expectantly at Isidore. 'What's the matter?' Touching his arm she said, 'You didn't lose anything; we'll pay you what that – what's it called? – that Sidney's catalogue says. Don't look so grim. Isn't that something about Mercer, what they discovered? All that research? Hey, answer.' She prodded him anxiously.

'He's upset,' Pris said. 'Because he has an empathy box. In the other room. Do you use it, J. R.?' she asked Isidore.

Roy Baty said, 'Of course he uses it. They all do – or did. Maybe now they'll start wondering.'

'I don't think this will end the cult of Mercer,' Pris said.

'But right this minute there's a lot of unhappy human beings.' To Isidore she said, 'We've waited for months; we all knew it was coming, this pitch of Buster's.' She hesitated and then said, 'Well, why not. Buster is one of us.'

'An android,' Irmgard explained. 'And nobody knows. No humans, I mean.'

Pris, with the scissors, cut yet another leg from the spider. All at once John Isidore pushed her away and lifted up the mutilated creature. He carried it to the sink and there he drowned it. In him his mind, his hopes, drowned, too. As swiftly as the spider.

'He's really upset,' Irmgard said nervously. 'Don't look like that, J. R. And why don't you say anything?' To Pris and to her husband she said, 'It makes me terribly upset, him just standing there by the sink and not speaking; he hasn't said anything since we turned on the TV.'

'It's not the TV,' Pris said. 'It's the spider. Isn't it, John R. Isidore? He'll get over it,' she said to Irmgard, who had gone into the other room to shut off the TV.

Regarding Isidore with easy amusement, Roy Baty said, 'It's all over now, Iz. For Mercerism, I mean.' With his nails he managed to lift the corpse of the spider from the sink. 'Maybe this was the last spider,' he said. 'The last living spider on Earth.' He reflected. 'In that case it's all over for spiders, too.'

'I – don't feel well,' Isidore said. From the kitchen cupboard he got a cup; he stood holding it for an interval – he did not know exactly how long. And then he said to Roy Baty, 'Is the sky behind Mercer just painted? Not real?'

'You saw the enlargements on the TV screen,' Roy Baty said. 'The brushstrokes.'

'Mercerism isn't finished,' Isidore said. Something ailed the three androids, something terrible. The spider, he thought.

Maybe it *had* been the last spider on Earth, as Roy Baty said. And the spider is gone; Mercer is gone; he saw the dust and the ruin of the apartment as it lay spreading out everywhere – he heard the kipple coming, the final disorder of all forms, the absence which would win out. It grew around him as he stood holding the empty ceramic cup; the cupboards of the kitchen creaked and split and he felt the floor beneath his feet give.

Reaching out, he touched the wall. His hand broke the surface; gray particles trickled and hurried down, fragments of plaster resembling the radioactive dust outside. He seated himself at the table and, like rotten, hollow tubes the legs of the chair bent; standing quickly, he set down the cup and tried to reform the chair, tried to press it back into its right shape. The chair came apart in his hands, the screws which had previously connected its several sections ripping out and hanging loose. He saw, on the table, the ceramic cup crack; webs of fine lines grew like the shadows of a vine, and then a chip dropped from the edge of the cup, exposing the rough, unglazed interior.

'What's he doing?' Irmgard Baty's voice came to him, distantly. 'He's breaking everything! Isidore stop—'

'I'm not doing it,' he said. He walked unsteadily into the living room, to be by himself; he stood by the tattered couch and gazed at the yellow, stained wall with all the spots which dead bugs, that had once crawled, had left, and again he thought of the corpse of the spider with its four remaining legs. Everything in here is old, he realized. It long ago began to decay and it won't stop. The corpse of the spider has taken over.

In the depression caused by the sagging of the floor, pieces of animals manifested themselves, the head of a crow, mummified hands which might have once been parts of monkeys. A donkey stood a little way off, not stirring and yet apparently alive; at least it had not begun to deteriorate. He started toward it, feeling stick-like bones, dry as weeds, splinter under his shoes. But before he could reach the donkey – one of the creatures which he loved the most – a shiny blue crow fell from above to perch on the donkey's unprotesting muzzle. Don't, he said aloud, but the crow, rapidly, picked out the donkey's eyes. Again, he thought. It's happening to me again. I will be down here a long time, he realized. As before. It's always long, because nothing here ever changes; a point comes when it does not even decay.

A dry wind rustled, and around him the heaps of bones broke. Even the wind destroys them, he perceived. At this stage. Just before time ceases. I wish I could remember how to climb up from here, he thought. Looking up he saw nothing to grasp.

Mercer, he said aloud. Where are you now? This is the tomb world and I am in it again, but this time you're not here too.

Something crept across his foot. He knelt down and searched for it – and found it because it moved so slowly. The mutilated spider, advancing itself haltingly on its surviving legs; he picked it up and held it in the palm of his hand. *The bones*, he realized, *have reversed themselves*; the spider is again alive. Mercer must be near.

The wind blew, cracking and splintering the remaining bones, but he sensed the presence of Mercer. Come here, he said to Mercer. Crawl across my foot or find some other way of reaching me. Okay? Mercer, he thought. Aloud he said, 'Mercer!'

Across the landscape weeds advanced; weeds corkscrewed their way into the walls around him and worked the walls until they the weeds became their own spore. The spore expanded, split, and burst within the corrupted steel and shards of concrete that had formerly been walls. But the desolation remained after the walls had gone; the desolation followed after everything else. Except the frail, dim figure of Mercer; the old man faced him, a placid expression on his face.

'Is the sky painted?' Isidore asked. 'Are there really brush-strokes that show up under magnification?'

'Yes,' Mercer said.

'I can't see them.'

'You're too close,' Mercer said. 'You have to be a long way off, the way the androids are. They have better perspective.'

'Is that why they claim you're a fraud?'

'I am a fraud,' Mercer said. 'They're sincere; their research is genuine. From their standpoint I am an elderly retired bit player named Al Jarry. All of it, their disclosure, is true. They interviewed me at my home, as they claim; I told them whatever they wanted to know, which was everything.'

'Including about the whisky?'

Mercer smiled. 'It was true. They did a good job and from their standpoint Buster Friendly's disclosure was convincing. They will have trouble understanding why nothing has changed. Because you're still here and I'm still here.' Mercer indicated with a sweep of his hand the barren, rising hillside, the familiar place. 'I lifted you from the tomb world just now and I will continue to lift you until you lose interest and want to quit. But you will have to stop searching for me because I will never stop searching for you.'

'I didn't like that about the whisky,' Isidore said. 'That's lowering.'

'That's because you're a highly moral person. I'm not. I don't judge, not even myself.' Mercer held out a closed hand, palm up. 'Before I forget it, I have something of yours here.' He opened his fingers. On his hand rested the mutilated spider, but with its snipped-off legs restored.

'Thanks.' Isidore accepted the spider. He started to say something further—

An alarm bell clanged.

Roy Baty snarled, 'There's a bounty hunter in the building! Get all the lights off. Get him away from that empathy box; he has to be ready at the door. Go on – *move him!*'

Nineteen

Looking down, John Isidore saw his own hands; they gripped the twin handles of the empathy box. As he stood gaping at them, the lights in the living room of his apartment plunged out. He could see, in the kitchen, Pris hurrying to catch the table lamp there.

'Listen, J. R.,' Irmgard whispered harshly in his ear; she had grabbed him by the shoulder, her nails digging into him with frantic intensity. She seemed unaware of what she did, now; in the dim nocturnal light from outdoors Irmgard's face had become distorted, astigmatic. It had turned into a craven dish, with cowering, tiny, lidless eyes. 'You have to go,' she whispered, 'to the door, when he knocks, if he does knock; you have to show him your identification and tell him this is your apartment and no one else is here. And you ask to see a warrant.'

Pris, standing on the other side of him, her body arched, whispered, 'Don't let him in, J. R. Say anything; do anything that will stop him. Do you know what a bounty hunter would do let loose in here? Do you understand what he would do to us?'

Moving away from the two android females Isidore groped his way to the door; with his fingers he located the knob, halted there, listening. He could sense the hall outside, as he always had sensed it: vacant and reverberating and lifeless.

'Hear anything?' Roy Baty said, bending close. Isidore

smelled the rank, cringing body; he inhaled fear from it, fear pouring out, forming a mist. 'Step out and take a look.'

Opening the door, Isidore looked up and down the indistinct hall. The air out here had a clear quality, despite the weight of dust. He still held the spider which Mercer had given him. Was it actually the spider which Pris had snipped apart with Irmgard Baty's cuticle scissors? Probably not. He would never know. But anyhow it was alive; it crept about within his closed hand, not biting him: as with most small spiders its mandibles could not puncture human skin.

He reached the end of the hall, descended the stairs, and stepped outside, onto what had once been a terraced path, garden-enclosed. The garden had perished during the war and the path had ruptured in a thousand places. But he knew its surface; under his feet the familiar path felt good, and he followed it, passed along the greater side of the building, coming at last to the only verdant spot in the vicinity – a yard-square patch of dust-saturated, drooping weeds. There he deposited the spider. He experienced its wavering progress as it departed his hand. Well, that was that; he straightened up.

A flashlight beam focused on the weeds; in its glare their half-dead stalks appeared stark, menacing. Now he could see the spider; it rested on a serrated leaf. So it had gotten away all right.

'What did you do?' the man holding the flashlight asked.

'I put down a spider,' he said, wondering why the man didn't see; in the beam of yellow light the spider bloated up larger than life. 'So it could get away.'

'Why don't you take it up to your apartment? You ought to keep it in a jar. According to the January Sidney's most spiders are up ten percent in retail price. You could have gotten a hundred and some odd dollars for it.'

Isidore said, 'If I took it back up there she'd cut it apart again. Bit by bit, to see what it did.'

'Androids do that,' the man said. Reaching into his overcoat he brought out something which he flapped open and extended toward Isidore.

In the irregular light the bounty hunter seemed a medium man, not impressive. Round face and hairless, smooth features; like a clerk in a bureaucratic office. Methodical but informal. Not demi-god in shape; not at all as Isidore had anticipated him.

'I'm an investigator for the San Francisco Police Department. Deckard, Rick Deckard.' The man flapped his ID shut again, stuck it back in his overcoat pocket. 'They're up there now? The three?'

'Well, the thing is,' Isidore said, 'I'm looking after them. Two are women. They're the last ones of the group; the rest are dead. I brought Pris's TV set up from her apartment and put it in mine, so they could watch Buster Friendly. Buster proved beyond a doubt that Mercer doesn't exist.' Isidore felt excitement, knowing something of this importance – news that the bounty hunter evidently hadn't heard.

'Let's go up there,' Deckard said. Suddenly he held a laser tube pointed at Isidore; then, indecisively, he put it away. 'You're a special, aren't you,' he said. 'A chickenhead.'

'But I have a job. I drive a truck for—' Horrified, he discovered he had forgotten the name. '—a pet hospital,' he said. 'The Van Ness Pet Hospital,' he said. 'Owned b-b-by Hannibal Sloat.'

Deckard said, 'Will you take me up there and show me which apartment they're in? There're over a thousand separate apartments; you can save me a lot of time.' His voice dipped with fatigue.

'If you kill them you won't be able to fuse with Mercer again,' Isidore said.

'You won't take me up there? Show me which floor? Just tell me the floor. I'll figure out which apartment on the floor it is.'

'No,' Isidore said.

'Under state and federal law,' Deckard began. He ceased, then. Giving up the interrogation. 'Good night,' he said, and walked away, up the path and into the building, his flashlight bleeding a yellowed, diffuse path before him.

Inside the conapt building, Rick Deckard shut off his flashlight; guided by the ineffectual, recessed bulbs spaced ahead of him he made his way along the hall, thinking, The chickenhead knows they're androids; he knew it already, before I told him. But he doesn't understand. On the other hand, who does? Do I? *Did* I?' And one of them will be a duplicate of Rachael, he reflected. Maybe the special has been living with her. I wonder how he liked it, he asked himself. Maybe that was the one who he believed would cut up his spider. I could go back and get that spider, he reflected. I've never found a live, wild animal. It must be a fantastic experience to look down and see something living scuttling along. Maybe it'll happen someday to me like it did him.

He had brought listening gear from his car; he set it up, now, a revolving detek-snout with blip screen. In the silence of the hall the screen indicated nothing. Not on this floor, he said to himself. He clicked over to vertical. On that axis the snout absorbed a faint signal. Upstairs. He gathered up the gear and his briefcase and climbed the stairs to the next floor.

A figure in the shadows waited.

'If you move I'll retire you,' Rick said. The male one, waiting for him. In his clenched fingers the laser tube felt hard but he could not lift it and aim it. He had been caught first, caught too soon.

'I'm not an android,' the figure said. 'My name is Mercer.' It stepped into a zone of light. 'I inhabit this building because of Mr Isidore. The special who had the spider; you talked briefly to him outside.'

'Am I outside Mercerism, now?' Rick said. 'As the chickenhead said? Because of what I'm going to do in the next few minutes?'

Mercer said, 'Mr Isidore spoke for himself, not for me. What you are doing has to be done. I said that already.' Raising his arm he pointed at the stairs behind Rick. 'I came to tell you that one of them is behind you and below, not in the apartment. It will be the hard one of the three and you must retire it first.' The rustling, ancient voice gained abrupt fervor. 'Quick, Mr Deckard. *On the steps*.'

His laser tube thrust out, Rick spun and sank onto his haunches facing the flight of stairs. Up it glided a woman, toward him, and he knew her; he recognized her and lowered his laser tube. 'Rachael,' he said, perplexed. Had she followed him in her own hovercar, tracked him here? And why? 'Go back to Seattle,' he said. 'Leave me alone; Mercer told me I've got to do it.' And then he saw that it was not quite Rachael.

'For what we've meant to each other,' the android said as it approached him, its arms reaching as if to clutch at him. The clothes, he thought, are wrong. But the eyes, the same eyes. And there are more like this; there can be a legion of her, each with its own name, but all Rachael Rosen – Rachael, the prototype, used by the manufacturer to protect the others. He fired at her as, imploringly, she dashed toward him. The android burst and parts of it flew; he covered his face and then looked again, looked and saw the laser tube which it had carried roll away, back onto the stairs; the metal tube bounced downward, step by step, the sound echoing and diminishing and slowing. The hard one of the three, Mercer had said. He peered about, searching for Mercer. The old man had gone. They can follow me with Rachael Rosens until I die, he thought, or until the type becomes obsolete, whichever comes first. And now the other two, he thought. One of them is not in the apartment, Mercer had said. Mercer protected me, he realized. Manifested himself and offered aid. She – it – would have gotten me, he said to himself, except for the fact that Mercer warned me. I can do the rest, now, he realized. This was the impossible one; she knew I couldn't do this. But it's over. In an instant. I did what I couldn't do. The Batys I can track by standard procedure; they will be hard but they won't be like this.

He stood alone in the empty hall; Mercer had left him because he had done what he came for, Rachael – or rather Pris Stratton – had been dismembered and that left nothing now, only himself. But elsewhere in the building; the Batys waited and knew. Perceived what he had done, here. Probably, at this point, they were afraid. This had been their response to his presence in the building. Their attempt. Without Mercer it would have worked. For them, winter had come.

This has to be done quickly, what I'm after now, he realized; he hurried down the hall and all at once his detection gear registered the presence of cephalic activity. He had found their apartment. No more need of the gear; he discarded it and rapped on the apartment door.

From within, a man's voice sounded. 'Who is it?'

'This is Mr Isidore,' Rick said. 'Let me in because I'm looking after you and t-t-two of you are women.'

'We're not opening the door,' a woman's voice came.

'I want to watch Buster Friendly on Pris's TV set,' Rick said. 'Now that he's proved Mercer doesn't exist it's very important to watch him. I drive a truck for the Van Ness Pet

Hospital, which is owned by Mr Hannibal S-s-sloat.' He made himself stammer. 'S-s-so would you open the d-d-door? It's my apartment.' He waited, and the door opened. Within the apartment he saw darkness and indistinct shapes, two of them.

The smaller shape, the woman, said, 'You have to administer tests.'

'It's too late,' Rick said. The taller figure tried to push the door shut and turn on some variety of electronic equipment. 'No,' Rick said, 'I have to come in.' He let Roy Baty fire once; he held his own fire until the laser beam had passed by him as he twisted out of the way. 'You've lost your legal basis,' Rick said, 'by firing on me. You should have forced me to give you the Voigt-Kampff test. But now it doesn't matter.' Once more Roy Baty sent a laser beam cutting at him, missed, dropped the tube, and ran somewhere deeper inside the apartment, to another room, perhaps, the electronic hardware abandoned.

'Why didn't Pris get you?' Mrs Baty said.

'There is no Pris,' he said. 'Only Rachael Rosen, over and over again.' He saw the laser tube in her dimly outlined hand; Roy Baty had slipped it to her, had meant to decoy him into the apartment, far in, so that Irmgard Baty could get him from behind, in the back. 'I'm sorry, Mrs Baty,' Rick said, and shot her.

Roy Baty, in the other room, let out a cry of anguish.

'Okay, you loved her,' Rick said. 'And I loved Rachael. And the special loved the other Rachael.' He shot Roy Baty; the big man's corpse lashed about, toppled like an over-stacked collection of separate, brittle entities; it smashed into the kitchen table and carried dishes and flatware down with it. Reflex circuits in the corpse made it twitch and flutter, but it had died; Rick ignored it, not seeing it and not seeing that of Irmgard Baty by the front door. I got the last one, Rick realized. Six today; almost a record. And now it's over and I can go home, back to Iran and the goat. And we'll have enough money, for once.

He sat down on the couch and presently as he sat there in the silence of the apartment, among the nonstirring objects, the special Mr Isidore appeared at the door.

'Better not look,' Rick said.

'I saw her on the stairs. Pris.' The special was crying.

'Don't take it so hard,' Rick said. He got dizzily to his feet, laboring. 'Where's your phone?'

The special said nothing, did nothing except stand. So Rick hunted for the phone himself, found it, and dialed Harry Bryant's office.

Twenty

'Good,' Harry Bryant said, after he had been told. 'Well, go get some rest. We'll send a patrol car to pick up the three bodies.'

Rick Deckard hung up. 'Androids are stupid,' he said savagely to the special. 'Roy Baty couldn't tell me from you; it thought you were at the door. The police will clean up in here; why don't you stay in another apartment until they're finished? You don't want to be in here with what's left.'

'I'm leaving this b-b-building,' Isidore said. 'I'm going to l-l-live deeper in town where there's m-m-more people.'

'I think there's a vacant apartment in my building,' Rick said.

Isidore stammered, 'I don't w-w-want to live near you.'

'Go outside or upstairs,' Rick said. 'Don't stay in here.'

The special floundered, not knowing what to do; a variety of mute expressions crossed his face and then, turning, he shuffled out of the apartment, leaving Rick alone.

What a job to have to do, Rick thought. I'm a scourge, like famine or plague. Where I go the ancient curse follows. As Mercer said, I am required to do wrong. Everything I've done has been wrong from the start. Anyhow now it's time to go home. Maybe, after I've been there awhile with Iran I'll forget.

When he got back to his own apartment building, Iran met him on the roof. She looked at him in a deranged, peculiar way; in all his years with her he had never seen her like this.

Putting his arm around her he said, 'Anyhow it's over. And I've been thinking; maybe Harry Bryant can assign me to a—'

'Rick,' she said, 'I have to tell you something. I'm sorry. The goat is dead.'

For some reason it did not surprise him; it only made him feel worse, a quantitative addition to the weight shrinking him from every side. 'I think there's a guarantee in the contract,' he said. 'If it gets sick within ninety days the dealer—'

'It didn't get sick. Someone' – Iran cleared her throat and went on huskily – 'someone came here, got the goat out of its cage, and dragged it to the edge of the roof.'

'And pushed it off?' he said.

'Yes.' She nodded.

'Did you see who did it?'

'I saw her very clearly,' Iran said. 'Barbour was still up here fooling around; he came down to get me and we called the police, but by then the animal was dead and she had left. A small young-looking girl with dark hair and large black eyes, very thin. Wearing a long fish-scale coat. She had a mail-pouch purse. And she made no effort to keep us from seeing her. As if she didn't care.'

'No, she didn't care,' he said. 'Rachael wouldn't give a damn if you saw her; she probably wanted you to, so I'd know who had done it.' He kissed her. 'You've been waiting up here all this time?'

'Only for half an hour. That's when it happened; half an hour ago.' Iran, gently, kissed him back. 'It's so awful. So needless.'

He turned toward his parked car, opened the door, and got in behind the wheel. 'Not needless,' he said. 'She had what seemed to her a reason.' An android reason, he thought.

'Where are you going? Won't you come downstairs and – be with me? There was the most shocking news on TV;

Buster Friendly claims that Mercer is a fake. What do you think about that, Rick? Do you think it could be true?'

'Everything is true,' he said. 'Everything anybody has ever thought.' He snapped on the car motor.

'Will you be all right?'

'I'll be all right,' he said, and thought, And I'm going to die. Both those are true, too. He closed the car door, flicked a signal with his hand to Iran, and then swept up into the night sky.

Once, he thought, I would have seen the stars. Years ago. But now it's only the dust; no one has seen a star in years, at least not from Earth. Maybe I'll go where I can see stars, he said to himself as the car gained velocity and altitude; it headed away from San Francisco, toward the uninhabited desolation to the north. To the place where no living thing would go. Not unless it felt that the end had come.

Twenty-One

In the early morning light the land below him extended seemingly forever, gray and refuse-littered. Pebbles the size of houses had rolled to a stop next to one another and he thought, It's like a shipping room when all the merchandise has left. Only fragments of crates remain, the containers which signify nothing in themselves. Once, he thought, crops grew here and animals grazed. What a remarkable thought, that anything could have cropped grass here.

What a strange place he thought for all of that to die.

He brought the hovercar down, coasted above the surface for a time. What would Dave Holden say about me now? he asked himself. In one sense I'm now the greatest bounty hunter who ever lived; no one ever retired six Nexus-6 types in one twenty-four-hour span and no one probably ever will again. I ought to call him, he said to himself.

A cluttered hillside swooped up at him; he lifted the hovercar as the world came close. Fatigue, he thought; I shouldn't be driving still. He clicked off the ignition, glided for an interval, and then set the hovercar down. It tumbled and bounced across the hillside, scattering rocks; headed upward, it came at last to a grinding, skittering stop.

Picking up the receiver of the car's phone he dialed the operator at San Francisco. 'Give me Mount Zion Hospital,' he told her.

Presently he had another operator on the vidscreen. 'Mount Zion Hospital.'

'You have a patient named Dave Holden,' he said. 'Would it be possible to talk to him? Is he well enough?'

'Just a moment and I'll check on that, sir.' The screen temporarily blanked out. Time passed. Rick took a pinch of Dr Johnson Snuff and shivered; without the car's heater the temperature had begun to plunge. 'Dr Costa says that Mr Holden is not receiving calls,' the operator told him, reappearing.

'This is police business,' he said; he held his flat pack of ID up to the screen.

'Just a moment.' Again the operator vanished. Again Rick inhaled a pinch of Dr Johnson Snuff; the menthol in it tasted foul, so early in the morning. He rolled down the car window and tossed the little yellow tin out into the rubble. 'No, sir,' the operator said, once more on his screen. 'Dr Costa does not feel Mr Holden's condition will permit him to take any calls, no matter how urgent, for at least—'

'Okay,' Rick said. He hung up.

The air, too, had a foul quality; he rolled up the window again. Dave is really out, he reflected. I wonder why they didn't get me. Because I moved too fast, he decided. All in one day; they couldn't have expected it. Harry Bryant was right.

The car had become too cold, now, so he opened the door and stepped out. A noxious, unexpected wind filtered through his clothes and he began to walk, rubbing his hands together.

It would have been rewarding to talk to Dave, he decided. Dave would have approved what I did. But also he would have understood the other part, which I don't think even Mercer comprehends. For Mercer everything is easy, he thought, because Mercer accepts everything. Nothing is alien to him. But what I've done, he thought; that's become alien to me. In fact everything about me has become unnatural; I've become an unnatural self.

He walked on, up the hillside, and with each step the weight on him grew. Too tired, he thought, to climb. Stopping, he wiped stinging sweat from his eyes, salt tears produced by his skin, his whole aching body. Then, angry at himself, he spat – spat with wrath and contempt, for himself, with utter hate, onto the barren ground. Thereupon he resumed his trudge up the slope, the lonely and unfamiliar terrain, remote from everything; nothing lived here except himself.

The heat. It had become hot, now; evidently time had passed. And he felt hunger. He had not eaten for god knew how long. The hunger and heat combined, a poisonous taste resembling defeat; yes, he thought, that's what it is: I've been defeated in some obscure way. By having killed the androids? By Rachael's murder of my goat? He did not know, but as he plodded along a vague and almost hallucinatory pall hazed over his mind; he found himself at one point, with no notion of how it could be, a step from an almost certainly fatal cliffside fall – falling humiliatingly and helplessly, he thought; on and on, with no one even to witness it. Here there existed no one to record his or anyone else's degradation, and any courage or pride which might manifest itself here at the end would go unmarked: the dead stones, the dust-stricken weeds dry and dying, perceived nothing, recollected nothing, about him or themselves.

At that moment the first rock – and it was not rubber or soft foam plastic – struck him in the inguinal region. And the pain, the first knowledge of absolute isolation and suffering, touched him throughout in its undisguised actual form.

He halted. And then, goaded on – the goad invisible but real, not to be challenged – he resumed his climb. Rolling upward, he thought, like the stones; I am doing what stones do, without volition. Without it meaning anything.

'Mercer,' he said, panting; he stopped, stood still. In front of him he distinguished a shadowy figure, motionless. 'Wilbur Mercer! Is that you?' My god, he realized; it's my shadow. I have to get out of here, down off this hill!

He scrambled back down. Once, he fell; clouds of dust obscured everything, and he ran from the dust – he hurried faster, sliding and tumbling on the loose pebbles. Ahead he saw his parked car. I'm back down, he said to himself. I'm off the hill. He plucked open the car door, squeezed inside. Who threw the stone at me? he asked himself. No one. But why does it bother me? I've undergone it before, during fusion. While using my empathy box, like everyone else. This isn't new. But it was. Because, he thought, I did it alone.

Trembling, he got a fresh new tin of snuff from the glove compartment of the car; pulling off the protective band of tape he took a massive pinch, rested, sitting half in the car and half out, his feet on the arid, dusty soil. This was the last place to go to, he realized. I shouldn't have flown here. And now he found himself too tired to fly back out.

If I could just talk to Dave, he thought, I'd be all right; I could get away from here, go home and go to bed. I still have my electric sheep and I still have my job. There'll be more andys to retire; my career isn't over; I haven't retired the last andy in existence. Maybe that's what it is, he thought. I'm afraid there aren't any more.

He looked at his watch. Nine-thirty.

Picking up the vidphone receiver he dialed the Hall of Justice on Lombard. 'Let me speak to Inspector Bryant,' he said to the police switchboard operator Miss Wild.

'Inspector Bryant is not in his office, Mr Deckard; he's out in his car, but I don't get any answer. He must have temporarily left his car.'

'Did he say where he intended to go?'

'Something about the androids you retired last night.'

'Let me talk to my secretary,' he said.

A moment later the orange, triangular face of Ann Marsten appeared on the screen. 'Oh, Mr Deckard – Inspector Bryant has been trying to get hold of you. I think he's turning your name over to Chief Cutter for a citation. Because you retired those six—'

'I know what I did,' he said.

'That's never happened before. Oh, and Mr Deckard; your wife phoned. She wants to know if you're all right. Are you all right?'

He said nothing.

'Anyhow,' Miss Marsten said, 'maybe you should call her and tell her. She left word she'll be home, waiting to hear from you.'

'Did you hear about my goat?' he said.

'No. I didn't even know you had a goat.'

Rick said, 'They took my goat.'

'Who did, Mr Deckard? Animal thieves? We just got a report on a huge new gang of them, probably teenagers, operating in—'

'Life thieves,' he said.

'I don't understand you, Mr Deckard.' Miss Marsten peered at him intently. 'Mr Deckard, you look awful. So tired. And god, your cheek is bleeding.'

Putting his hand up he felt the blood. From a rock, probably. More than one, evidently, had struck him.

'You look,' Miss Marsten said, 'like Wilbur Mercer.'

'I am,' he said. 'I'm Wilbur Mercer; I've permanently fused with him. And I can't unfuse. I'm sitting here waiting to unfuse. Somewhere near the Oregon border.'

'Shall we send someone out? A department car to pick you up?'

'No,' he said. 'I'm no longer with the department.'

'Obviously you did too much yesterday, Mr Deckard,' she said chidingly. 'What you need now is bed rest. Mr Deckard, you're our best bounty hunter, the best we've ever had. I'll tell Inspector Bryant when he comes in; you go on home and go to bed. Call your wife right away, Mr Deckard, because she's terribly, terribly worried. I could tell. You're both in dreadful shape.'

'It's because of my goat,' he said. 'Not the androids; Rachael was wrong – I didn't have any trouble retiring them. And the special was wrong, too, about my not being able to fuse with Mercer again. The only one who was right is Mercer.'

'You better get back here to the Bay Area, Mr Deckard. Where there're people. There isn't anything living up there near Oregon; isn't that right? Aren't you alone?'

'It's strange,' Rick said. 'I had the absolute, utter, completely real illusion that I had become Mercer and people were lobbing rocks at me. But not the way you experience it when you hold the handles of an empathy box. When you use an empathy box you feel you're *with* Mercer. The difference is I wasn't with anyone; I was alone.'

'They're saying now that Mercer is a fake.'

'Mercer isn't a fake,' he said. 'Unless reality is a fake.' This hill, he thought. This dust and these many stones, each one different from all the others. 'I'm afraid,' he said, 'that I can't stop being Mercer. Once you start it's too late to back off.' Will I have to climb the hill again? he wondered. Forever, as Mercer does . . . trapped by eternity. 'Good-by,' he said, and started to ring off.

'You'll call your wife? You promise?'

'Yes.' He nodded. 'Thanks, Ann.' He hung up. Bed rest, he thought. The last time I hit bed was with Rachael. A violation of a statute. Copulation with an android; absolutely against the law, here and on the colony worlds as well. She must be back in Seattle now. With the other Rosens, real and humanoid. I wish I could do to you what you did to me, he wished. But it can't be done to an android because they don't care. If I had killed you last night my goat would be alive now. There's where I made the wrong decision. Yes, he thought; it can all be traced back to that and to my going to bed with you. Anyhow you were correct about one thing; it did change me. But not in the way you predicted.

A much worse way, he decided.

And yet I don't really care. Not any longer. Not, he thought, after what happened to me up there, toward the top of the hill. I wonder what would have come next, if I had gone on climbing and reached the top. Because that's where Mercer appears to die. That's where Mercer's triumph manifests itself, there at the end of the great sidereal cycle.

But if I'm Mercer, he thought, I can never die, not in ten thousand years. *Mercer is immortal.*

Once more he picked up the phone receiver, to call his wife.

And froze.

Twenty-Two

He set the receiver back down and did not take his eyes from the spot that had moved outside the car. The bulge in the ground, among the stones. An animal, he said to himself. And his heart lugged under the excessive load, the shock of recognition. I know what it is, he realized; I've never seen one before but I know it from the old nature films they show on Government TV.

They're extinct! he said to himself; swiftly he dragged out his much-creased Sidney's, turned the pages with twitching fingers.

TOAD (Bufonidae), all varieties. . . . . . . *E.*

Extinct for years now. The critter most precious to Wilbur Mercer, along with the donkey. But toads most of all.

I need a box. He squirmed around, saw nothing in the back seat of the hovercar; he leaped out, hurried to the trunk compartment, unlocked and opened it. There rested a cardboard container, inside it a spare fuel pump for his car. He dumped the fuel pump out, found some furry hempish twine, and walked slowly toward the toad. Not taking his eyes from it.

The toad, he saw, blended in totally with the texture and shade of the ever-present dust. It had, perhaps, evolved, meeting the new climate as it had met all climates before. Had it not moved he would never have spotted it; yet he had been sitting no more than two yards from it. What happens when you find – if you find – an animal believed extinct? he asked himself, trying to remember. It happened so seldom. Something about a star of honor from the UN and a stipend. A reward running into millions of dollars. And of all possibilities – to find the critter most sacred to Mercer. Jesus, he thought; it can't be. Maybe it's due to brain damage on my part: exposure to radioactivity. I'm a special, he thought. Something has happened to me. Like the chickenhead Isidore and his spider; what happened to him is happening to me. Did Mercer arrange it? But I'm Mercer. I arranged it; I found the toad. Found it because I see through Mercer's eyes.

He squatted on his haunches, close beside the toad. It had shoved aside the grit to make a partial hole for itself, displaced the dust with its rump. So that only the top of its flat skull and its eyes projected above ground. Meanwhile, its metabolism slowed almost to a halt, it had drifted off into a trance. The eyes held no spark, no awareness of him, and in horror he thought, It's dead, of thirst maybe. But it had moved.

Setting the cardboard box down, he carefully began brushing the loose soil away from the toad. It did not seem to object, but of course it was not aware of his existence.

When he lifted the toad out he felt its peculiar coolness; in his hands its body seemed dry and wrinkled – almost flabby – and as cold as if it had taken up residence in a grotto miles under the earth away from the sun. Now the toad squirmed; with its weak hind feet it tried to pry itself from his grip, wanting, instinctively, to go flopping off. A big one, he thought; full-grown and wise. Capable, in its own fashion, of surviving even that which we're not really managing to survive. I wonder where it finds the water for its eggs.

So this is what Mercer sees, he thought as he painstakingly tied the cardboard box shut – tied it again and again. Life which we can no longer distinguish; life carefully buried up to its forehead in the carcass of a dead world. In every cinder of the universe Mercer probably perceives inconspicuous life. Now I know, he thought. And once having seen through Mercer's eyes I probably will never stop.

And no android, he thought, will cut the legs from this. As they did from the chickenhead's spider.

He placed the carefully tied box on the car seat and got in behind the wheel. It's like being a kid again, he thought. Now all the weight had left him, the monumental and oppressive fatigue. Wait until Iran hears about this; he snatched the vidphone receiver, started to dial. Then paused. I'll keep it as a surprise, he concluded. It'll only take thirty or forty minutes to fly back there.

Eagerly he switched the motor on, and, shortly, had zipped up into the sky, in the direction of San Francisco, seven hundred miles to the south.

At the Penfield mood organ, Iran Deckard sat with her right index finger touching the numbered dial. But she did not dial; she felt too listless and ill to want anything: a burden which closed off the future and any possibilities which it might once have contained. If Rick were here, she thought, he'd get me to dial 3 and that way I'd find myself wanting to dial something important, ebullient joy or if not that then possibly an 888, the desire to watch TV no matter what's on it. I wonder what is on it, she thought. And then she wondered again where Rick had gone. He may be coming back and on the other hand he may not be, she said to herself, and felt her bones within her shrink with age.

A knock sounded at the apartment door.

Putting down the Penfield manual she jumped up, thinking, I don't need to dial, now; I already have it – if it is Rick. She ran to the door, opened the door wide.

'Hi,' he said. There he stood, a cut on his cheek, his clothes wrinkled and gray, even his hair saturated with dust. His hands, his face – dust clung to every part of him, except his eyes. Round with awe his eyes shone, like those of a little boy; he looks, she thought, as if he has been playing and now it's time to give up and come home. To rest and wash and tell about the miracles of the day.

'It's nice to see you,' she said.

'I have something.' He held a cardboard box with both hands; when he entered the apartment he did not set it down. As if, she thought, it contained something too fragile and too valuable to let go of; he wanted to keep it perpetually in his hands.

She said, 'I'll fix you a cup of coffee.' At the stove she pressed the coffee button and in a moment had put the imposing mug by his place at the kitchen table. Still holding the box he seated himself, and on his face the round-eyed wonder remained. In all the years she had known him she had not encountered this expression before. Something had happened since she had seen him last; since, last night, he had gone off in his car. Now he had come back and this box had arrived with him: he held, in the box, everything that had happened to him.

'I'm going to sleep,' he announced. 'All day. I phoned in and got Harry Bryant; he said take the day off and rest. Which is exactly what I'm going to do.' Carefully he set the box down on the table and picked up his coffee mug; dutifully, because she wanted him to, he drank his coffee.

Seating herself across from him she said, 'What do you have in the box, Rick?'

'A toad.'

'Can I see it?' She watched as he untied the box and removed the lid. 'Oh,' she said, seeing the toad; for some reason it frightened her. 'Will it bite?' she asked.

'Pick it up. It won't bite; toads don't have teeth.' Rick lifted the toad out and extended it toward her. Stemming her aversion she accepted it. 'I thought toads were extinct,' she said as she turned it over, curious about its legs; they seemed almost useless. 'Can toads jump like frogs? I mean, will it jump out of my hands suddenly?'

'The legs of toads are weak,' Rick said. 'That's the main difference between a toad and a frog, that and water. A frog remains near water but a toad can live in the desert. I found this in the desert, up near the Oregon border. Where everything had died.' He reached to take it back from her. But she had discovered something; still holding it upside down she poked at its abdomen and then, with her nail, located the tiny control panel. She flipped the panel open.

'Oh.' His face fell by degrees. 'Yeah, so I see; you're right.' Crestfallen, he gazed mutely at the false animal; he took it back from her, fiddled with the legs as if baffled – he did not seem quite to understand. He then carefully replaced it in its box. 'I wonder how it got out there in the desolate part of California like that. Somebody must have put it there. No way to tell what for.'

'Maybe I shouldn't have told you – about it being electrical.' She put her hand out, touched his arm; she felt guilty, seeing the effect it had on him, the change.

'No,' Rick said. 'I'm glad to know. Or rather—' He became silent. 'I'd prefer to know.'

'Do you want to use the mood organ? To feel better? You always have gotten a lot out of it, more than I ever have.'

'I'll be okay.' He shook his head, as if trying to clear it, still bewildered. 'The spider Mercer gave the chickenhead, Isidore; it probably was artificial, too. But it doesn't matter. The electric things have their lives, too. Paltry as those lives are.'

Iran said, 'You look as if you've walked a hundred miles.'

'It's been a long day.' He nodded.

'Go get into bed and sleep.'

He stared at her, then, as if perplexed. 'It is over, isn't it?' Trustingly he seemed to be waiting for her to tell him, as if she would know. As if hearing himself say it meant nothing; he had a dubious attitude toward his own words; they didn't become real, not until she agreed.

'It's over,' she said.

'God, what a marathon assignment,' Rick said. 'Once I began on it there wasn't any way for me to stop; it kept carrying me along, until finally I got to the Batys, and then suddenly I didn't have anything to do. And that—' He hesitated, evidently amazed at what he had begun to say. 'That part was worse,' he said. 'After I finished. I couldn't stop because there would be nothing left after I stopped. You were right this morning when you said I'm nothing but a crude cop with crude cop hands.'

'I don't feel that any more,' she said. 'I'm just damn glad to have you come back home where you ought to be.' She kissed him and that seemed to please him; his face lit up, almost as much as before – before she had shown him that the toad was electric.

'Do you think I did wrong?' he asked. 'What I did today?'

'No.'

'Mercer said it was wrong but I should do it anyhow. Really weird. Sometimes it's better to do something wrong than right.'

'It's the curse on us,' Iran said. 'That Mercer talks about.'

'The dust?' he asked.

'The killers that found Mercer in his sixteenth year, when they told him he couldn't reverse time and bring things back to life again. So now all he can do is move along with life, going where it goes, to death. And the killers throw the rocks; it's they who're doing it. Still pursuing him. And all of us, actually. Did one of them cut your cheek, where it's been bleeding?'

'Yes,' he said wanly.

'Will you go to bed now? If I set the mood organ to a 670 setting?'

'What does that bring about?' he asked.

'Long deserved peace,' Iran said.

He got to his feet, stood painfully, his face drowsy and confused, as if a legion of battles had ebbed and advanced there, over many years. And then, by degrees, he progressed along the route to the bedroom. 'Okay,' he said. 'Long deserved peace.' He stretched out on the bed, dust sifting from his clothes and hair onto the white sheet.

No need to turn on the mood organ, Iran realized as she pressed the button which made the windows of the bedroom opaque. The gray light of day disappeared.

On the bed Rick, after a moment, slept.

She stayed there for a time, keeping him in sight to be sure he wouldn't wake up, wouldn't spring to a sitting position in fear as he sometimes did at night. And then, presently, she returned to the kitchen, reseated herself at the kitchen table.

Next to her the electric toad flopped and rustled in its box; she wondered what it 'ate,' and what repairs on it would run. Artificial flies, she decided.

Opening the phone book she looked in the yellow pages under *animal accessories, electric*; she dialed and when the saleswoman answered, said, 'I'd like to order one pound of artificial flies that really fly around and buzz, please.'

'Is it for an electric turtle, ma'am?'

'A toad,' she said.

'Then I suggest our mixed assortment of artificial crawling and flying bugs of all types including—'

'The flies will do,' Iran said. 'Will you deliver? I don't want to leave my apartment; my husband's asleep and I want to be sure he's all right.'

The clerk said, 'For a toad I'd suggest also a perpetually renewing puddle, unless it's a horned toad, in which case there's a kit containing sand, multicolored pebbles, and bits of organic debris. And if you're going to be putting it through its feed cycle regularly I suggest you let our service department make a periodic tongue adjustment. In a toad that's vital.'

'Fine,' Iran said. 'I want it to work perfectly. My husband is devoted to it.' She gave her address and hung up.

And, feeling better, fixed herself at last a cup of black, hot coffee.

Philip K. Dick was born in the USA in 1928. His twin sister Jane died in infancy. He started his writing career publishing short stories in magazines. The first of these was 'Beyond Lies the Wub' in 1952. While publishing SF prolifically during the fifties, Dick also wrote a series of mainstream novels, only one of which, *Confessions of a Crap Artist*, achieved publication during his lifetime. These included titles such as *Mary and the Giant* and *In Milton Lumky Territory*. During the 1960s Dick produced an extraordinary succession of novels, including *The Man in the High Castle*, which won a Hugo award, *Martian Time-Slip, Dr Bloodmoney, The Three Stigmata of Palmer Eldritch, Do Androids Dream of Electric Sheep?* and *Ubik*. In the 1970s, Dick started to concern himself more directly with metaphysical and theological issues, experiencing a moment of revelation – or breakdown – in March 1974 which became the basis for much of his subsequent writing, in particular *Valis*, as he strove to make sense of what had happened. He died in 1982, a few weeks before the film *Blade Runner* opened and introduced his vision to a wider audience.